STORM LOG-0505

A DETECTIVE DEANS MYSTERY

JAMES D MORTAIN

MANVERS PUBLISHING

Edited by Cornerstones Literary Consultancy
Cover design by Laura Clayton
ISBN: 978-0-9935687-0-1

STORM LOG-0505

A DETECTIVE DEANS MYSTERY
- BOOK ONE -

JAMES D MORTAIN

www.jamesdmortain.com

For my girls, Rachael and Gracie.

PROLOGUE

What made someone the ideal victim? he speculated.

Were they created that way, right from the start? Was it a case of nature or nurture? On the other hand, was it all down to luck, perhaps? Maybe they were simply in the wrong place at the wrong time. He chuckled. There was no such thing as the wrong time. Everyone had a time, regardless of how it may play out.

He stared down intently at the washed-out family snap as if it was the first time he had seen it. The truth was, he had studied this photo many times before and with equal fascination.

He was alone. There was no noise from the TV or radio, only the sound of his own trancelike, metronomic breathing, eyes refusing to deviate from the photo as he gazed down at Mum, Dad and himself.

To anyone else it would be a classic family photograph: two children, a boy of about six and a girl of about eight, wearing woolly hats and scarves, frolicking in the snow with their parents. For him, though, it was more. It had always meant much more.

Back, then, to the question. He smiled, and closed the two halves of the black faux-leather photo album, carefully placed it into the box and slotted it in the correct position, the right way around, between number 3 and number 5.

He snorted joss stick-scented air through his flared nostrils and cast his mind back. The first was easy – he had been left with little alternative. The second fell somewhere between curiosity and education. And what of the next? He had been counting down her final days since they first met. She was... ideal, but she was not going to be alone. The one after her, he would leave to fate, and for the sporting hell of it.

CHAPTER ONE

Carl considered himself fortunate to be with Amy. She was widely regarded as the university babe, especially amongst his mates. He would just smile, go along with what they would say, join in the banter so as not to lose face. If only they knew.

She was stunning, and fun – too stunning, and much too fun. He wished she were less popular, especially with the blokes. He despised the heads that would turn, the eyes that would undress her, the endless attempts to lure her. He carried a snail's shell of doubt and suspicion. They had been together almost a year, and each month, each week and each day was increasingly destroying who he used to be. Who he *should* be.

His last conversation with Amy was on Friday afternoon in the university's east car park.

'So, you're off to Devon again tonight,' he said glumly.

She frowned. 'You know I am.'

'I was just wondering if something might have changed.'

'No. But you know I'm back on Monday. We can meet up at lunchtime, if you like?'

Carl looked away.

'God, what's wrong with you?' Amy nipped.

Carl knew that Amy loathed his silent treatment. 'Nothing,' he said quietly. The warm, gentle breeze snatched away his answer, adding to its misdirection.

'Carl, what's wrong? You have to tell me,' she said, her face increasingly tight and unforgiving.

He turned to her with a fake smile. 'Nothing,' he said again, but inside all he could think about was Amy meeting up with Scotty, and his imagination was filling in all sorts of undesirable detail.

'Fine!' she snapped and walked to her side of his car, climbed inside and slammed the door with a thud and rattle.

He waited ten or more seconds. Now he was the baddie. He clenched his jaw and joined her inside the car. 'Come on,' he mumbled. 'I'd better drop you back.'

They hardly spoke during the three-mile drive to Amy's student home. Carl steered with his left hand, his arm acting as a barrier between them. It didn't matter to Amy, though, because she spent the entire journey looking out of her window.

When they arrived, she looked over at Carl, but he continued staring ahead.

'I'll see you on Monday then,' Amy said.

'Yep.' Carl had not moved. His left hand still gripped the wheel.

'Okay,' she said, crestfallen. 'Bye then.'

'Yep.'

Amy pulled quietly at the door handle, but before stepping out, she turned to Carl, sank her head and stepped silently onto the pavement.

· · ·

As Carl pulled away with a squeal of rubber and a scattering of gravel, his gaze met hers for a transitory moment in the rear view mirror.

'You fucking whore.'

CHAPTER TWO

Amy Poole arrived at her parents' home in the early evening and carefully manoeuvred her car into one of the last available spaces on the street. She used her sunglasses to sweep hair from her face, slid her phone into the front pocket of her back-pack, and strolled the short distance uphill to her parents' house.

She had called ahead, and her mother was already waiting at the open door as Amy crunched her way up the shingle pathway.

'How was the drive, darling?' Mum asked, holding out an arm to take Amy's bag.

'Pretty good actually,' Amy said, and embraced Mum on the doorstep.

'How have you been, my love?'

'Yeah, good.' Amy looked into the hallway. 'Where's Daddy?'

'Have a wild guess.'

'At the window?'

Mum laughed. 'How did you know?'

They both giggled and Amy followed mum through to the

kitchen. Amy smiled to herself as Mum's heels echoed off the old flagstone flooring. She was nothing if not glamorous, even at home.

Mum removed a bottle of white wine from the fridge and topped up an already half-full glass sitting alone on the breakfast bar.

'Glass for you, darling?' she asked.

Amy shook her head, noticing the purposefulness of the pour.

'Cheers,' Mum said, taking a long swig.

Mum was not a big drinker. Amy waited.

'I'm afraid Aunty Jayne isn't well. Your dad and I have arranged to visit her tomorrow.'

'Oh no! What's wrong?'

'We don't yet know for sure,' Mum said, 'but because she's alone, we thought she might appreciate a little help for a while.'

'Of course. We can all go up tomorrow.'

'We've already discussed it. We want you to stay here but Dad and I will be leaving after breakfast.' Mum took a longer guzzle. 'You've a hard year coming up. These times of relaxation won't come around that often, so enjoy it while you have the chance.'

Amy complied silently with a nod.

'It's probably nothing,' Mum said, with a reluctant smile. 'How's everything going with that new boyfriend of yours, darling?'

'Fine,' Amy replied, but did not feel much like talking about Carl right then.

'Why don't you meet up with Scotty? You always have a nice time when you see Scotty.'

'Already sorted,' Amy said. 'I'm supposed to be seeing him tomorrow night.'

Amy's dad came into the kitchen.

'I thought I heard your voice, sweetheart.' His weighty hands rounded her shoulders and he gave her the gentlest of kisses on the forehead. 'How are you doing, love?'

'Hi, Daddy,' Amy purred. 'Mum just told me about Aunty Jayne.'

A frown creased his brow, but before he had the chance to say anything else, Mum interjected.

'Come on, darling, let's eat. You must be starving. We've got beef stroganoff and homemade bread.'

'How's the studying going this week?' Dad asked.

'Yeah, fine. We started on firearms legislation. I can't believe how complicated it is.'

'I'm not sure I can assist you much there, sweetheart. It was never my forte either.'

'Come on, you two,' Mum encouraged, 'you can have your solicitor-talk after food.'

'We'll chat later,' Dad said with a wink. 'Let's not keep Mum waiting.'

Next day Mum and Dad had gone by ten. They wouldn't be back to see Amy off. In fact, they thought they could be in Gloucester for most of the week, which suggested that they knew more about Aunty Jayne's health than they were letting on.

It was another glorious October morning in North Devon. Amy spent the first minutes of her time alone gazing out of 'Dad's window' towards Adamsleigh and the yachts clustered near to the sailing club, dancing gently on the incoming tide. She had long since realised she was blessed to live in such beautiful surroundings.

She took Mum's advice and spent the day lounging around

the garden, reading a chick-lit book, and soaking up the sun on a recliner. Anyone could be forgiven for thinking it was July, with the warmth.

She had arranged to meet with Scotty around eight, at the quay in Torworthy, and by seven thirty, she was almost ready and glanced at herself in the hallway mirror. She was feeling good. She had no makeup to check, she rarely needed any. Her short denim skirt accentuated her long tanned legs, and she finished the look with her favourite O'Neill short-sleeved blouse.

It was time to leave.

She raced up to her bedroom and scrabbled around for her dependable helpers. Drawing her platinum-blonde mane away from her face she ducked beneath the tap and washed the pills down in one. Deciding against taking a jacket, she set off on the five-minute walk to the bus stop on the quay.

He was waiting for her, motionless inside his car, driver's seat tilted back so that he was barely visible above the window line. Inconspicuously watching her yellow Beetle, with which he was so familiar.

He first spotted Amy as she walked downhill towards the quay, passing her car in the process. She was moving away from him now, maybe twenty metres ahead. He sat upright, eyes watching every step intently. His pulse rate quickened and the windscreen began to fog with his hot breath.

He had been biding his time for almost three hours now and the air outside had become moist and cool. Deciding against keeping the engine running, he did not want anyone, especially Amy, to know he was there. The hairs on his forearms stood rigid amongst the goose bumps, but that was not entirely down to the temperature.

He stretched forward and wiped the screen with the side of his hand leaving a band of smeared glass through which he was now straining to see, and consciously slowed his breathing. Twenty more seconds and she would be out of his view.

He did not take a second glance away from his quarry and lowered the driver's window, just enough, and smoothly wound the car seat back to a more appropriate driving position, and the moment she was lost from sight he started the engine.

Lights out, he rolled the car downhill.

He saw her again as she crossed over the main road towards a bus stop, and he looked for a space to pull in. It had to be quick; she must not see his car or else the plan would fail.

Amy turned in his direction as she sat down on the bus stop bench, just as he killed the engine and cruised slowly to a stop behind a silver Smart car. He held his breath, dare not even blink. She looked away, not seeing him. It was still on.

She was sitting alone, one leg folded over the other, looking down at her mobile phone; the glow from the screen illuminated her face. Damn, she was looking good!

The corner of his mouth twitched and he licked his upper lip as her left thigh strained and bulged softly as it pivoted over the other knee. *Tonight is the night*, he thought.

A street lamp cast a faint umbrella of brightness around the bus stop roof encapsulating Amy. He considered his options: go across and take the initiative, or sit tight and wait for the right moment. He rocked in his seat – the right moment – whenever that would be.

A glance at the dash showed **19:51** in bright green square digits. He had no idea how long he had before the bus was due to arrive.

The longer he observed, the less of a choice he seemed to have. His legs were getting restless, his hands growing clammy and his breathing was no longer under his control. He knew what he had to do and it had to be now.

He quickly rehearsed the stages in his mind: what he was going to do and how he was going to deal with her reaction. He could not mess it up. He had waited a long time for this.

He smirked. Amy still was not looking his way. He had maintained the element of surprise, and so he stepped out from the security of his car. She was no more than fifty metres away, obliviously engrossed with her mobile phone.

Blood surged through his veins, and his hearing buzzed dimly with building adrenalin and excitement.

A car pulled slowly to a stop alongside the bench, partially blocking his line of sight. Only Amy's head and shoulders were now visible above the roofline. He needed a clearer view.

A man climbed out from the car and walked towards Amy who noticed and waved to the man. She was now standing up, smiling and laughing, and the man was standing close to her, just inches away. Who was he?

Struggling to catch a glimpse of the man's face, he moved further into the road but still only saw the back of the man's beanie.

'Scott?' he breathed, recognition dawning. His shoulders and arms stiffened and his chest filled with air. He stood planted to the spot as he watched their interaction.

Amy leant forward, giving Scott a lasting hug.

'Bitch,' he snarled. She had it coming to her.

He drew a sharp breath, his surroundings came back into focus – he was exposed, and he darted back to his seat.

It was too late. The other car was gone and so was Amy.

He noticed the time: **19:53**, and sat motionless, gaping ahead at the now empty bus stop.

Several minutes went by, and then he caught his eyes in the rear view mirror. 'You fucked that right up.'

CHAPTER THREE

Detective Constable Andrew Deans was sitting despondently at his desk. From his second floor vantage point, he had a clear view of the people below going about their daily routines, most of them leading normal lives in comparison to his own. He sucked in deeply and expelled a long, coffee-fuelled breath as he watched with envy the public below. Tuesday afternoon, and this was his third day of six on duty, his morning confined in the small and overcrowded custody unit helping his colleague, Daisy Harper, interview a smug maggot of a man, arrested for stealing a large quantity of cash from his employer. Hours had wasted away as they waited for the solicitor to conduct his consultation, only to receive a half-page, barely legible, prepared statement at interview.

Few things bothered Deans much, but lingering around a stuffy, fluorescent-lit dungeon was certainly high up on the list, particularly as it was a beautiful day and especially as the brief was Johnson.

Deans secretly hoped that Johnson would one day become the unwitting victim of one of his own clients. Nothing serious, of course. Maybe a shed break-in or sat-nav theft from his car, but enough. Enough to see if Johnson would come bleating to the cops for help. Deans bet Johnson would rather suffer in silence than seek the help of his colleagues.

It was now three forty p.m. and the day had started at eight. There was an hour and a quarter to go before he could head off home, and it could not come soon enough. Harper had already gone for the day; had some family commitment or something. She had three kids to juggle as well as the job. They had been the only two detectives on duty that morning, but the skipper, who was himself enjoying some time off, had granted Harper the leave in advance. Now, Deans was solo in the office.

'Great,' he muttered under his breath as he continued to stare wistfully out of the window, considering whether to make his thirteenth coffee of the day.

DC Young from the late shift had been expected in at three but was commencing a crown court trial in the morning, so was pretty much written off from any meaty jobs that might arise. Deans was acutely aware that as it stood he was all that was left of the CID cover that day. The radio just had to stay 'Q' for a short while longer and then he could be at home with his wife and maybe even enjoy some fading autumn sunshine. He had learnt very early into his career never to use the word 'quiet' while on duty. Not only would his colleagues berate him, but it also had a nasty propensity of dishing up quite the opposite.

He sighed and flicked back through the recent pages of his blue A4 daybook – indispensable CID issue. No self-respecting detective could be without one. Those hard-backed matt covers safeguarded every investigative scribble. He had been working on a dubious robbery report from the early hours of yesterday; a young male victim, walking home at gone two a.m., alleging that he was followed by hooded kids on pushbikes who surrounded him, pushed him to the ground, produced a flick knife and stole his mobile phone and 'probably about eighty pounds cash'. 'Probably' was never a good starting point and even more of a challenge with a hammered victim, unable to recall any significant detail about the offence, or the offenders.

Deans had already re-interviewed the complainant, sussing him out, testing his account, and four DVDs from the Council CCTV system were still sitting in his pending tray. No matter how many times he had tried to avoid noticing them, they were not going away.

CCTV was potluck, and sometimes a thankless task. Deans already had a slightly defeated mindset, and suspected the student had lost his phone whilst on the piss and been told by the phone company to get a crime number before they would offer a replacement. The eighty pounds would be mere embellishment.

He eventually mustered a degree of motivation with the aid of another strong brew and began reviewing the first disk, but it was not long before his eyes started feeling heavy with the lack of action from the computer screen.

DC Young sauntered into the office wearing civvies and humming along to headphones.

'Dress down day?' Deans said, looking Young up and down.

'I'm at court tomorrow,' Young replied, as he scoured the office. 'Something going on, Deano?'

'No. I'm it.'

'Who else is on lates?' Young asked more attentively.

'You're it.' Deans smiled and turned back to his computer screen that was still showing dark and grainy images of a faraway park. Reflected in his monitor Young was pleading silently; arms out at his side.

With only a short time to go before his shift was due to end, Deans checked the log of ongoing calls for anything requiring CID attention. Though sixteen outstanding jobs showed nothing obvious to be concerned about, one made him take a second look. Medium Risk MISPER, LOG-0505.

CID did not normally deal with missing persons unless someone with pips on their shoulders deemed they were high risk. Deans knew that with a starting point of medium risk, this particular job had potential to ascend the stairs to the suits and so he read on.

Third party informant is reporting a missing housemate. MISPER – Amy Poole last seen on Friday afternoon. MISPER has not returned home over the weekend and has not attended lectures this week. Informant has spoken to MISPER'S boyfriend who has not had contact with her since Friday. Alternative telephone numbers are unknown.

The log now had Deans' full attention and he continued reading.

MISPER is a 20-year-old female student of Minerva University, Bath, living in privately rented accommodation. MISPER last seen with boyfriend, Carl Groves, on Friday 3rd October after final lectures. MISPER not answering calls texts or social media.

A lacklustre voice from behind interrupted Deans' concentration.

'Anything I need to know about, Deano?'

'Not really. There's a medium risk MISPER – female student – probably one to keep an eye on.'

'Oh great, not another bird shacked up somewhere? She'll return once she's had enough.'

It was not unusual for MISPERs to return of their own accord but the problem with them, especially when they were higher risk, was that they absorbed significant resources and time. Considering there were any number of MISPER logs every day, and this was the third that Deans knew of during his shift alone, only occasionally did one come along that grabbed the attention, and this was a case in point.

'It seems a little strange to me,' Deans said.

'Well, it's medium risk. Leave it for the woodentops to deal with.' Young was always so complimentary about his uniformed colleagues.

Deans chortled and grabbed his bag. 'I'm out of here,' he said, tapping Young's desk with his knuckle as he passed. 'Have a good one.'

'Remember I can't get involved in anything, I've got court tomorrow.'

Deans did not reply. His stint was over.

Walking home, Deans continued to think about the MISPER log, and it bothered him. Friday afternoon to Tuesday lunchtime was a significant period with no contact. The boyfriend must have heard from Amy Poole at some point, some other family member, or a friend. But he knew the job would probably be waiting for him next day, along with God knows what else, so he continued his journey home and did not give it another thought that night.

CHAPTER FOUR

Wednesday lunchtime and Deans was at home with his wife, Maria. She had been off sick from work since Monday. He was making her beans on toast, which was all she fancied. He made himself the same but double the amount. He was starting late-turn that day and wanted to know he had some food inside him just in case he did not get another chance to eat.

Despite Maria feeling unwell, they had at least spent some unexpected time together although she was not particularly forthcoming.

They were enduring an anxious time. No one else knew other than close family; no one else needed to know – yet. It was taking a toll, especially on Maria. For Deans it was slightly different. It was not diminished ownership, perhaps less self-imposed responsibility. They were both aware of the stats: twenty-five to thirty per cent, the experts had quoted. Not great odds if you were putting money down, but more than a glimmer of hope to cling onto if you dreamed of becoming a parent. Work was his coping mechanism, his fleeting release from the anguish. Maria had a part-time hairdressing job with her best friend from school days, who had two children herself. Deans did not think Maria resented the fact he could *escape*, but it certainly did not help that he was often at work when she was at her most fertile. The three a.m. attempts to conceive off the back of a long shift because Maria was ovulating, were anything but romantic.

He left the house having cocooned Maria within a duvet in front of the TV and a boxed set of *Sex and the City* and walked his usual route to work.

Bath was shaped like a bowl, with the majority of action taking place at the heart. He likened it to the crater of a volcano, not only in appearance but also for its quiescent energy with undertones of irrepressible ferocity. He had lived in Bath all his life, and becoming a cop had tainted his image, but not his love for his home.

He arrived at the office well before his shift was due to begin. The team on days were sitting around their desks, faces glued to their screens.

'Hey, guys, how's it going?' Deans said as he walked past them towards his own desk. He fired up the computer and tried the room again. 'All right, guys? How's it been?'

'Busy,' DC Saunders replied, still looking at his screen.

'Anything to hand over?' Deans asked.

'Need to speak with you about that MISPER from the weekend, Deano,' DS Boyle, the day shift skipper said. 'No problems. Uniform have disowned it and I see you were on duty when the job first came in.'

'MISPER?' Deans hesitated; he had been dealing with the robbery. 'Are we talking about the student?'

'You've got it,' Boyle replied. 'Grab yourself a brew and come on over.'

'Not sure what I can offer,' Deans said. 'CID didn't have any involvement. She was medium risk.'

'Not any more, Deano,' Boyle said dejectedly. 'High risk and we're all tucked up.'

Deans looked at Boyle's team, each of them avoiding eye contact. It was their first day on duty from rest days – how could they all be unavailable already?

Boyle handed Deans a wad of papers. The top sheet was a contemporaneous transcript of the 999 call, showing the timings, caller details and all subsequent police enquiries – the STORM LOG; the starting point of most investigations. And this one had been the five hundred and fifth call of that day. When Deans first saw this log there were only several lines of information. Now it was four A4 pages long.

'We need a detective on this now, Deano,' Boyle said. 'Uniform have done everything they can but this needs a comprehensive investigation.' He clutched Deans' shoulder and leant in. 'The Boss is starting to kick up about this at prayers. We need progress and we need it pronto.'

Deans sighed, and looked over at the case files on his desk stacked like a game of Jenga. 'Yeah, no worries. Last I heard, she hadn't returned to her digs after the weekend. Surely someone's had contact with her by now?'

'Not according to uniform,' Boyle replied. 'It seems no one knows where the girl is. Can you or someone from your team get back onto the housemate, Jessica Morrison, and track down the boyfriend? Somebody must know something. Pin them down to specifics. Oh, and we need contact with the family, ASAP, compliments of the boss.'

'Yeah. Sure.' Deans nodded half-heartedly, and shuffled over to his desk to review the enquiries.

PC Wilder of Team 1 had spoken to Jessica Morrison by phone yesterday. She still had not heard from Amy. Deans scanned the rest of the bundle and was disappointed to see telecoms and banking enquiries had not been arranged. Historic cell-site activity could at least show the phone's location at a given time, and similarly with cash withdrawals, and that would have made for a useful starting point. A Police National Computer (PNC) report showed the boyfriend, Carl Groves, had received a caution back in the summer for a public order offence in the city centre. The officer in the case was PC Hill, a foot patrol officer whose arrest rate was significantly higher than the rest of his team, or the station, come to that. The bosses loved him for it and he regularly received performance awards. The reality however, was that Hill was an average officer who had an unbelievable knack for getting under the skin of the late-night revellers. Those stupid enough to engage or argue got nicked. Hill was like a Venus fly trap, indiscriminate and uncompromising, and Deans imagined Carl Groves had flown just too close for his own good.

He noted with interest that Amy's family were from Hemingsford. He had been to Cornwall with Maria several times but was less familiar with North Devon. He hunted for the contact details and punched the home number into the desk phone. Being a Wednesday afternoon he did not know whether to expect an answer or not, but the skipper had said the call needed making, and so be it. Deans understood this contact was important and potentially difficult. It had been several days since Amy went missing, with no significant progress. That was unsatisfactory from an investigative perspective, but nothing compared to the anguish her parents must be feeling.

He failed to gain a response from the landline; however, a mature-sounding woman with a soft, warm voice answered the mobile number.

'Hello. Mrs Poole?' Deans asked.

'Yes.'

'Hello, my name is DC Deans. I'm calling from Falcon Road CID in Bath. I just wanted to make contact with you and introduce myself.'

There was a silence for a few moments, and then Mrs Poole replied, 'Yes.'

'I'd like to pass you my direct contact details and let you know that I'm the officer in the case for Amy's disappearance.'

There was a longer silence.

'Hello?' Deans said again, but heard nothing. He pressed on. 'I've only been allocated the job today, but I can assure you that I'll do all I can to find your daughter, Mrs Poole.' He stopped talking and waited for some sort of response. It was unusual in these circumstances to be having a one-way conversation, but then again, he would usually be visiting the family in their home. He pressed the phone tightly to his ear and then the magnitude of his error struck him: Mrs Poole didn't know.

'Mrs Poole,' Deans said quickly. 'Mrs Poole, are you okay?'

Instead of an answer, Deans heard heartbreak and pain. He flicked through the handover papers to the STORM LOG and immediately saw what he had missed. *NOK have not been informed.*

A surge of blood rushed to his head, his cheeks flushed, and he fought in his mind to construct the right words to rectify his balls-up.

'Mrs Poole, I'm very sorry. It was my belief that you'd already been informed. I'm terribly sorry to have given you the news in this way.'

He stopped, but heard nothing.

'We received a report on Tuesday from one of Amy's housemates that she was missing. It's suggested that Amy hasn't been answering her phone or social media. Have you had any contact with her since the weekend, Mrs Poole?'

A shadowy sound of gasping breath was all he could hear in the earpiece.

'Okay, Mrs Poole,' he said softly. 'I'll take it you've had none.' He paused, heard snivelling. 'Do you have someone else there with you at the moment, Mrs Poole?'

'Y-yes. My hus-husband… and… s-sister.'

'I'm glad you're not alone. Would it be possible to speak to either of them, please?'

The line went quiet for a moment. 'Who is this?' a male voice boomed.

'Hello, sir. My name is Detective Constable Andrew Deans of Falcon Road CID in Bath. Am I speaking with Mr Poole?'

'Yes.'

'I'm sincerely sorry to have upset your wife, Mr Poole. I'm afraid I have some difficult news to pass to you. Your daughter, Amy, has been reported missing by a university housemate.'

'What? When?' he barked.

'She apparently hasn't attended any lectures so far this week, sir.'

'What? Why didn't someone tell us this before?'

'Please accept my apology for that, Mr Poole. I've only been allocated this case today and it was my impression that family would've been contacted from the outset. I will look into that for you, and I'll be making my own complaint to my supervisor.'

'I don't give a shit about your supervisor. Where's my daughter – is she alright?'

'I'm afraid I can't answer that right now, but I'll ensure we'll do all we can to find your daughter, sir.'

'What about her AEDs? Has she got them with her?'

'I'm sorry, her AEDs?'

'Her medication. She is epileptic. Does she have them with her?'

Deans bunched his eyes and threw his head backwards. The stakes had just risen.

'I didn't know,' he replied gingerly. 'Her friends didn't mention anything to—'

'Amy doesn't broadcast her affliction. She's very private about it.'

Deans did not know much about epilepsy and had to think on his feet.

'How often does Amy take her medication?' he asked.

'Every day.'

'What would happen if she didn't take it?'

Mr Poole did not answer immediately, and then spoke with a sullen voice. 'The chance of a seizure increases.'

'Could you describe her seizures for me, please?'

'Amy hasn't suffered from one in quite some time, thankfully, but without her AEDs the risk increases and she could quickly become disorientated... or have a full on attack.'

'When was her last seizure?'

'When she was fifteen. She has been on gabapentin ever since.'

'Gabapentin, her medication?'

'Yes.'

Deans scribbled the name in his daybook. He would worry about the spelling later.

'Has she ever missed taking them before?'

'When she was younger, yes.'

'And what happened?'

'Nothing too untoward, thankfully. But we intervened.'

'So, if she's missed a few now, there's a possibility she would be okay?'

'Well, yes, that's a possibility. But the longer she goes without her AEDs, the higher the risk of an event.'

Deans noticed he had underlined the word gabapentin in his daybook so much that he was almost through the paper. 'Mr Poole, when did you or your wife last have contact with Amy?'

'We left her at the house on Saturday morning. My wife spoke to Amy on Saturday afternoon and was going to call again later tonight. We're still in Gloucester, you see.'

'So… you haven't been home since Saturday?'

'No.'

'Okay,' Deans said, formulating a scenario in his head. 'I tried the landline, but couldn't get a reply. That doesn't necessarily mean Amy was not there, but I'll contact my colleagues in Devon and request an urgent send-to.'

'Meaning?'

'Sorry. A local police officer will attend your home address to see if they can get a reply. It's possible they'll need to force an entry, unless there are spare keys with someone?'

'Yes. Derek next door – Williamson. Number eleven.'

'I'll contact my Devon colleagues as soon as I'm free from this call and I'll let you know the moment I hear an update.'

'Right, make sure you do. Your name. Give me your name again?'

'DC Andrew Deans, sir. Falcon Road CID, in Bath.'

At the end of the call, Deans sank his head into his hands and then realised that nobody in the office was talking. He looked up through his fingers and saw everyone gazing back at him.

CHAPTER FIVE

Deans spent the next hour and a half attempting to make contact with the informant, Jessica Morrison, and Amy's boyfriend, Carl Groves. He did not chat with anyone else in the office and he did not intercept any other phone calls. Completely focused, he felt the need to remedy his earlier error. He had immediately contacted comms following the call to the Pooles, requesting an officer check the home address. His money was on them finding Amy unconscious on the floor somewhere at home, but now it was out of his hands and he would just have to be patient and wait for Devon to do their thing. He was realistic though, and did not expect an answer for a good few hours.

He gnawed at his nails as he watched the phone. He had put in eight calls; one each to Morrison and Groves, every half an hour. The incessant chatter of his colleagues was making him increasingly agitated and he was going to snap eventually, and so he took a tactical time out and wandered through the nearby streets of the Southgate shopping development.

The voice of Mrs Poole played over in his head, and the bustling shoppers around him faded to smudges.

His phone vibrated in his trouser pocket. It was a text from Daisy Harper telling him there had been a phone call.

He sprang up the two-storey flight of stairs, and found Harper sitting at her computer.

'Who was it Dais?' Deans asked.

'Some girl.' Harper shrugged. 'Details are on your desk. Are you getting the brews in?'

Deans did not answer and soon he was speaking with Jessica Morrison. They arranged to meet at her house at five p.m., but Deans refused to discuss any more over the phone. Once bitten, as the saying goes.

His partner for the day was DC Damien Mitchell – one of those people who delight in sharing their personal life, especially sexual activities – grunts and all – in vigorous detail with anyone willing to listen. He could be extremely amusing with his anecdotes but there was a time and a place and Mitchell did not seem to worry about either. He possessed natural investigative flare and would no doubt ascend the rungs of rank in time. If anything were to hold him back, it would likely be a combination of his age, inexperience and having the hormone levels of a rampant rhinoceros.

Deans filled Mitchell in with the job details as they drove to the address, a mid-terraced Victorian house in the student quarter of town. A short concrete pathway bisected a small, wildly overgrown garden that had maybe once passed as a lawn.

A pretty girl in her early twenties opened the front door. She had a pensive but friendly smile. Deans focussed immediately on her vibrant, asymmetrical, red-dyed hair, and then noticed the shiny metal stud in her top lip and a small black spike protruding out of her right nostril.

'Jessica?' he asked.

'Jess.' She nodded. 'Come in please.'

They followed her inside, through a poky hallway to a kitchen area at the rear of the property that was surprisingly clear of clutter, for a student home.

Deans offered his right hand. 'I'm DC Andy Deans. I spoke to you on the phone. And this is—'

'Hi, I'm Mitch,' DC Mitchell interjected with a broad smile.

Jess invited them to sit around the kitchen table but she remained standing.

'Thanks for seeing us,' Deans said. 'Do you know why we're here?'

'Amy?' she replied, softly.

Deans nodded and gave a consoling smile. 'When did you last see Amy?'

Jess pushed back a pile of unfolded clothing that smelt recently washed and leant back against the edge of the worktop.

'Last Friday. At the uni car park.'

'Do you know what time?' Deans asked.

'About three thirty, I think. I had just finished. So yes, it was around three thirty.'

'Thank you, Jess,' Deans encouraged. 'What was Amy doing when you last saw her?'

'She was with Carl. They must've been heading off to his car.'

'Boyfriend, Carl?'

'Yes.'

'How do you know it was to his car?' Deans asked.

'Because it was my turn to drive us in that week. So she would have taken a lift back with him, or jumped on the bus, because she didn't come back with me.'

'What car does Carl have?' Mitchell asked. He was finally

concentrating on something else other than the pile of skimpy underwear next to Jessica's left hand.

'I don't know the make but it's an orange colour with a black bonnet.'

'What time in the morning did you and Amy arrive at uni?' Deans asked.

'Around nine. We usually get there around that time.'

'Does Amy drive a car?'

'Yes.' Jessica half-smiled. 'A really cute VW Beetle.'

Deans was taking notes in his daybook. 'What colour?'

'Yellow. Bright yellow, with large white flower stickers.'

'Do you happen to know the registration number?'

'No. Sorry.' She hesitated. 'But I know it starts WK because we nickname it "wicked bug".' She tittered and looked away.

'Thank you, Jess. Go on, what did you and Amy talk about on the way to uni on Friday?'

'The usual kind of stuff really. She was heading down to see her parents for the weekend again.'

'Her family in Devon?' Deans asked, noticing Mitchell straining his neck to view a framed photo on the wall of three tanned and bikini-clad girls. 'Why did you feel the need to report her missing if you knew she was at her parents' house?'

'She was due back by Sunday evening. We both had job interviews in town. And she was supposed to be driving us to uni this week.'

Deans shook his head. 'Ever done this before?'

'No. Never.' Her face was anxious. 'It's so unlike Amy. She's the most reliable person I know.'

There was a moment of silence.

Jess looked down at her feet. 'Do you know where Amy is?' She suddenly appeared vulnerable and fragile.

There were a couple of ways Deans could answer the question: give the corporate spiel or be blunt.

'I'm going to be honest, Jess. I have no idea. That is why we are here. I'm leading the investigation and I need to piece together as much information as I can. You may know more than you realise, but that's down to me to work out.'

Jess gently bobbed her head, still staring at her bare feet.

'Have you spoken to anyone else about this since last week?'

'Sarah and Billie and Carl,' she replied.

'Carl, Amy's boyfriend?'

Jess nodded.

'Who are Sarah and Billie?' Mitchell asked.

'They live with us here. We all go to uni together.'

'Where are they now?' Mitchell continued.

'Sarah doesn't stay here much. She has the smallest room so stays with her boyfriend most of the time and Billie broke her leg last week and has gone back home with her parents. I don't know when she's coming back.'

'You didn't contact Amy's parents?' Deans asked, but he already knew the answer.

'No,' she hesitated. 'I don't have their number.' She caught Deans' eye briefly, then looked away again.

'Who's in this photo?' Mitchell asked, using the excuse to peer closer at the bikinied trio.

'Me, Billie and Ames,' Jess replied without looking at the photograph.

Deans turned to face the picture. He recognised Jess standing in the middle of the other two girls, although her hair was darker in the picture. There was another dark-haired female – Billie presumably, because Amy was reported to be blonde, and the only blonde-haired person in this photo was much taller and completely reigned over the others. However, it was not just her stature. Even from this picture, Deans could tell she was… exceptional.

'We may need to take this,' Mitchell suggested.

'We may not have to,' Deans countered and forced himself to break away from the photograph. He looked over at Mitchell and flashed him a look. 'If there's another recent photo of Amy, as she looks now, that'll be just fine.'

'Sure. I've loads of photos upstairs from a couple of weeks ago.'

As Jess left the kitchen, Deans shook his head at Mitchell.

'I mean, come on, Deano?' Mitchell grinned.

There was no denying it. Amy was an extraordinary looking girl, but Deans figured that made the disappearance a whole lot more significant.

Jess returned from upstairs and handed Deans a five-by-seven close-up of Amy's face. She had a wide smile of beautiful white teeth and the most incredible blue eyes that sucked him deeper into the picture.

'Tell me about Carl,' Deans said, still studying the photo.

'He's nice, I suppose. Pretty fit if you know what I mean. Not my type, but definitely Ames'. She seems to attract the sporty ones.'

'How long have they been together?'

'A year, I guess, kind of properly.'

'Did you see him after last Friday at the car park?'

'No. But I called him on Monday when Ames didn't come home.'

'What did he say?'

'Um, he hadn't seen her all weekend, and didn't know where she was either.'

'Did you think there was anything strange about that?'

'Not really.' She paused. 'Well, a bit, I guess.'

'How so?'

'Because Carl's always with Ames. It's like he's her shadow or something.'

'Do you speak to Carl much?' Deans asked.

She shrugged nonchalantly. 'Sometimes. We're kind of mates because of Ames. We're friends on Facebook.'

'Is he hard to get hold of, on the phone?' Deans asked.

'No, I don't think so.'

Deans nodded and jotted a note in his daybook, and then asked if he could look around the house and at Amy's room in particular. Jess was happy to accommodate and offered them a cup of tea. Mitchell accepted. Deans asked for coffee.

Amy's room was typical of a young female student. Deans scanned the room taking in the detail: a double bed below the window with newish-looking unmade sheets, a wooden bedside table, a recessed area on the far wall stacked with trendy clothes hanging from a metal rod, and a desk with a laptop plugged into the wall socket. A large poster of a girl surfing a ridiculous-sized wave dominated the wall to his left. Beneath the poster, piles of clothing, magazines, textbooks and shoes covered the floor space. From his cursory scan, there were no obvious messages or suicide notes, and nothing out of the ordinary to indicate that this was anything other than a normal student's bedroom.

Deans opted to take the laptop and a diary that was on the desktop. It was better to secure potential evidence now rather than have to come back at some point in the future. If she returned, she could simply have them back.

On the bedside cabinet, he noticed a phone charger without the phone.

'Does Amy have an iPhone?'

'Yes.'

'Any other phones?'

'No, I don't think so.'

Not a good sign.

'Would you happen to know if Amy is into anything, drug-wise?'

'No. She hardly even drinks.'

'Does she have any debts; does she owe money to anyone?'

Jess shook her head. 'No, I don't think so. Amy always has money.'

Deans was satisfied that he could do no more at this time, but had developed a throbbing pain in his head. He left Jess with a business card and thanked her for her help. Mitchell winked and left her with a 'See you later.'

CHAPTER SIX

Back at the station, Deans booked his exhibits onto the detained property registry, and there was still no contact from Carl Groves. Deans' suspicion was becoming increasingly piqued the longer time went by.

Deans' sergeant, DS Michael Savage beckoned him into the empty DI's office, pointed to a chair pushed up against the wall, and took the inspector's chair for himself.

'Fill me in, Deano,' he said.

'Still early days, Mick. We just got back from speaking with Jessica Morrison. She doesn't have much to offer, she's pretty spaced out by this whole thing. I really need to speak to Carl Groves, but he's proving elusive.'

'Why do you suppose that is?'

'That's what I'd like to know. I tested Jessica. She said he wasn't hard to get hold of.'

'What are you thinking, Deano?'

'I'm not happy, Mick, to be honest. I'm playing catch-up and having to find out things that should already be known. Did you know the MISPER is epileptic?'

'No. Christ that could change things.'

'Tell me about it. I had to find out from her old man while he was giving me earache.'

'I'm sorry, Deano. Boylie gave me an update before he went off-duty. Thanks for taking this on. I know you have plenty of other real crime to be getting on with, just make sure you don't sacrifice your existing workload for this crock of shite. Do enough to keep the bosses at bay, and then sack it off back to Devon and Cornwall. Let it become their headache. Anyway, I'm sure at some point she'll materialise.'

'Honestly, Mick? I just can't see this being that straightforward. The more I hear, the more concerned I'm getting. She's already been missing four days.'

Savage sank into his seat. 'Well, what do we know, Deano?'

'Not much.' Deans shrugged. 'Mum and Dad left her on Saturday, and it appears no one's seen her since.'

'What about her addresses?'

'I've requested an urgent send-to in Devon, but haven't heard back yet. Her bedroom in Bath is typical of her profile. I checked it out for signs of an extended absence but there was nothing. If anything, it is more indicative of unusual behaviour. I seized a laptop and a diary from her room, but only to cover all bases.'

'Good,' Savage replied. 'The laptop will just have to sit in DPR for now. There is no way we will get authority to examine that. This is only a MISPER enquiry after all.'

Deans had been here many times before. He knew the score.

'Update the log with everything you've done, Deano, and consider contacting her GP if you think we need to know more about her epilepsy.'

'Her old man played it down mostly. I got the impression her condition is generally well controlled, but she's on daily meds, if she has them with her.'

'Document everything he said to you. Make sure you cover your arse.'

Deans nodded.

'If you need help with anything else, grab Mitch or Harps. Have you got a photo of the MISPER?'

Deans rooted around in his file and handed Savage the photograph Jessica had given him earlier.

'My God!' Savage said.

'Yep.'

'Wow.'

That reaction said it all. So far, every bloke that had seen her picture had responded similarly. It made Deans think about one of his favourite films, *There's Something About Mary*. Perhaps, he wondered, there was something about Amy.

They decided to use the photograph for a local press release, to be mirrored in North Devon. They agreed that if she had been sighted, she would be remembered. A low-key message would suffice for now – *Amy Poole, 20-year-old student. Missing since Saturday the 4th of October. Any information regarding her whereabouts to Falcon Road CID on 101 or anonymously via Crimestoppers.*

Deans returned to his desk and cleared away an open space. He slugged a large mouthful of cold coffee and placed a blank sheet of white A3 paper on the desktop. He drew a straight black horizontal line across the entire width of the page and stared at the middle, and wondered how far along they were, and then considered whether he would need more sheets before the end of the investigation. It was the makings of an investigative timeline.

He drew a red box above the horizontal line, roughly a third of the way in from the left. Inside the box, he wrote, *University car park with Carl GROVES*. He drew a connecting line to the horizontal and beneath wrote, *Friday 3rd October –*

15:30hrs. He drew a green box below the horizontal, towards the left-hand side of the page, penned *University I/C Jessica MORRISON. Friday 3rd October – 09:45hrs.* The next box was red, three-quarters of the way along and dated *Tuesday 7th October,* and simply titled, *Reported missing.*

He stared down at the timeline and the mass of white empty space burned into his eyes like snow blindness. At the top of the page in bold red letters, he wrote *EPILEPTIC.*

CHAPTER SEVEN

It was usually a social meeting place for Carl Groves but this time he spoke to no one at the gym. He had already finished lectures and had spent the last couple of hours pushing his body to the limits. He had a lot on his mind, and no one he could tell. His parents, with whom he still lived, had commented on his mood change over the weekend. They had not pushed him about it, but he guessed they knew he had relationship issues.

Carl had already listened to the four voicemail messages from the copper. He understood why he wanted to speak to him. What troubled him was how much the copper knew. He had not replied to the calls because he was buying himself some time to think, to get his story right. The gym session had helped to a degree but only by burning up some of the nervous energy he had been suffering since the calls. He knew he would have to speak to the police at some point. It was obvious they wouldn't just go away.

His hand was trembling as he clutched the copper's name and number on a small scrap of paper. He had already taken himself outside for some fresh air. Few people walked to this area, so he would be undisturbed. His stomach muscles twitched as he dialled the number and he took a quick peek over his shoulder.

Deans' job mobile phone vibrated on his desk.

'DC Andy Deans speaking.'

There was silence.

'Hello?' Deans said firmly. He huffed and was about to terminate the call but then heard a tentative voice.

'Um, hello. This is Carl Groves. I've got a message to call this number.'

'Mr Groves,' Deans said faking gratitude, 'so good of you to call back.' He fumbled around his desk for a pen and his daybook. 'You're an elusive man.'

There was no reply.

'I'd like to see you today,' Deans said.

'Uh, I can't today, I'm afraid,' Groves replied.

'Tell me why,' Deans said quickly, giving Groves no opportunity to hide in his answer.

'I've got to go out later.'

Deans snorted, probably loud enough for Groves to hear. 'Let's put it this way, Carl. I am either seeing you today, or I'm coming over to your house in the middle of the night, waking up whoever else may be there, and we can all have a conversation about things then. Alternatively, I could come to your university and get you out of a lecture. But of course I'd have to explain the reason why. So, what is it to be? Your choice.'

There was a period of silence. 'Carl?'

'Okay,' he replied sheepishly.

'Okay what, Carl? Am I seeing you today?'

'I suppose.'

Deans arranged to meet Groves at the station front office at seven. He would have preferred to meet him at his home address but Groves seemed keen to avoid that and Deans had no reason to force the issue.

Carl Groves' one and only experience of the police was not a fond one. He had spent the entire night in a small, cold cell having been arrested for no apparent reason. All he had to sleep on was a thin, worn, mattress. It was miserable. The only natural light came in through a small window of grubby opaque glass blocks, and to top it off, he was not released until gone six p.m. next day. They told him they had been busy but he did not believe them. He guessed the copper who had nicked him told the others to leave him because he had called that copper a bald-headed twat.

He had no idea how long he was going to be at the station this time, so he dressed in a warm top just in case he would be spending another long night in the cells.

He left his parents, saying he was heading out to see a mate and might be back late. They had not questioned him.

He drove to the station, arriving shortly after seven, and parked on the subterranean level of the twin-storey car park next door. The parking meter was free between six p.m. and seven a.m. He was in luck. Even so, he hoped he would be out before the charges started again in the morning.

Walking up the steps to ground floor level, he looked up at the police station building. Row upon row of windows stared back at him. He imagined faces were watching him from behind the glass. It did not look much like a police station from the side but at the front there was no mistake, thanks to the cop cars and riot vans in their parking bays.

He dawdled towards the main entrance and ran the story through in his head, one final time.

Two coppers came out of a side door and approached him. He snatched at his breath. Were they coming for him? Did they know who he was?

One of the coppers looked directly at him. Carl slowed to a half-pace and tensed up, but the cops continued towards one of the waiting cars. His heart was pounding as if he had just finished a training run. He moved towards the entrance and stepped gingerly into the foyer. Ahead of him, a black counter spanned the entire width of the room. A glass screen partitioned the counter top and ceiling with beige-coloured blinds pulled down low. Behind the only opened blind stood a middle-aged woman staring attentively in his direction.

Carl instinctively checked behind himself and looked around the room. He was alone.

The glass screen was now creeping slowly upwards under the power of a buzzing motor.

He inched forward.

'May I help you, sir?' the woman behind the counter asked.

'Um, yeah.' Carl dithered. 'I've been told to come for seven.'

The woman raised her eyebrows. 'Do you know who asked you to come for seven?'

She made a point of looking at the clock on the wall.

Carl followed her gaze and noticed it was almost seven fifteen.

'Um, a detective,' he replied, just as a stern-looking man wearing a grey suit and holding a blue book came into view from behind the woman.

Deans had been waiting in the front office since six fifty. He did not like inactivity.

'Carl Groves?'

'Yeah,' Groves replied, taking a half step backwards.

'Stay there. I'll be right over.' Deans gave a subtle *lock the door if he makes a bolt for it* nod to the officer at the desk, and entered the foyer via a side door and bound his way towards Groves, who was paying attention to the exit.

'Hi, Carl, thank you for coming in.' Deans held out his right hand and Groves looked at it suspiciously.

'I'm DC Deans. I spoke with you on the phone earlier.'

Groves nodded and tentatively shook Deans' hand.

'Follow me.'

Deans turned and walked towards another door, and signalled to the officer behind the counter. The door buzzed and opened inwards into a small interview room and Groves stepped inside.

Deans offered him a seat nearest the entrance and he sat opposite. The door closed on a stiff spring and a secure clout of the latch. This was it for Groves. No going back. Cards on the table.

Deans noticed Groves checking out the room. He had already felt the clamminess of his hand. Groves did not know it but Deans was taking everything in. Every little anxious reaction. Every jumpy twitch. Every furtive body movement.

'Thanks for coming in tonight, Carl. Have you parked next door?'

Groves nodded and looked away towards the window.

Deans waited until Groves looked at him again. 'I'm a detective from the CID department, and I'm investigating the disappearance of Amy Poole, who I understand is your current girlfriend.'

Groves' head drooped and he stroked the hair at the nape of his neck.

'Carl, is Amy your current girlfriend?'

'Yeah,' he replied, sharply.

'Carl. You are aware that Amy is missing?'

Groves shrugged and nodded, but did not look Deans in the eye.

Deans' knee began to bounce beneath the desk. 'What do you know about the CID, Carl?'

Groves shifted in his seat and his eyes flicked up to meet Deans' for the briefest of moments.

'Um, you deal with the serious stuff.'

'That's right, Carl. And we, the police, are taking Amy's disappearance very seriously.'

Deans waited for a reaction, and received one when a response vehicle on the forecourt lit up the room with blue strobe light and blazed away with howling sirens. Groves damn near jumped out of his skin and stared wildly out of the window as more vehicles came to life with equal urgency.

Deans would usually turn up the volume on his Airwave radio and monitor the action, but right at that moment, Groves' responses fascinated him far more. Unluckily for Groves, nothing was evading Deans' attention.

He had only just met him but a number of factors already niggled Deans about Groves. Why had he been so hard to contact? Why did not he report his own girlfriend missing, and why was he being so edgy?

To start the interview with anything too heavy would undoubtedly make Groves unreceptive and that would do no good for either of them. Deans needed to earn some trust. He needed common ground, and he found it in the shape of rugby.

Deans was a life-long Bath rugby fan and had played rugby himself for many years, before too many injuries swung the balance towards common sense and the need to acknowledge that he was getting older. Groves was a physically imposing lad and happened to be wearing a Minerva University rugby-training top.

'So, I see you're wearing a drill top. What are you, Centre, fullback?'

For the first time Groves looked at Deans for more than a second or two, and after a short delay replied, 'Fullback.'

'I guess you're either good with the boot, in defence or a pretty handy runner?'

Groves squinted and tilted his head. 'All of the above, I guess.' This time he did not look away.

Deans grasped the connection.

'I bet you're the last person the oppo want to see hurtling towards them. You're a pretty big unit.'

Groves nodded, looked Deans up and down. 'I look after the boys.'

He was now not only facing Deans square on, but had also leant very slightly towards him, engaging in the conversation.

'So how many tries have you scored over the past few seasons?' Deans asked.

Groves' eyes almost smiled as they darted up to his left.

He did not answer immediately but Deans was not about to say anything else until Groves next spoke.

'This season's only just got started, so none, yet. Last season I had… fifteen, and the season before twelve or thirteen, I think.' He stared directly at Deans for the longest time in their brief contact. He was seeking approval and recognition.

Deans indulged him. 'Good stuff, mate. That's pretty impressive.'

'Plus, something around three hundred points with the boot.'

Groves' head was now tilting slightly backwards, exposing

more of his throat. He was clearly feeling increasingly confident.

Test over.

'Tell me about last Friday with Amy.'

Groves immediately lowered his head and looked anywhere but at Deans, who waited until the next eye contact.

'Go on.'

'Like what?'

'How about how things were left with Amy?'

'We were fine. She was off to see her family.'

Groves had placed a gentle emphasis on the word 'family', which did not evade Deans' attention.

'Family?' he mirrored.

'In Devon.'

As Groves spoke, he looked down at the table and simultaneously scratched the side of his neck.

Deans made a mental note, some kind of issue with the family. Alternatively, with Devon, or with Amy going away to Devon. He scribbled *Devon* in his daybook and circled it.

'Ever been there yourself?'

Groves rubbed his nose, partially covering his mouth as he gave his answer. 'No.'

Deans allowed a pregnant pause to do some work for him, covering his own mouth with the back of his hand, not once breaking his focus away from Groves.

Groves sneaked eye contact once again and stirred in his seat. The silence was getting to him. Deans counted to seven slowly in his head.

'Tell me about the last time you saw Amy.'

Groves' eyes darted around the tabletop, and Deans noticed his right hand was squeezing the fingers of his other hand.

Interesting, Deans thought.

'I dropped her home after uni,' Groves said, finally.

'Any arrangements?'

'Um.' He blinked rapidly. 'She said to meet up at uni on Monday.'

'Any contact since then?'

'No. I haven't had any contact since then.'

Groves' response was robotic.

'What did Amy say she would be doing over the weekend?'

Groves dropped his head once more and imperceptibly rocked left and right in his chair.

'She didn't,' he replied, quietly.

'Did Amy say who she would be meeting up with in Devon apart from her parents?'

'No.'

Deans leant back in his chair, slid his daybook onto his lap and took his time to write something inside. He stared at the page.

'Tell me, Carl, what have you done to find out where Amy is?'

'Well, I'm here, aren't I?' Groves snarled, displaying a previously restrained hostility.

Deans grinned and then looked up. 'You are indeed.'

Groves turned away.

'Does Amy have a car?' Deans asked. He of course already knew the answer but he needed a soft way in to his next real question.

'Yeah – course,' Groves hissed, screwing up his face.

'What is it?'

'Beetle.'

'Cool. What colour?'

Groves curled his upper lip. 'Yellow.'

'Thank you, Carl. Ever been in it?'

'Course.'

'Where is it now?'

Groves turned sideways and scratched the back of his neck.

'I guess it's where she left it.'

'Any ideas where?' Deans was watching him closely.

'I guess it's at her parents'.'

There was so much Groves was not saying, but was it enough to think there was anything sinister about him? Deans pondered it a while, creating another uncomfortable silence. Intrigued by a couple of the answers, he doodled in his daybook.

The repeated use of 'I guess' was a nothing answer. Flippant, juvenile even. Not 'I don't know' or 'I can't answer that because I haven't seen it since Friday', but 'I guess'. Then there was the repeat to the question, 'Any contact since then?' Groves' answer: 'No, I haven't had any contact since then.' Not simply 'No', which would have been the easiest and quickest way to answer. Instead, he chose to repeat the question. Was that because responding parrot-fashion saved him from admitting to the truth? Whatever truth that might be?

Deans mulled it over, his pen tapping his book as if he was tattooing the page. Was Groves' slippery disposition enough to have him nicked? Moreover, for what offence? After all, this was only a MISPER enquiry.

'I'm almost finished, Carl, for now. Jess – you know Jess don't you?'

Groves nodded, looked Deans up and Down.

'Well, Jess mentioned that she thought you'd given Amy a lift home from uni.'

'Yeah, I already said that,' Groves said cuttingly.

'Ah, yes,' Deans said, looking into his book. 'My mistake. What car do you have?'

46

Groves backed up, just a fraction, but enough to display that he was growing increasingly wary.

'Saxo.'

'What colour?'

'Orange.'

'Standard-looking orange Citroen Saxo?'

'Yeah,' Groves said, his beady eyes giving away his own questioning mind.

'Good,' Deans said, closing his daybook with a dull thud. 'Well, thank you, Carl. Unless you've any questions for me, I think we're done here today.'

Deans did not ask for the registration number of the Saxo. He did not need to, he had already seen a vehicle report on the intelligence database. He could get all the information he needed from that.

Groves did not have any questions, stood up, and made for the door handle when Deans dropped in the all-important question.

'So, Carl. Where do you think Amy is?'

It stopped Groves in his tracks. He turned and neatly placed his chair tightly under the desk.

'Beats me.'

'Just before you go then,' Deans said, 'I think to be thorough, as neither of us knows where Amy is, I'll complete a statement from my notes. But I need you to understand that any formal evidence you provide needs to be the truth and if you knowingly make a false declaration you could be prosecuted or even end up in prison.' Deans smiled broadly. 'Is that all right?'

Groves did just enough to nod.

'So, shall I catch up with you again tomorrow with a typed statement?'

Groves nodded again and let himself out of the room.

CHAPTER EIGHT

Deans watched Groves leave the building, then made his way quickly up to the office and looked out of the window to the council car park below. It was dark outside but the domed streetlamps did a reasonable job of lighting up the parking bays.

Headlight beams in the far corner grabbed his attention. A vehicle was coming up the ramp. He tracked the car and as it passed below his window, he confirmed it was an orange Citroen Saxo, complete with black bonnet. He also noticed two yellow stickers on either side of the windscreen and a familiar Bath rugby club sticker on the back window. Although he could not see Groves from this angle, he had no doubt this was his car.

The office was empty. The clock on the wall showed 9:10 p.m. A Post-it on his computer screen informed him of two missed calls from Janet Poole.

He took a deep breath, held the phone to his ear and dialled the number.

'Hello,' she answered after the first ring.

'Hello, Mrs Poole?'

'Yes,' she replied hurriedly.

'Mrs Poole, this is DC Deans. I am very sorry for the lateness of the call. Is it convenient to speak?'

'Yes. Do you have some news?' Her voice was brittle.

'No… I'm afraid there's no update. I'm sorry I missed your calls. Was there something specific I can help—'

'Have you spoken to Scotty?'

'Scotty?'

'Amy was meeting Scotty on Saturday night.'

Deans sat upright. 'No. Who is Scotty?'

'Amy's best friend.'

'Do you know where they were meeting?' he said, turning over a fresh page.

'Um, Torworthy, I assume.'

Deans scribbled *Torworthy* in his daybook.

'And Scotty's last name, please?'

'Parsons. Scott Parsons.'

Deans wrote the name in capitals further down the page and circled it several times.

'And his address?'

'Oh, I'm afraid I don't know. He moved, but is still in the area.'

'Phone number?'

'Sorry.'

Deans circled his name a few more times.

'Can you think of anyone else who may know his address or contact number?'

'Sorry.' There was a pause.

'Don't worry, Mrs Poole. There are other ways I can find out.'

She did not answer.

'Am I right in thinking Amy drives a yellow VW Beetle?'

'Yes.'

'Do you happen to know the registration number?'

'Oh, gosh! Um... I'm sure I could have it for you tomorrow.'

Deans hoped he could short cut the process by striking lucky on the Intel database.

'Would you happen to know if Amy's car is still parked at the house?'

'Oh, no, it wouldn't be at the house as we only have a small driveway. Amy usually parks on the road at the front.'

'Thank you, Mrs Poole. I'm unfamiliar with the area. If I requested a local officer to attend that road, do you think Amy's car would be easy to locate?'

'Oh, yes. Parking is only allowed on one side because the road is so narrow.'

Deans' mind drifted and he imagined Amy's Beetle neatly parked beside a slim pavement in front of a row of semi-detached houses.

Amy's car might present a forensic Nirvana: traces of blood, semen or other bodily fluids. Maybe signs of a struggle or fight. Foreign fibres of clothing. Even a body in the boot, although that would be unlikely – the local critters would be paying more than a passing interest after this number of days.

'Do you know if there are any spare car keys at the house?'

'I'm afraid I don't know, but Amy would normally hang her keys from the hook in the hallway.'

Deans nodded knowingly. That was standard practice for people inexperienced at home security. He had lost count of the number of burglaries he had attended over the years that also involved the vehicles being taken because the keys were readily available.

'Okay, Mrs Poole, I think I've troubled you enough for tonight. Thank you for your help. Would you mind if I contact you again in the morning, please?'

'No. That is absolutely fine. We're returning home very early tomorrow morning, but you can still contact me in the night if you hear anything.'

'I'm very grateful.' He paused. 'Have you managed to get any rest yourself, Mrs Poole?'

'Oh, I shall probably fall asleep at some point later. It will no doubt sound rather silly to you, but I don't want to sleep, in case Amy tries to call me. I wouldn't want to miss her.'

'That doesn't sound silly at all. I understand.'

Deans pictured Mrs Poole waiting beside the phone, longing for it to ring. It would be a scene of utter torture.

'Well, goodnight, Mrs Poole.'

'Goodnight. And thank you for everything you're doing to find my little girl.'

'You are most welcome, Mrs Poole. Take care.'

Deans replaced the receiver gently, kept his hand on the phone and stared right through it.

He blinked and broke away. Despite the late hour, Deans made a coffee. He did not need caffeine. It was part of working long and late shifts.

He pulled on a pair of blue vinyl gloves and removed Amy's diary from the forensic bag. He was being cautious – could not afford any cross-contamination if this exhibit was required for analysis at some point in the future.

The diary was the current year, too large for a pocket, but just right for a handbag. He took a long gulp from his mug and stared at the plain purple cover before opening it up.

Seeking out the current date, he flicked the pages back to the week Amy disappeared. He was in luck – there were entries. Friday showed *M&D* with an arrow passing through Saturday and into Sunday – Mum and Dad, presumably. Saturday also showed *Scotty*.

He made a note and looked at the other entries. Wednesday

showed *Carl Rugby* and there were other references to university, he guessed. Deans continued looking backwards through the pages; more references to Carl, and another that puzzled him; *DM*, shown several times that month, the most recent being Saturday 27th of September, between two and three p.m.

He pondered the initials as he emptied his mug, and followed the DM trail back to the middle of summer where it appeared to start. He checked his notes. There had been eleven DMs – mostly, but not exclusively at weekends.

'DM,' Deans breathed.

There were two impending DMs, one next Saturday, and the Saturday after. He chewed his lip and glanced at the clock.

'Shit,' he shouted. He had not realised the time, and he had not contacted his wife to say he would be home late. He hoped she would understand, and understand again tomorrow.

CHAPTER NINE

Amy had the best of both worlds. She was a student living away from home, enjoying the independence that brought, but also close enough to be able to drive home and back in a weekend. So many of her university friends were less fortunate.

She had called Mum the previous Wednesday night for their usual midweek catch-up and mentioned that she would be down again at the weekend.

The North Devon coastline had been a fantastic place for a child's upbringing. Some of Amy's friends found it all a bit too boring, but from a young age, she had taken advantage of the environment and had become a competent surfer. It was during those early teen years that she first became close to Scotty. He was the same age and lived nearby. They would meet up most days, and more often than not, would end up on the beach. The more time they spent in each other's company, the more they wanted to be together, and it was not long before their friendship grew into a closer bond that developed further with age and intimacy. By the time they were young adults they both expressed openly their love for each other.

Unfortunately, the bubble of young love burst for Scotty

when Amy received her placement at university. Even before the first academic year was over, Scotty said that he could not continue the relationship while she was away from him. Amy was devastated, but he maintained it was the only way to manage his emptiness.

As a result, Amy deliberately limited her home visits during that first year, which hurt her more than she was willing to express. She wanted to see more of Mum and Dad. She wanted to see more of Scotty but had to accept and understand his pain, but she was bitter. After all, the relationship was not just about him.

Over the recent summer break, Amy had forged reconciliation with Scotty, and they had spent good time together. Amy still loved him, and their regenerated harmony provided her with inner warmth that had been missing for too long.

Three weeks before her return to university, Amy invited Scotty to the house. It was time he knew about Carl.

Mum and Dad were downstairs when Scotty arrived. Amy had been in her room, enacting the scene, preparing her lines.

'Amy. Scotty's here,' Mum shouted up the stairs.

'Okay.' Amy swept her hair back and tied it with a band. 'Oh God,' she mumbled as his footsteps clunked louder on the wooden steps. She smoothed down her clothing and waited for the door to open.

'Ames?' Scotty said from behind the door.

Amy drew breath as the door opened inwards and the moment she saw Scotty she thrust herself into his arms, almost knocking a frothing beer bottle from his hand.

'What's up with you tonight?' he asked.

Amy squeezed a little tighter.

'I only saw you yesterday,' he said chuckling.

Amy released her grasp, sat on the edge of the bed, and

hugged a large pillow, as she used to do when they were teenagers.

'Come on Ames, what's up?'

'Um, there's something I need to talk to you about,' she muttered into the material.

'Ames?'

'Don't rush me, Scotty. I need... I need to tell you something.'

Scotty stopped smiling.

Despite her preparation, this was proving tougher than she had anticipated.

'I'm truly sorry, Scotty...' She paused and tears welled in her eyes.

Scotty snatched at his breath.

Amy met his fixed stare and her stomach heaved as her voice surrendered to the truth.

'I... I've been seeing someone at uni.' She turned away; could not bear to see his reaction.

Stillness beset the room.

Amy found the courage to open her eyes and gradually lifted her head.

Scotty's expression said everything; maybe more than any words he could have spoken. She had just broken his heart and the wave of guilt was overpowering.

She did not know how long they both remained in that acrid silence before he placed his beer on the bedside cabinet and walked out of the door without saying another word.

Saturday night was to be their first meeting since that evening. Amy needed to finish her conversation, end her torment and tell Scotty in person that her relationship with Carl was not serious, and she was going to end it, for him.

CHAPTER TEN

Deans was a conscientious and sensitive man. This job bothered him. The phone call to Mrs Poole had bothered him. Groves bothered him and the fact that ninety-six hours had passed without progress seriously bothered him.

Maria was barely speaking to him at breakfast. He appreciated that working all those hours was affecting their relationship and at times recently, it felt they were bound by a pressure cooker. Lack of sleep was a major issue. When he got the chance to – he couldn't, and when he wanted to – he was working.

He watched her spoon in her cornflakes without looking back at him. She looked worn out, her hair dishevelled. At times like these, he almost resented being a detective.

He ran a hand through his long, dark hair and his fingertips lingered on the ridge of the partially hidden, scythe-shaped scar behind his left ear – his souvenir from a night that was to become the catalyst for a career as a detective. It was like pressing a replay button, but this repeat was one that he had battled for a decade to forget.

• • •

Echo control. Any mobile units, please? Arthur Street, fight in progress. The voice of comms broke the monotonous sound of Deans' squad car engine. He had just entered into Milsom Street, he was seconds away and jumped at the chance to see some action.

'Echo Six-three, solo crewed.' Although it was approaching 2:30 a.m., and the streets were all but deserted, he put on the strobes, and floored the accelerator.

Thank you, six-three. Update from the informant; multiple groups of males now fighting in the street. Any other units to back-up six-three, please?

Deans sucked in, wished he had been less hasty to volunteer and activated the sirens. They should hear him coming from this distance and he hoped it would disperse at least some of the shit-bags.

Echo Six-one, making ground from Newbridge, the response from Deans' colleagues came over the wailing sound of their own sirens.

Six-two, from Odd Down.

His back-up was travelling from the extremities of the city. That meant Deans was going to be on his own for at least the next few minutes.

'CCTV please,' Deans requested urgently. He guessed the disorder would be somewhere between The Mint Club and the late-night takeaway, and consequently under the watchful eye of the cameras.

As the road widened onto Arthur Street and the needle hit fifty, he saw the chaotic situation spread over an unmanageable distance on the right hand pavement – three, possibly four separate fighting groups.

'Fuck!' Deans said drawing breath. 'Six-three, on scene.' His pulse raced as he decided where to position his vehicle.

Roger. Early update please, six-three.

'Priority,' Deans bellowed, as he watched one prone male on the pavement surrounded by a group, having his head jumped upon as if he was a bouncy castle. 'Urgent assistance required.'

Roger. Units are making to your location, came the calm voice of comms.

Deans brought the car to a rapid halt, but kept the sirens howling – that way the offenders might not immediately twig that he was alone.

Deans fumbled for his CS canister amongst his stab vest attachments, and then noticed Jordan Finch standing over another horizontal male. Finch was a nineteen-year-old bag of skin and bones, but he was a nasty bastard with a liking for knives, probably to make up for his lack of physical presence.

Deans had to make a snap-decision. He looked over at the bouncy castle male. He was not moving, and the others were still working it into him.

Deans sprinted beyond one fighting faction, and as he neared the stamping group, he gave up trying to pull out his CS and hurled himself towards them with wide swinging arms, taking at least two of them out as he came to a sprawling halt on the damp pavement. He could only hope that CCTV was watching and recording everything that was unfolding.

It took a second to gain his orientation and as he lifted his upper body from the floor, he looked over his shoulder. The victim on the ground was no longer surrounded. A startling blow to the back of his head forced Deans to the ground. He instinctively rolled away and up to his knees, just as a swinging leg caught him square in the chest forcing him to rock onto the back of his heels. He activated the emergency button on his Airwave radio and the faint sound of approaching sirens temporarily lifted his spirits, but as he brought himself up to his haunches, still suffering blows from all sides, he then heard a familiar, animated voice above the chaos. It was Finch.

'Let's do the cunt, come on. Come on, let's do the fucking pig.'

Deans looked up to where the voice was coming from and saw Finch, with hatred in his eyes, bounding towards him, prodding a broken wine bottle in Deans' direction.

The police vehicles were growing louder from both sides, but another knee to the head felled Deans like a sick oak tree. In desperation, he tried to raise himself to his feet, but an impossibly heavy weight pinned him down from behind. He scraped his nose on the paving slab to search for Finch, and found him standing right beside him. Deans buried his face into the concrete, but felt no pain, as at that precise moment, Finch plunged the jagged wine bottle into the back of Deans' head.

Deans was already unconscious by the time his teammates arrived. He awoke with a crescent of medical staff and bosses around his bedside. The job had been great, not only to him, but also to Maria. His physical recovery took a few months, but the mental healing – much longer. He had managed to avoid viewing the CCTV until the cold-blooded brutality of Finch was dissected in painstaking detail at the trial. It was soon after that Mick Savage approached Deans to join his team, on the basis that he passed the selection criteria. Maria had wept at the thought of Deans escaping the frontline, and that was all he needed to drive him on to succeed.

Looking across the table now at Maria he realised how fortunate he was. She was a good woman. He knew she was not happy with the time he spent at work but she would never force ultimatums upon him. They had often discussed where they would live when he retired. It gave them hope, albeit temporarily, as he still had nine years of service to go before he could draw his thirty-year pension.

Deans noticed Maria wiping her eyes.

'Hey, what's up?'

She shook her head and trailed strands of her long dark hair through her milky bowl.

He pushed back his chair, knelt beside her and put his arm around her shoulders. 'Come on, sweetheart.'

'Sam's pregnant.' Maria looked at Deans, her eyes red and desperate.

He waited fifteen, maybe twenty seconds. 'Work Sam?'

Maria bobbed her head.

'Well… that's great news.' He did his best to sound as disarming as possible.

'They've only been married for seven months,' she whimpered.

Deans dropped his head, closed his eyes and clenched his teeth

'Six years.'

'I know, Maria'

'Six years, Andy. If someone else tells me not to leave it too long, I'll bloody blow. "You're not getting any younger",' Maria mimicked, 'Oh can't you just all fuck off.'

'They don't know the score…' Deans stopped himself. '… I'm pleased for Sam. She's a nice girl.'

'I know, and that's what makes it harder. I should be delighted for her, but instead… well, it only highlights my own failure.'

'You're not a failure, Maria,' Deans said quickly. 'Remember we're in this together. It will happen. We're good people.'

'Oh come on, Andy. You know better than anyone, that's utter bollocks.'

He did. Experience had proved that repeatedly.

'Look, I need to run.' He gave Maria a kiss on the cheek. 'You try to keep positive. We've done everything we can. We're going to know ourselves in less than a week.'

She nodded and reached for his hand.

'I don't know when I'll be back. I have to travel to Devon today.' He squeezed her hand, but she was already letting go.

Deans made his way to work with leaden feet. He wanted to do something nice for Maria, but it would be another full set of shifts before his next complete weekend off.

He arrived at the office and immediately obtained authorisation from the DI to make enquiries in Devon.

The missing person report originated in Bath and so it would remain a Bath enquiry, although technically, her mother in Devon last saw Amy. The Police National Computer had not provided Deans with any answers regarding Scott Parsons – he was no trace, so given the circumstances, the DI allowed a degree of licence with the proviso that Deans inform the CID in Devon of his intentions.

Deans gathered up his kit and checked out the location on Google Maps. He could be there for around eleven thirty, traffic permitting. He had arranged for a colleague to take Groves' statement for signing, and bagged himself one of the unmarked pool-cars. It was a burgundy Ford Focus, which might as well have had *CID* printed along the side for all its conspicuousness. To the regular 'customers', as the bosses liked them to be called, the unmarked cars were just as noticeable as the brightly adorned response vehicles, which was frustrating to say the least during covert operations.

. . .

The journey lasted just short of three hours, most of which felt as if it had been taken up by the North Devon link road with its forty-something miles of endless undulating, tree-lined roads, remote moors and wide open spaces.

Finally, a large bridge appeared before him and beneath, he saw a wide, glistening estuary drenched in sunshine. Dozens of small white craft bobbed on the waters below and the tightness in his shoulders softened noticeably.

According to the satnav, the Pooles' house was not far away and he approached with anxious anticipation.

He drove slowly up a narrow incline, the estuary in view to his right, beyond the stepped rooftops of the closely packed, whitewashed houses of the village. Cars parked in a line, leaving just enough space to pass. A high stone wall on his left extended ahead with a small void breaking the continuity of this old-looking, solid structure.

The satnav repeated, 'You have reached your destination' in a female American voice, so he continued up the hill and finally found a space to park. He gathered up his papers and his thoughts and made his way back along the high wall, gazing all the while towards the estuary.

A nameplate on a six-foot high wooden gate spanning the void in the wall showed him he had arrived at the Poole residence, Tradewinds. He stretched his back, rolled his neck, and then noticed a yellow Beetle just a short distance away, sandwiched between a Campervan and a Land Rover. He approached it and peered inside but there was nothing obvious to get excited about. He tugged on the door handles but they were secure. At least he could scrub that one thing off the list.

He returned to the gate and climbed the fifteen or so slate

steps that opened out onto a decorative stone pathway and well-kept lawns. The size of the house surprised him. He was not expecting to see such an imposing property. Amy clearly came from money and he wondered what was waiting for him behind the grey stone walls and church-like wooden front door.

A large black cast-iron knocker signalled his arrival and he waited pensively for a reply.

A man with salt-and-pepper hair opened the door. 'Hello,' he said with a hollow voice. He appeared washed out and pained.

'Mr Poole?' Deans asked.

'Yes,' he replied as if apologising for the fact.

'I'm DC Deans. I have been speaking with you and your wife about Amy. I wonder if I could discuss the matter further with you both. Is Mrs Poole around?'

At that, Mrs Poole came into view from behind her husband. 'Please come in. Ian, let the officer through.'

Mr Poole seemed trancelike, vacant and dim. He dutifully moved to the side allowing Deans to enter.

'I was expecting a phone call from you rather than a personal visit,' Mrs Poole said, straightening a slumped umbrella beside the door.

'I've other enquiries in the area and I wanted to be more than just a voice on the end of a phone.' Deans shook both their hands in turn. 'I'm so sorry that we're meeting under these circumstances.'

Mr Poole shuffled off into a side room and Mrs Poole smiled fleetingly then guided Deans in the direction that her husband had just gone. They entered a living room and as Deans gaped out through a vast panoramic window, he suddenly appreciated the full extent of the outlook. Being a city lad, he was not used to seeing the coastline and he became temporarily distracted.

'It's a special view,' Mrs Poole said.

'I'm so sorry,' Deans replied quickly, turning back towards them. 'Yes, yes, it is. You're very lucky to live here.'

Neither of them answered.

They all took a seat, Mr and Mrs Poole together on the sofa and Deans on a single chair that was further away from them than he would have liked.

Deans half-smiled awkwardly, and then began.

'I'm the officer in the case for Amy's disappearance, and responsible for the overall missing person investigation, even though I'm based in Bath.'

Both faces stared blankly at him.

'I'm involved because the original report was made in Bath, so the investigation remains with us, although I'll be liaising with local officers here.' He stopped to allow an opportunity for any questions. There were none.

'As well as formally introducing myself to you today, I'd like to ask you some questions about Amy, if that's okay?'

Mr Poole did not respond but Mrs Poole nodded compliantly and said, 'Yes, of course.'

'I take it that you've had no further contact from Amy since we last spoke?'

'No,' Mrs Poole said softly.

'How often would you normally expect to hear from Amy?'

'I wasn't expecting to hear from her until yesterday evening,' Mrs Poole said, glancing over to her husband. 'That's why we had no idea she had gone missing.'

Deans imagined they were both feeling an element of guilt for not knowing Amy was missing.

'Please, don't think that you could've done anything differently to avoid this situation.'

Mrs Poole acknowledged the gesture with a subtle nod of the head. 'Thank you.' Mr Poole did not move.

'Tell me more about Scott Parsons.'

'Well, he's a lovely boy,' Mrs Poole replied. 'They used to be an item actually, for many years.' She paused and looked towards her husband again. 'Long-distance relationships rarely work in my experience, and it wasn't doing either of them any good.'

'He hasn't tried to contact you?'

Mrs Poole leant forward, and gripped her knees. 'No. Do you think he should have?'

'I don't know,' Deans replied. 'I'm just trying to gather all the information I possibly can at the moment, Mrs Poole.'

Truth was, he thought it was strange Scotty had not shown any concern given his alleged closeness to Amy. Unless he did not know she was missing either.

'Would Amy have met up with anyone else while she was down in Devon?'

Mrs Poole shrugged. 'No, I don't think so. She has many other friends but I wasn't aware that she intended meeting anyone specifically, other than Scotty, of course.'

'I noticed a yellow Beetle out on the road. Is that Amy's?'

'Yes,' she replied.

Deans detected that Mrs Poole was becoming distracted.

'Mrs Poole, would it be possible to see Amy's bedroom, please?'

'Yes, of course. I've already looked around it, I hope that's okay?'

'Of course, Mrs Poole.'

She raised herself up from the sofa but Mr Poole remained seated. Deans stood up simultaneously and followed her upstairs to the first floor and a closed door.

Deans pulled on a pair of vinyl gloves and noticed alarm in Mrs Poole's face.

'Standard practice,' he said in a reassuring tone.

Mrs Poole turned the handle, opening the door a fraction and then moved to the side allowing Deans to do the rest. It was a large, pristine bedroom with views to the front of the house and an en suite stone-tiled wet room. Deans had always wanted a wet room himself but Maria was less keen, so that meant they did not have one.

It was far bigger than his own bedroom and contained expensive-looking furniture. Framed photographs were dotted around. One caught his eye on the bedside cabinet. It showed Amy with a male of around her age and both looked very happy. Probably taken several years before, going by the picture Jessica had shown him. They were both wearing beach gear and looked well suited. He was a handsome-looking lad, and the position of the photograph in relation to others in the room suggested he must have been special to Amy.

'Amy and Scotty,' Mrs Poole said. 'Taken at Sandymere Bay.'

Deans answered only with a nod and a smile but he was taking everything in. A daypack buried beneath an untidy pile of clothing in the corner of the room caught his attention.

'May I look inside?' Deans asked, exposing the bag.

'Yes, of course. Oh my, it looks like Amy's university bag.' Mrs Poole held her hand to her mouth as Deans bent down beside the bag and unzipped the main compartment. He removed several law books and then found Amy's student ID attached to an O'Neill lanyard. He looked closely at the badge. It was current.

'Is it okay to take a look in the bathroom?'

Mrs Poole followed Deans into the en suite. He took a quick glance around, and then saw what he was after: Amy's toothbrush and a hairbrush. He also saw a wash bag containing various other makeup and toiletry items, and a medicine box. He picked it up and saw that it was the gabapentin. Inside he discovered seven complete blister strips of ten small, white pills, plus four others. He checked the prescription label – 26th September. A hundred capsules dispensed. Three per day, twenty-one per week. Twenty-six missing from the box. He performed a quiet calculation in his head. That would take them up to the night Amy went missing, unless she had others in reserve.

He cleared his throat and pointed to the toiletries and brushes. 'Do you mind if I keep these all together and take them away with the bag? Amy will probably need them when she returns to university.'

'Yes, yes, of course, please do,' Mrs Poole willingly obliged.

It was devious but given the state of Mrs Poole's emotions, he did not feel it appropriate at this stage to explain that both brushes could be rich sources of Amy's DNA.

Having spent almost two hours with the Pooles, Deans concluded that he liked them very much and genuinely felt for them. They were a likeable couple and he imagined Amy would be no different.

'Just before I go,' he said, as they said their goodbyes, 'I found a diary in Amy's bedroom in Bath. There are references to a DM. You wouldn't happen to know what or who that could be?'

Mrs Poole put her hand to her face and looked puzzled for a while. She did not ask her husband.

'I think it could be something she does whilst she is here, looking at the dates in the diary,' Deans said. 'Could it be something she was doing for a hobby, or part of her coursework?'

'How about Denise?' Mr Poole suggested in a downcast voice.

They both stopped and looked over at him.

'Denise?' Deans mirrored. Mirroring was usually an effective technique of obtaining more information without having to ask for it. This was more than appropriate in Mr Poole's case.

Instead, Mrs Poole once again resumed conversation duties. 'Denise. Yes. She has been helping Amy with her coursework. I believe her surname is Moon. Yes, there we go. DM.' She took a step towards her husband and touched the back of his hand. He did not respond.

'Okay,' Deans said, 'how does Denise Moon help Amy?'

'She's a medium or something,' Mrs Poole said, apologising for her husband with her eyes. 'I don't understand what they do. I know Amy has been working on the suggestion that mediums can help the police with their investigations. It was all part of her thesis.'

Deans had certainly never experienced such involvement at first hand, and as far as he knew, it was something fabricated for TV entertainment.

'Interesting,' he said, trying not to sound dismissive. 'What do you know about this woman, Denise Moon?'

'She has a shop in town and I think Amy sees her there. They get along rather well, evidently. I know Amy was enjoying their meetings.'

'Is Amy into all that mystical, fortune-telling stuff?' Deans asked.

'No, it's not like that at all,' Mrs Poole said defensively. 'Denise is a therapist. She helps people. She's not some fairground attraction.'

'I'm sorry, I meant no disrespect. I'm ignorant on such matters.'

Deans noticed Mr Poole nodding.

'Would you happen to know where I can find the shop?'

'I haven't been in there myself,' Mrs Poole replied, 'but I know it's off the High Street, behind the bank. There is a small walkway leading away from the cashpoint. Follow that and you'll eventually come to it.'

Satisfied that he had covered all angles, Deans left the Pooles, glad that he had been given an opportunity to spend valuable time with them. Their grief was palpable and he felt happier that some much-needed bridge building had taken place between them.

Back inside his car, he studied the notes he had made in his book. He turned over to a blank page and drew two large circles, one above the other. Inside the top circle, he wrote *Scott Parsons* and inside the second, he wrote *Denise Moon*.

CHAPTER ELEVEN

A glance at his watch only confirmed to Deans that time was pressing. Desperate for caffeine, he found a homely-looking coffee shop on the quayside. The Pooles had been lovely company but understandably a little lax on the hospitality stakes. He ordered a double shot espresso and a door-wedge piece of homemade flapjack from the young server, and sat at a small round table at the back of the room, which was something he subconsciously always did. Maybe all cops did the same. It was better to know who was around you than not, although here he knew no one and no one knew him.

It always amused Deans that, no matter where he was, the local shit-bags would sense he was a cop. Some would give a little nod of recognition or a toothy grin. Their way of saying, *I know what you are*. It was a strange occurrence, but then again, he could tell they were shit-bags, so it was fair game.

In this town, specifically in this little coffee house, Deans must have stood out like a sore thumb dressed in his grey pinstriped suit, salmon-pink shirt and matching tie, however the espresso tasted good, and he savoured the bitterness with two full gulps, then opened his daybook and read over his notes. It was already his intention to track down Scott Parsons, but now he had generated an additional enquiry: to locate and interview Denise Moon.

He picked at the remaining crumbs from his flapjack and with a smile handed the empties back to the server as he left.

Fifteen minutes later, he was standing outside of Rayon Vert Therapy and Treatment Studio, on the backstreets of Torworthy town centre.

He had never given the idea of mediums any thought before and now he was about to speak to one. He did not know what to expect and struggled to rid his mind of the classic image of an older woman with a silk bandana and crazy eyes.

'If only the guys could see me now,' he muttered beneath his breath, pushing at the small entrance door, and stepping inside.

He was surprised to be greeted by a man in black spectacles that were too large for his head, seated behind a narrow stone counter top.

'May I help you, sir?' the man asked gently.

'I'm looking for Denise Moon,' Deans said, wondering if Dennis Moon was more accurate.

'She's with a client at the moment.'

The man had a deadpan look and said no more.

After an awkward delay, Deans asked, 'Do you happen to know how long she'll be?'

'Have you made an appointment, sir?'

'No,' Deans chuckled, and then cleared his throat. 'No, no, I haven't.'

The man watched Deans with a humourless, poker-faced expression.

God, he is one intense cookie, Deans thought. He whistled a muted tune and looked around the room.

The man's eyes were still upon him.

'I'm sorry,' Deans said. 'I'm Detective Constable Andrew Deans. I need to speak to Ms Moon about a police matter.'

The man looked over his right shoulder towards a closed door, and then turned his focus back on Deans.

'I tell you what,' Deans said. 'I'll sit down here and wait until she's free. I'm doing fine for time,' he lied. It was getting late and he still had lots to do.

As Deans bided his time, he noticed a small CCTV camera positioned in the corner of the wall behind the counter, pointing towards the front door. It looked real enough but could easily be a dummy, which was exactly how Deans was feeling right then. This place was certainly out of his comfort zone.

Eco-warrior music played softly in the background, and glass shelving displayed exotic-looking crystals and stones as if they meant something. To him they were just curious rocks. He looked closer. Each one had a black label with gold hand-writing describing the stone's powers and the price. 'Jesus,' he whispered. Eighty-five quid for a small black pebble.

Deans shook his head at the desperation people must feel to spend so much money, and the exploitative ways in which some were willing to cash in on the vulnerabilities of others.

After twenty more minutes of awkward silence, the rear door opened and a pretty, young woman full of verve and smiles entered the room. Deans sat up straight and adjusted his tie. She noticed him and smiled pleasantly back. Deans was about to ask if she was Denise when another woman walked in behind her. Denise Moon, he presumed.

She was not as he had expected. In her late forties, with long dark hair, pale skin and a friendly, almost familiar face.

Although she was still quite young, she was mumsy at the same time.

The smiling woman paid with a card and left the shop, announcing that she would return next week. Deans looked over to the man, expecting him to relay his message, but instead he said nothing and remained seated behind the counter. Needing to take the initiative once again, Deans stood up.

'Hello,' he said, 'Denise Moon?'

'Yes. Hello. How may I help you?' She was holding out her hand to shake. Deans noticed that she had near-flawless skin. She was naturally attractive with large, brown intelligent eyes. A black, sparkly stone around her neck on a long slender chain caught his eye, and he wondered what it was. He could only imagine how much it would cost going by the prices of the other pebbles on display.

'Hello,' he said again, taking her outstretched hand. 'I'm Detective Constable Andrew Deans. I was wondering if I could trouble you for a short while. You may be able to help me with an investigation I'm conducting.'

She had a look of surprise. 'Yes, of course.' She turned to the man behind the counter. 'How's the diary looking, Ash?'

'Next appointment in fifteen minutes,' he replied, without taking his eyes away from Deans.

Denise smiled warmly and welcomed Deans through to the back. He followed her into a low-arched hallway and through to a room similar in appearance to a spa salon. There was a treatment bed in the centre, leather seating was against one wall and peaceful music playing in the background.

'I do hope you haven't been waiting long, Detective?' she asked. 'I'm afraid Ash can be a little protective of my schedule.'

'No, no, not at all,' he lied again and she gave him a knowing smile. 'Please, call me Andy,' he said.

'How may I be of assistance to you?'

'Do you know a Miss Amy Poole?'

'Yes, I do,' Denise replied without hesitation. 'She is a wonderful girl and extremely bright. I have been helping her with some work. She's interested in the power of mediumship.'

Ms Moon was clearly skilled in non-verbal communication and subtly encouraged Deans to expand.

'I'm afraid Amy is missing,' he reciprocated.

She half-stepped backwards and covered her mouth. 'Oh my God! Since when?'

'Saturday last week. I am trying to trace her movements to establish where she may be or whom she may be with. I found a diary with what I believe to be your initials beside certain dates and I'd just like to check these out and ask you about Amy.'

'Yes, of course. Poor Amy.' She waved towards the sofa. 'Her family must be beside themselves. Yes, of course, I'll help you all I can.'

'Thank you. When did you last see Amy?'

'Would you excuse me a moment while I get the diary from outside? I know it was sometime within the last few weeks but I'm not sure when exactly.'

'Of course.'

As Denise left, Deans studied the room.

She returned carrying a desk diary and started to flick through the pages.

'Tuesday, three weeks ago,' she said. 'That's right; we had a quick thirty-minute session.'

'What exactly would you do with Amy?'

'Well, just talk really. Amy has a very sensitive soul and the potential to develop the gift. We mostly discuss her thesis. And how she can harness the gift to enrich her life. She's an excellent student and a pleasure to be around.'

'The gift?' Deans mirrored.

Denise smiled. 'How long do you have, Detective? Your fifteen minutes wouldn't begin to scratch the surface even if I tried to explain.'

Deans liked Denise. He felt comfortable in her presence. Not at all how he thought she would be.

'Would it be possible to have a list of the dates and times you met with Amy please? It might be beneficial for me to piece together her movements over a period of time,' he said.

'Of course. I can't let you have the book for client confidentiality reasons, but I can jot down the relevant details for you, if that would be okay?'

'Thank you.'

'I've only been seeing Amy for a few months, so it shouldn't take long.'

Denise swivelled in her chair and started to write on a sheet of headed paper. Deans politely waited. A provocative question kept rebounding inside his head. Would it be rude of him to ask? He did not know. He leant forward, about to speak, then stopped just short of the words coming out.

'Something you want to ask?' Denise said without turning around to face him. She was good.

Deans paused before speaking. He did have one vitally private question to ask, but at the same time, he did not want to hear the answer. Instead, his query sounded amateurish.

'So, do you read people's future and stuff?'

Denise chuckled. 'You're thinking of a clairvoyant. I'm not necessarily a clairvoyant, so I suppose I do "stuff" as you put it. But there is so much more to it.' She turned back to face him. 'Perhaps if you have a couple of hours free sometime you could experience some *stuff* for yourself?'

Deans leaned back. 'Oh, I'm afraid I'm not local. My patch is in Somerset.' He noticed Denise had a quizzical expression. 'Amy's reported missing from Bath.'

Denise shook her head. 'It's such a shock. What a dreadful, dreadful shock.'

She held out a sheet of paper, which Deans took with thanks.

'It's been a pleasure to meet you, Detective. I'm pleased Amy is in good hands.'

Deans wafted the compliment aside. 'Thank you for your help. It was very nice to meet you too.' He removed a business card from his wallet and handed it to Denise. 'Would you call me if you hear anything from Amy?'

'Without question,' she said and placed the business card onto her treatment couch.

Deans led the way back to the shop entrance. Ash was still behind the counter. Deans exchanged a handshake with Denise, nodded to Ash and went on his way to his next task.

A ten-minute stroll later, he found the police station at a picturesque setting overlooking the old town bridge and estuary. The entrance was locked and the front office in darkness. A laminated notice to the public was stuck to the inside of the glass informing them of front office closures and restrictions to opening hours, effective from nine months ago. *Cost cutting*, Deans thought. The same thing had happened in Bath.

A uniformed officer emerged from the side of the building, and Deans jogged over to her before she stepped into a marked vehicle.

'Hi,' Deans said, catching his breath. 'I'm DC Deans from

CID in Bath. Would you know if there are any DCs around I can chat to please?'

'They've already gone,' she said opening the door hurriedly, her Airwave radio chattering nonstop on the front of her body armour. 'Try tomorrow. Early turn.'

Deans checked his watch; it was nudging five.

'How do I get in?' Deans asked before she slammed the door closed.

'Front office opens at nine,' she shouted through the glass, turning over the engine and hitting the 999 button on the emergency equipment display panel.

'Thanks,' he shouted with a wave, but she was already on her way.

He was now at an impasse. He looked at his watch again, through his gritty, strobe-blinded eyes. He only had two options: drive back home to return in the early hours of the morning, or find somewhere to stay the night. Tomorrow was looking like another long day.

A call to Savage and then home to his wife confirmed that he was staying the night in Devon, and soon he was driving around the area looking for a B&B to throw onto job expenses.

He discovered a small car park set on a hillside overlooking a vast bay. The Atlantic Ocean was pounding into a long ridge of grey rocks way off to his right. He watched, captivated, as growling waves glided gracefully across his path before smashing into wispy white plumes on the shore. The repetitive sequence was sleep inducing. Womblike. It was the first time that day he allowed his mind to rest.

He blinked away his lethargy and focused on a cluster of small black dots in the distant water. Surfers.

The creases of his face softened as the image evoked memories of holidays with Maria, lounging on a beach and messing about in the sea. *Those were the days*, he thought.

CHAPTER TWELVE

It had been a reasonably comfortable night's sleep and Deans woke early. The sun was yet to rise fully but he was feeling increasingly claustrophobic in the poky B&B bedroom he had occupied since about eight thirty the night before. Breakfast was not for another hour and a half, and so he decided to head back to the small car park overlooking the bay to make the most of whatever peaceful opportunity he had.

This time, the tide had retreated, exposing a large bed of glassy, golden sand and a bank of jagged black rock beneath him. It was a calm morning. The rising sun over the hills had transformed the gossamer clouds into a bed of fire, and aircraft jet-wash left silvery traces against the pure cyan sky high above. Everything he saw was in stark contrast to the mornings he encountered back home, and he liked it.

After breakfast, he settled the bill and tucked the receipt away in a special flap of his wallet kept aside for expenses. He would have to go through a rigmarole of paperwork when he returned to the office to reclaim his costs. Sometimes he felt it was hardly worth the hassle – maybe that was the idea.

He set off and made his way to the police station once again, arriving just after nine. He met up with the two duty detectives: Ranford and Mansfield. It was not the friendliest of welcomes, but it was a start. He established CCTV was well covered in the area and some had automatic number plate recognition – ANPR capability. Ranford provided him with Intel on Scott Parsons, and they agreed to keep in contact through the day.

Deans drove the short distance to Fore Street and found Scott's address with little effort. A tatty brown VW Transporter adorned with surfer graffiti was parked nearby and he wondered if this belonged to Scott. To be fair though, Deans had never seen so many camper vans as over the past twenty-four hours.

If the Intel was correct, the last time the police had anything to do with Scott he was unemployed and so Deans was hopeful of a response.

He did not have long to wait before the door was opened by a man in his early twenties, wearing baggy shorts and a hoody top. He was more overweight than Deans had expected, but the photograph he had seen next to Amy's bed was a good few years old.

'Scott?' Deans asked.

The man studied Deans' suit, then yelled back into the house, 'Scotty, the Feds are here for you.' He turned away, leaving Deans outside the open door.

'What are you going on about, you knob-head?' Deans heard from the first floor, and watched as a man bounded down the stairs, two steps at a time.

'What is it?' he queried again before noticing Deans standing at the door. 'Oh, all right, mate? Did you want me?'

He was only wearing baggy shorts. He was lithe, muscular and heavily tattooed. There was no mistaking; this was Scott.

'I'm DC Deans. Can I come in for a private chat, please?'

Scott pulled a face and looked like he was about to debate the question.

'Scott, it's important, and I'd rather we chatted inside than on the doorstep.'

'Hold on,' Scott said and closed the door three-quarters of the way, leaving Deans once again standing alone.

He returned a few moments later and nodded Deans inside. Scott led the way through to the kitchen. He walked with short, stabbing steps as if he was walking on broken glass. Deans imagined that was from years of negotiating hot sand and stones to get to the surf.

Deans entered the kitchen, looked at the clutter and made an early decision not to accept any drinks, if offered.

'Scott, I understand that you are Amy Poole's ex-partner and you are still good friends?'

'Yeah, me and Ames is tight, man.' He screwed his face. 'What's this all about?'

'Amy is missing.'

Scott lurched forward. 'What? Where is she? Is she all right?'

'That's what I need to find out, Scott.'

'What do you mean?' Scott's voice was getting louder. 'Where is she?'

'Missing.'

'Missing? How, when?' Scott asked impatiently.

'That's exactly what I'm trying to find out.' Deans employed a calm voice. The last thing he needed was to be isolated in an unfamiliar house, in a town he did not know, with an over-excited man half his age, built like the proverbial shithouse.

'When did you last see her, Scotty?'

'Saturday night.'

'Where?'

'Joe's'

'Joe's?' Deans mirrored.

'Jumping Joe's.'

Deans shrugged and shook his head.

'In town, mate. It's our usual hangout.'

'Is it a club?'

'Yeah, well, more of a late-night bar than a club. Ames doesn't do clubs.'

'Why not?'

'The lights affect her head.'

'You know about her condition?'

'Course I do.'

'Do you know if she had her medication with her on Saturday night?'

Scotty shrugged and shook his head. 'No idea.'

'What time did you last see Amy?'

Scott shrugged again. 'Maybe about one, something like that.'

His eyes were wide, he was leaning back and holding the underside of the worktop as if to let go would cause him to fall. Reminiscent of Jessica.

'Who else was with you?'

'Jacko, Gemma and Soph.'

'Did anyone leave with Amy?'

'No,' he replied softly. 'She went home and we all stayed at Joe's.'

'Did you see where she went after leaving the club?'

Scott scratched at his ribs with a scraping noise.

'I think she went to the rank.'

'Scott, have you had any contact from Amy since Saturday night?'

His head dropped. 'No,' he said softly. 'She was heading back to uni, so that was it until the next time.'

'Can you remember what Amy was wearing on Saturday night?'

Scott puffed out his cheeks. 'Uh… a white and green O'Neill top, and probably jeans or a skirt, or something like that.'

Deans made a note in his book and gave Scott a moment or two without questions.

Scott then spoke with urgency, 'Have you been to her house? I can take you there.'

'There's no need thanks, Scott. I've already been there.'

'Oh my God! Janet and Ian.' Scott gripped the sides of his head, elongating his eyes. Clearly, this man genuinely cared not only for Amy, but also for the entire family.

'Scott, I need to you sit down with me, please,' Deans said, trying to deflate the ever-growing emotion spilling out from the lad. 'It's possible that you were the last person to see Amy…' He fell short of the word he felt compelled to say. He was so used to dealing with more serious cases that he temporarily forgot that Amy was still just a simple MISPER.

'What, alive?' Scott said, his face full of horror.

'No, I'm not saying that. Look, to the best of my knowledge you were the last person to see Amy.'

Deans observed Scott wiping his face and saw a glistening bead stream down his left cheek.

'I tell you what, Scotty,' Deans said gently, 'you're my best chance at the moment of getting a clearer picture of what happened on Saturday night. I think I will need a statement, but right now isn't the best time. You have a lot to take in. Could you meet me in a few hours at the station?'

'What, the police station? Are you going to nick me?'

Deans raised his hands. 'No. I promise. I need you focused that's all. We can find a quiet room. I need to know everything that happened on Saturday night, no matter how insignificant you may think it is. Can we do that?'

Scott nodded. 'Yeah, yeah, of course.'

'Okay, good. Bring any phones or cameras you may have had with you on Saturday night in case we need to look through them, all right?'

'Yeah, thanks, man,' Scott said, wiping his running nose with the top of his left forearm.

Deans headed for the front door. 'And do me a favour as well, Scotty?'

Scott nodded.

'Leave the weed at home, mate, we don't need that causing unnecessary complications at the nick, okay?'

Scott turned away.

'It's in the air. Don't put me in a position I can't get out of. See you later.'

CHAPTER THIRTEEN

The thrill of excitement was overwhelming, as he extracted box number 9 from the shelf. There was no one else around, but he still checked furtively behind. His cheeks glowed and he could feel a pulse in his neck as he gently held a leather-bound album, removed from the box, in both hands.

He was sitting perfectly still, and opened the album cover, slowly turning the pages to his latest creation. He drew sharp breath and his eyes rolled behind their lids. Pleasure oozed through him like a narcotic hit.

She was a beautiful girl and the images brought the moments they had experienced together back to life. He turned the page excitedly. Another sequence of photographs accelerated his breathing.

His smile narrowed as his thoughts took him back several weeks. She was the kind of girl who would never know suffering. Always be accepted. Always be popular. Never have to fight to be noticed. Never be constantly compared and judged. *Not any more*, he thought, *the little slut deserved everything she got.*

The side of his face broke into spasm.

'Go away,' he screamed through a warped grimace, gripping his head with both hands, and knocking the album onto the floor.

Mummy loves me more than you.

He cowered and dropped to his knees, squeezing his skull between his hands.

Mummy loves me more than you.

'Go away,' he fumed. 'Just, fuck off you little shit.'

The voice ended.

He lifted his head tentatively, his entire body trembling. He knew it was not over. He waited. Scanned the room frantically.

'No,' he whined. 'Please…' He bunched his eyes and curled his body as tightly as possible, using all his willpower to stave off the accompanying apparition. Nevertheless, the vision of his doting mother invaded his senses.

Don't you have beautiful eyes, Douglas? Who is my extra-special one?

'Go away, bitch,' he bellowed. 'Fuck you both.'

She was dead. They both were, but the torment was as fresh now as all those years ago.

He snorted deeply, filling his lungs with air and his throat with mucus. He shielded his face, held his breath, and bobbed to comfort himself. His chest burned to release the trapped air, but he had found this was the only way.

The voices had fallen silent, but had they really gone? He snatched the album from the floor, held it tightly against his chest. This was his reality now. This was what made *him* special, and this would set him apart.

He spluttered and heaved, and his thoughts shifted to the detective. There was something about him, something… extraordinary.

A wide smile returned to his face. He could not wait for the games to begin.

CHAPTER FOURTEEN

Deans weighed up the possibilities of Amy's location. There was so much that did not sit comfortably in his stomach. She was not in any of the local hospitals and her bank account and social media sites had not altered. He had also been checking out the taxi companies from Intel. His instinct was telling him to probe deeper, although there was nothing out of the ordinary from the reports he had read so far.

Several years before, Deans had been OIC on a case that had terrorised his home community. Six women sexually assaulted under extreme levels of violence, and then dumped on the roadside like disused commodities. Seventeen months of investigation, endless hours at the office and countless sleepless nights finally brought the offender, a late-night taxi driver, to justice. All his victims were heavily intoxicated, all of them lone female students on their way home late at night, and now all of them emotionally scarred for life.

Deans had put out a media warning following the attack on the second victim, and it haunted him to think that perhaps the subsequent victims had tried to do the right thing by getting a taxi, rather than walk home.

It was hard not to have a prejudiced opinion from time to time. Impartiality was rammed home from day one of training school. It was an easy concept to deal with until a job came along that tainted and distorted all reasoning. Perhaps his thoughts were being misled now. All he knew was that he did not fancy getting into another investigation like that, and certainly not when it was not on his patch.

The police logs relating to the taxi company over the last six months were not throwing much up. There was not a huge amount to go through; it was a small town. He discovered the usual kind of complaints: non-payment of fares, criminal damage to fleet vehicles and the taxi booking office. Several reports of aggressive driving by taxi staff, but nothing suggesting a rogue operative.

Mansfield was apparently out for the morning, so Deans was using his desk. From his limited contact with the bloke, Deans imagined Mansfield was out on some social, domestic chore or off shopping on job time.

The phone next to him erupted with a loud electronic chime. There was no one else around so he answered.

'DC Mansfield's phone. How can I help please?'

It was the front office and there was a visitor – for Deans.

He was surprised to see Denise Moon waiting for him. He offered a wave but she did not reciprocate. She looked tense. He found a vacant interview room, motioned her inside, but before he had the chance to close the door Denise asked, 'How much do you know about Amy so far, Detective?'

'Please, take a seat,' he said, and watched attentively as she took her position opposite without breaking eye contact.

He smiled and took his own seat. 'It's still early days, Miss Moon.'

'Amy is deceased, Detective,' she announced with stout conviction.

'I'm sorry?'

'To be exact, she has been murdered.'

Deans placed his pen slowly on the desk, folded his arms, took a moment, and studied her face. She seemed different to the first time they had met – starchy.

After a moment more, he opened his daybook to a fresh page, and gave Denise a tilted stare. 'Go on.'

'When you left me, I did some work around Amy,' she said.

Deans narrowed his eyes, said nothing and nodded for her to continue.

'I made contact with Amy.'

'Contact?'

'I asked the guardians to guide me to Amy. To show me she was safe.' She paused and looked away. 'Regrettably, I made contact with her.'

'Guardians?'

She stared forcefully at Deans. 'Amy is dead, Detective.'

'Okay,' Deans said, trying hard to suppress his frustration. 'Are you saying she's in the afterlife and you had some kind of chat with her?'

'No. She is not in the afterlife. She is trapped between this life and the next life. And she needs your help.'

Deans smiled politely, shook his head and shrugged.

'Believe her and believe me,' Denise said. 'Use me like a transmitter to communicate with her.'

'Okay,' Deans said holding a hand up. 'Miss Moon, I thank you for coming in today, but I'm sure you can appreciate that I'm a busy man right now. I am not sure how I can help, given the information you have provided. Unless you know where she is, how she died or even who killed her, I can't see what else we can do here today.'

Denise frowned and slowly nodded her head as if it was on a stiff spring. It was obvious she believed this stuff.

Deans looked at the wall clock and then back at Denise. Her glare was penetrating. He wearily ran his fingers down his cheeks and brought his hands together at the tip of his nose as if in prayer. 'All right,' he said from behind his cupped hands. 'What did she say?'

Denise delayed her response. It was obvious she was sussing him out equally as much.

Eventually, she spoke. 'It was confused.'

Deans felt like a judge on a TV talent show with a large red plunger beneath his palms, waiting for his moment to end the suffering.

'She's been betrayed,' Denise said.

Deans nodded; gestured with his hand for her to continue.

'She accepted a lift.'

Deans lifted his head. *She accepted a lift.* 'Go on.'

Denise shook her head. 'There was confusion. My contact was for some reason… limited. I can't explain how or why.'

'Tell me more about the lift.'

'That's all I know right now. It was vague… but I do know she got into a car.'

'Describe the car,' Deans said impatiently.

'I can't. My connection to Amy faded. I need more time with her.'

'Where are you saying Amy is?'

'I don't know. I couldn't make out specific detail. She was… she was in darkness.'

Deans sat motionless. *Is this for real?* he thought. A part of him hoped that it was; that Denise could in some way make contact with the afterlife, or whatever life she was claiming that Amy was occupying right then.

'I'm offering you my services, Detective. I don't expect payment, however I do demand respect and trust in all I say.'

'Miss Moon, I thank you for coming to see me. Please, you must appreciate this is a rather strange occurrence and one that I'm not overly comfortable with.'

She nodded.

He ran a hand through his hair. 'Let me consider what you've told me. I still need to find Amy and I hope to God that you're wrong.'

He held out his hand to shake and the conversation was over.

Back at his acquired desk, he continued checking through the taxi logs. Outside the window a bank of angry dark clouds were gathering ominously on the hills beyond the estuary. He tried his best to concentrate on the job in hand but became wildly distracted by his conversation with Denise Moon.

Ranford glided into the office clutching a brown A4 envelope and slid it across the table towards Deans, who stopped it before it fell off the edge of the table.

'Your CCTV,' Ranford said.

'Excellent,' Deans replied, more than surprised at the gesture. 'Thank you.'

'I saw your timeline,' Ranford explained. 'We don't use them much here so I had a nosey at it and thought I'd help out a little. I took the dates and times and worked out the cameras from the locations you described.'

Deans removed the six CDs from the envelope.

'Everything's good to go,' Ranford said cheerfully.

'Thanks. I appreciate it.' Deans racked his memory for the last time anyone back at his own station had willingly gone out of their way to such a degree, and he did not even know Ranford.

Deans checked the clock on the wall: 11:43 a.m. He still had not given any update to his wife but he was hoping to be heading back home that night. The taxi driver line of enquiry had so far gotten him nowhere, so he decided to break away from that and start on the CCTV.

Six cameras, one conveniently covering the quay where Amy lived, two incorporating the streets either side and over-lapping the taxi rank in Torworthy, and one other comprising the pedestrian street where Jumping Joe's was situated. Ranford had also collected two others including late-night fast food outlets. He had done a good job. It was close to perfect coverage from what Deans knew of the events of that night.

So what did he know? He looked at his timeline. Little point commencing at the start, best to work backwards.

Deans always worked CCTV in thirds of an hour. The perception of time through the eyes of a witness was often distorted, not only in the length of time an incident took, but also exactly what time it happened. Thinking about his conver-sation with Scott, he readied the computer and in his daybook wrote *Sunday 5th Oct – CCTV Camera 2 (Taxi queue left)*. Beneath he started a log with *00:40 hours*.

The footage was delayed between frames, by only a second or two, but enough to make viewing problematic. He groaned and sucked in cold air behind his teeth. At this setting, it was challenging to distinguish whether someone was running or walking. What else might be missed?

After reviewing eighty minutes of footage in just about ninety minutes of real time, he had drawn a blank on camera two. He had done the same for camera three (taxi queue right) with the same result, and thanks to a canopy overhanging the front of Jumping Joe's, seventy percent of the screen was obscured by overexposed glare.

It was now 2:52 p.m. by his watch. Scott Parsons still had not shown. He rapped the edge of the desk with his fingertips. If he left for home now he would avoid the worst of the rush hour and could make alternative arrangements with Parsons over the phone. Nevertheless, there was still one CCTV camera left to view, and that was at Amy's home village, Hemingsford.

He huffed and tutted and again checked his watch. Deep down he knew he was better off completing all the viewing today. Another task to tick off the list.

Scott mentioned that he had met with Amy around eight p.m. at the bus stop in town, so she must have made her way to him, because he lived close-by and wouldn't need a bus, unless he was travelling from elsewhere.

Deans set the viewing clock to 19:40 hours and jotted the time in his book with an underscore.

Already jaded by viewing the previous disks, his eyes were professionally reluctant. It was helpful that he had been to the location shown on the footage; at least it was somewhere he recognised. The camera faced across the road from the quay-side towards the small row of businesses; including the quaint coffee shop he had visited when he first arrived.

Fifteen minutes went by without incident, and it was then that a briefest moment in time gripped him by the balls and wrenched his senses into action.

'What the...' he squealed, and in that instant, all his plans needed to change.

CHAPTER FIFTEEN

Thinking quickly, Deans established the immediate priorities, and soon he was speaking to DS Savage back in Bath.

'Deano, enjoying our little jolly, are we? Make sure you come back when you're good and ready,' Savage jested, clearly in a playful mood.

'Mick, listen,' Deans said. 'I need Carl Groves lifted for the kidnap of Amy Poole. And we need his car, pronto.'

'Hold-up, Deano. Have you been doing some work while you've been away? You'd better tell me what's going on.'

Deans explained the grounds for the arrest and Savage agreed.

'Get your arse back up here, Deano, you're in for a long night.'

That was something Deans did not need telling.

Ranford had come into the office while Deans was on the phone and was obviously interested in the conversation.

'Progress?' he asked.

Deans hastily updated him, gathered up his things and exchanged mobile numbers with Ranford. He made a quick phone call putting off Scott Parsons, and less than ten minutes after ending the call with Savage he was back on the North Devon link road and eating up the journey time.

As he pulled into the rear yard of his own station, the time was nearing seven thirty. He spent a silent moment and then dialled home.

'Hi, love,' Deans said. 'I'm back in Bath again, but I'm going to be a bit tied up for a while at the office.'

'Where've you been?' Maria responded in a deadened tone.

'Devon, but I'm back now.'

'When are you coming home?'

'Are you alright, love?'

Maria did not reply.

'Look,' Deans said checking his watch. 'It was just a quick call to say I'm back and I'll be home a little later, so don't wait up, okay?'

There was a delay before Maria spoke again.

'I've been to the hospital today.'

'What?' Deans fell still. 'Why, love… Everything's alright isn't it?'

'I had to go to the EPAC clinic,' Maria said slowly.

'What's that?'

'Early pregnancy assessment clinic.'

'Why?'

Deans could hear Maria snivelling.

'Maria, what is it? Please tell me.' He could feel his chest pounding.

'I'm spotting, Andy. We're losing the baby.'

'Are you sure? I mean… did they use those words?'

'I didn't stay around to speak to anyone.'

'What, why the hell not?'

'Don't you criticise me,' Maria snapped, her voice trembling. 'You're in no position to judge me. You couldn't even be here to support me.'

'It wasn't a criticism, that's not what I meant.'

'It was horrible, Andy. I was herded into the waiting room with all the other mums. Had to sit there for ages, watching them being called …seeing their faces again as they left.'

'I'm so sorry, love.'

'I was the only one alone, Andy. The only one. The only one who didn't have someone to talk to… someone I could hug.'

He bunched his eyes and dipped his head. 'Maria, I—' He knew the next words were empty; 'I could have got away. Why didn't you say something?'

'Huh,' she grunted. 'You were in Devon, remember?'

Chin on chest, he bobbed his head. Culpability echoed through his muteness.

He blew a long breath. 'So, what now? I mean, what can we do?'

'They're going to find me an appointment. Maybe tomorrow. Maybe the day after.'

'It could still be alright, Maria. We're only a couple of months—'

'Ten weeks, three days,' she said mechanically.

Deans puffed out his cheeks. 'Have you told your mum?'

'Not yet, I mean, what can I say? Sorry, Mum, I'm losing your first grandchild.'

'We don't know that.'

Maria was silent.

'Look,' Deans said softly, 'I'll get away as soon as I can, but I know it's not going to be for a few hours, at least. I'm sorry.'

Maria's reply was slow in coming. 'Yeah.'

'Love you, babe.'

'Yeah. I know.' Her voice trailed away.

Deans ended the call and sat inactive for the next five minutes.

Mitchell had been tasked by Savage to work with Deans through the night and he was not looking happy about it.

'Is Groves in the bin?' Deans asked, not interested in his colleague's discontent with the situation.

'Damn right,' Savage replied. 'Bless him. He hasn't stopped bawling since he arrived.'

'What's the state of play with forensics?' Deans asked.

'All taken care of,' Savage reassured him. 'Grab yourself a brew and let's have an O-Group in ten. Okay?'

Deans had not come across O-Groups until he joined the CID, but they were invaluable forums for thrashing out ideas during complicated or serious cases. Rank and experience counted for nothing: any suggestion could be the golden solution.

Deans sprawled out in his chair. Ten minutes did not give much time to prepare, so he would have to wing it. Nobody knew as much about the job as him and most people thought he had been on a jolly for the last couple of days, so this would be a revelation for them, if nothing else.

They went through to the darkened conference room. There were five of them present: Deans, Mick, Harper, Mitchell and DC Bairstow from the day shift who had been late off from dealing with an earlier custody case.

Savage opened the briefing. 'As a result of information received from Deano, Carl Groves was arrested at eighteen fifty-four hours at his home address by PC Bright on suspicion of kidnap. He was compliant throughout but very emotional. He has made no significant comments. He couldn't, from what I've been told, because he was blubbing so much.'

Everyone else, apart from Deans, laughed.

Savage continued, 'People, we have until eighteen fifty-three hours tomorrow to get some kind of result. Deano is OIC and I am Deputy SIO. DI Feather will be the Senior Investigating Officer. He's aware of the progress but couldn't be here tonight.'

Savage turned to Deans. 'Deano, tell us what we are dealing with, please.'

Deans took the lead and ran through the case from the start of medium risk MISPER through to the present kidnap investigation. He explained the relationship between Groves and Amy Poole, Groves' apparent reluctance to open up, the victim's family status in Devon and her connection to Scott Parsons. He deliberated a beat with the name of Denise Moon on his lips, but decided to play safe and not mention her, even though his contact with her was bugging him like crazy.

'The reason I've asked for Groves to be arrested is quite simple really. Two days ago, before I went on my "jolly" to North Devon, he provided me with an account of his final day with Amy. A very convenient and generally believable account, until I saw him on CCTV, on the night of Amy's disappearance, driving along the quayside in her home village. He failed to tell me he had visited Amy that night, in fact he clearly stated he had never been to her home in Devon.'

The faces around the room looked positive and concerned all the same.

Deans carried on. 'I'd suggest he knows a lot more than he told me, and he has clearly lied. We need to find out why, and what he knows of Amy's current whereabouts.'

'Nick him for perverting the course of justice,' Savage suggested. 'That should concentrate his mind.'

The heads around the room nodded, as if kidnap was a mere triviality.

Savage continued, 'CSI are working on Groves' wagon as we speak, but given the time, we're not likely to get any results until tomorrow. Time-wise, Deano, what do you need to be interview-ready? Mitch will be your number two.' Savage appeared keen to progress.

Deans looked away, his thoughts turned to Maria waiting for him at home. He shrugged. 'I don't know. I have to prepare the CCTV for interview, work on disclosure—'

'Deano, did I mention that Johnson's the brief?' Savage said with a dry smile.

The room groaned in unison. Everyone felt the same about Johnson.

Deans slapped his hands loudly on the table. 'In that case, I can't see this getting off the ground any time this side of midnight. Seriously, Johnson is a joke. He thinks nothing of a two-hour chitchat with the shits for the simple stuff. How long's he going take for a kidnap?'

'Now, now, Deano. I know you don't see eye-to-eye with Johnson, but we also can't afford any unnecessary hold-ups. Are you saying it'll be the early hours before you can stick it into Groves?'

Deans nodded, prayed Mick saw it the same. 'Probably, if it is Johnson. He'll be the hold-up.'

Savage stared at his watch. 'Okay, I'll speak to the custody sergeant and suggest a lie-down on the grounds that you've just returned from Devon and need to get interview-ready. In any event, we have to wait for the forensic results, not to mention that Groves needs his eight hours beauty sleep. Leave it to me,' Savage said, winking at Deans.

The others left the room, leaving Deans slumped in his chair. Savage came alongside him. 'Deano, you look like crap. Tidy up what you can and get home to your wife.'

At just gone half past midnight, Deans headed off home.

CHAPTER SIXTEEN

Saturday 11th October. Five forty-five a.m. Seventh and final day on duty.

Four hours' rest was not a great starting point for what was going to be another taxing day. Deans dragged his hand across his mouth and stared wearily at Maria's back as she lay on the other side of the bed. The large tumbler of whisky had seemed like a good idea in the middle of the night. He was less sure now. Even with the liquid sedative, he'd had a rough few hours. Thoughts of the investigation had raved away in his head and the harder he tried to clear his mind to sleep, the more determined the thoughts became. Each time he was close to dropping off, vivid notions lit up his eyelids, as if someone was shining a torch at his face. It had been a hellish night.

He took a deep breath and rolled his creaky shoulders. His prisoner still had two of his compulsory eight hours' rest ahead of him before Deans could even think about making him feel uncomfortable.

Deans gently slid out of bed, doing his best not to disturb Maria, dragged himself to the bathroom and stared at the jaded face peering back at him in the mirror. An OIC can toil, to the verge of exhaustion, but a suspect has human and legal rights. Of course, HR would say each officer should get eleven hours' rest between shifts as per the working directive. That was all well and good when they had a cushy eight-to-four job and every weekend off. If Deans did not do the work, who else was going to do it for him, the DC fairy?

He had shuffled his way into the kitchen and was clutching a strong black coffee in the largest mug he could find when Maria walked over to the kettle.

'Morning, babe. I wasn't expecting you up so early,' Deans said.

Maria slammed a mug down on the worktop and turned angrily to face him. 'For God's sake, Andy. When will all these hours end?'

He lowered his head and stared into his mug.

'What happened to our bloody life?' she foamed. 'It's all about your sodding work. What are you going to do if we *do* have a baby, just expect me to bring it up alone? When will you say no, and start putting me somewhere in your bastard list of priorities?'

Deans subtly nodded, chewing the inside of his cheek. He glanced up and caught her glare.

'You'd better be around for the scan.' She stormed out of the kitchen, slamming the door behind her.

'That went well,' Deans said into his coffee with the sound of her footsteps reverberating around the kitchen as she pounded back up the stairs.

He did not have the energy to follow, or try to explain why work was currently so demanding. She was perfectly right, of course. He knew the demands of the job were unfair on her and on their family unit, but what other choice did he really have? The reality was there were not enough detectives to handle the workload. For as long as he had been in the office the constabulary had been running on minimal staffing levels and they were all facing the uncertainty of further government cutbacks.

He was lucky in many respects. His department was small, unlike the Bristol office, but they had the resources to cope. In Bath, it only took a few decent jobs to throw the delicate equilibrium between a work and home-life balance.

He allowed a cushioning few minutes to elapse before following upstairs. Maria had taken herself to the second bedroom. The door was closed, and the TV booming. Deans thought for a second about going inside, but he could not deal with a further barrage and time was pressing. He opened his wardrobe – there were no ironed shirts. Looked in the wash basket – Maria had not touched his dirties. He emptied his laundry onto the bed, sniffed the armpits, and selected the least offensive option. Ten minutes later, without further conversation with Maria, he quietly left the house for work.

As always, he was the first into the office. The freakishly fine weather had completely changed. Looking out, cobalt blue and grey clouds were rapidly pushing through on the chilly easterly breeze. Beyond them, a bleak obsidian horizon was heralding further hostilities. This was one day he did not mind being stuck in the office. There was no denying it: this set of shifts had been tough. He did not know exactly, but estimated that he had already worked eighty-plus hours before the start of whatever today had to bring.

Computer fired up, he began typing Johnson's disclosure and imagined he would be on the phone soon enough to pressurise him for the information.

He can get stuffed, Deans thought. *It's my bloody interview, and it'll start when I'm good and ready.*

Even so, delays had already eaten heavily into the custody clock, and as it stood, they would be hard pushed not to need a superintendent's extension of time. The office clock read 7:35 a.m. Deans' mind slowly processed where the maximum of twelve additional hours would take him up to.

'Maria's going to love me,' he muttered beneath his breath.

Deans' mobile phone went off in his pocket. He quickly answered, but it was not Maria. It was an unrecognised mobile number.

'Hello,' he said assertively.

'Good morning, Detective Deans. This is Denise Moon.'

'Good morning, Miss Moon. Or should I say good early morning?'

'Amy's been found,' she said without hesitation.

'Oh, fantastic,' Deans said, throwing himself back into his seat. 'Where's she been?'

'I received a message this morning, not fifteen minutes ago. She needs you,' Denise said.

'I am sorry, Miss Moon. A message from…?'

'Amy.'

'Great. Do you know where she is? I still need to speak with her.'

'I already told you, Detective. Amy is dead.'

Deans fell limp, flopped his head over the back of the chair, and stared up at the ceiling.

Denise filled the silence. 'She was stuck between the here and now and the afterlife.'

Deans rocked his head from side to side, as Denise continued. 'She needed to be found and now that she has, she can move on, but she wanted me to help the detective find her killer.'

'Killer?' Deans finally interjected, standing aggressively

from his chair. 'Just hold on a minute. What are you talking about?'

'You must believe me, Detective. For the sake of Amy.'

'For the sake of Amy, I'm ending this conversation. Thank you for your valuable time, Miss Moon.' Deans terminated the call before she could say any more.

'Jesus,' he vented, slamming his phone down onto the desk. 'Fucking nut-job.' He reached for his mug, found it drained and stormed off to the canteen for a refill.

When he returned to the office, others from the team had arrived. He was calmer, and settled back to the job in hand: Johnson's disclosure. It was going to be brief. After all, the details were sketchy and the evidence against Groves was limited, at best.

Forty-five minutes later, Deans was with Mitchell in the quiet of the conference room preparing for the interview. His mobile phone rang again. It was Savage.

'Two things, Deano: A, the brief is already giving custody earache about an ETA for interview and B, there's a message on your desk from Devon.'

'Okay. Thanks,' Deans replied wearily. 'We'll be back in the office soon.' As it was, he felt no urgency to dance to the beat of Johnson or Denise Moon.

It was 10:35 a.m. when Deans was back at his desk.

Savage joined him. 'I've given custody a heads-up of eleven.' Meaning Deans had twenty-five minutes before he had to dive down to the depths of the custody suite. He picked up a scrawled note from the table.

'Who took this message?' he asked, his irritation obvious.

'I did,' Daisy Harper replied.

'Why the hell didn't someone tell me it was Ranford trying

to contact me?'

'Easy, Deano. What does it matter?' Harper answered, quite happy to up the ante if required, but Deans was already on the phone.

'Paul, it's Andy Deans. Sorry I missed your call. We've got one in the bin for this MISPER job, so we're a bit snowed under at this end, mate. What can I do to help?'

'I hope it's a murder suspect,' Ranford said. 'We discovered a body on the beach this morning, and my money's on it being your girl.'

A sudden chill passed through Deans causing his entire body to judder.

Ranford was still talking. 'I haven't got to the scene yet but I understand it's a young woman buried beneath a large pile of rocks.'

Deans' mind flashed to the long, grey boulder ridge he had seen at the bay. 'Jesus,' he said sternly, 'what's the state of play?'

'Uniform are on scene. Apparently, a bunch of potwallopers found her at around seven twenty this morning.'

'Pop wally who?'

'Potwallopers. You know... volunteers who look after the land, repair natural sea defences, that sort of thing. Dates way back. We've got about a dozen of them at the nick waiting to give statements as we speak.'

'Good,' Deans said, closing his eyes, imagining the scene. 'Have we got containment on the body?'

'Already taken care of. I'm heading down now.'

'Please tell me I'm wrong,' Deans said, screwing-up his eyes, 'but is the body on Sandymere Bay?'

'Certainly is,' Ranford said.

That was the beach Deans had fallen in love with – what were the chances of that?

CHAPTER SEVENTEEN

Deans faced a crossroads. A body, possibly that of missing person Amy Poole, had been found on a North Devon beach, with Amy's boyfriend, Carl Groves, being held at Bath on suspicion of kidnap, for a job reported in Somerset but now more likely to have occurred in Devon. It was a jurisdiction muddle and it wanted to be resolved ASAP if Deans was going to progress the investigation effectively. However, it was not down to someone from his pay scale to determine. He would have to rely on the DI to thrash it out with his counterparts in Devon.

If the body transpired to be Amy with foul play suspected, then a murder enquiry would commence in Devon and their murder squad would take the investigative lead. If the body was not Amy then North Devon Police would proceed accordingly and Somerset Police would continue the missing person enquiries. So much depended on the scene, the state of the body, whether or not it was Amy and inter-constabulary politics.

Armed with Ranford's update, the supervisors went off to discuss a plan of action in the DI's office and closed the door.

Deans waited quietly at his desk, chewing the tip of his pen lid as he watched the second hand of the clock slowly tick onwards. His prisoner had already used over fourteen hours of his custody time limit. Every minute spent talking was a minute less doing. If the interview took a total of five hours, including legal briefings and faffing about, Groves could still get bail with five hours in the bank for some point in the future. If the North Devon body turned out to be Amy, then Deans would need to see her and examine the scene, but he could not do that and deal with Groves at the same time.

This was a high stakes situation, without the added impediment of the intervening distance, or the fragility of his domestic situation.

Even the clearest-cut of murders involved a high demand on resources and complete dedication on the part of the OIC, and it would take months of grafting for the case to become trial-ready. How could he provide that level of service from one hundred and twenty miles away?

He was torn. His head told him not to get involved any further because family had to be his priority. His heart was telling him to fight his corner and keep the case. After all, he informed the family of Amy's disappearance and took the time to comfort them and establish the bond of trust that was so important in these investigations. He had tracked down the witnesses, obtained the statements and established that Groves was a prime suspect when no one else seemed that bothered about the investigation.

Something else was nipping away at him: Denise Moon. It felt abnormal for Deans to think it, but if there was the faintest element of truth in what she told him then he owed it to Amy and her family to continue. If only it was his decision.

The clock continued to tick away. Another seventeen

minutes gone. Seventeen minutes less to deal with Groves. Seventeen minutes less to get himself down to Devon. Seventeen minutes less time at the end of the day to be at home with Maria.

Deans began to pace the floor. He had picked up a ball of Blu-Tack from Harper's desk and was working it eagerly in his hand as he trod a channel in the carpet tiles. His makeshift stress-reliever was doing a reasonable job, however his thoughts kept returning to Denise Moon. How had she known that Amy took a taxi, and why was she suggesting Amy's dead body had been found. She had called Deans at just gone seven thirty. According to Ranford, the body at the beach had been discovered at seven twenty. If it turned out to be Amy, there was no possible way Denise could have known.

The DI's door opened and out walked the boss with Savage following close behind.

'Deano, I've contacted my equivalent in Devon,' the DI said. 'They obviously need to establish the identity of the deceased before they'll give me a final decision about the extent of your involvement.'

Deans nodded.

'As it stands, they're happy for you to be on board, but they've also made it clear you're not to tread on any toes, you get me?'

Deans raised his brows with a twitch.

'Obviously a lot of their resources will be tied up at the scene and with statement-taking so I think they'd be grateful for a little help. If this turns out to be sinister, they'll be pulling additional resources from County HQ to supplement the local DCs. And that's certainly how it's looking.'

Deans gently nodded again. He was waiting for a 'but'.

'Our problem, Deano, is the young lad locked up downstairs. His eggs are already hard-boiled and I feel we should definitely wait for more news before we interview him.'

Deans finally spoke up. 'Our options are limited, boss.'

'I know, Deano. I know.' The DI put a hand on Deans' shoulder. 'Good work so far, Deano. Well done.'

'Thanks, boss.'

CHAPTER EIGHTEEN

Deans punched a number into his desk phone, and after a long delay, Ranford answered the call.

'Paul, it's Andy Deans again.'

'Hello?' Ranford bellowed back, causing Deans to recoil. 'You'll have to speak up. I can't hear very well.'

Ranford might have been having difficulty hearing him, but Deans and anyone else in the immediate vicinity had no problems hearing Ranford.

'Paul, it's Andy Deans again,' he said at hands-free-volume. 'Can you hear me now?' This time Deans pre-empted the booming reply and held the receiver away from his ear.

'Just about,' came the distorted reply. 'You can probably hear it's like a bloody hurricane down here.'

'Are you at the scene yet?'

'Sorry?'

Deans huffed and spoke louder still. 'Are you at the scene?'

'Yes.'

'Are you with the body?'

'Sorry, I got something about the body?'

Deans looked across the desk at Mitchell, who appeared to be enjoying his obvious frustration.

'Are you with the body?' Deans was now shouting his question, as if semaphorically.

'Nearby, yes.'

'I need you to describe any clothing.'

'Clothing?'

'Yes.'

'Hold on. Let me go back into the tent.'

There was a long delay and Deans waited with the phone held at arm's length for Ranford to speak again.

'Hello, Andy.'

This time, Deans could just about make out Ranford's voice.

'Yeah, go on. That's better.'

'Yeah, I'm inside now. You wanted to know something about the clothing?'

'Can you describe any, please?'

There was another short delay.

'I can see a bit. Looks like an elbow sticking up out of the rocks, and some white and green material.'

That was enough; Deans did not need to hear any more. He knew it was Amy and he knew he had to be at the scene. He quickly ended the call and dashed off to find the skipper who was chatting in the DI's office.

Deans interrupted their conversation. 'Excuse me, boss. Sorry to disturb you. I've a further update from the scene in Devon.'

Two faces looked attentively his way.

'My contact from D and C is at the scene. The body is still in situ and I believe it could be Amy.'

Their expression simultaneously became quizzical.

Deans carried on. 'From the accounts I've been given it sounds like there are similarities in the clothing.'

The DI nodded.

Deans grasped the moment. 'We've roughly ten hours left on Groves' clock. Let me go back down to Devon, suss out the scene and the body. If it is Amy then...' He paused. 'Well, then Groves has an awful lot to answer for. If not, then no harm done. I could know definitively within three hours from now, including travelling time. Best case scenario, we then request an extra few hours from the Superintendent. Worst case scenario, we go for the full twelve and fill our boots.'

Savage was the first to respond. 'Deano, I admire your determination with this job, I really do, but we don't yet know if it's our MISPER.'

'My gut's telling me it is, Sarge.' Deans had last called him 'Sarge' on the first day he joined the team. 'I can't just sit around and wait for the phone to ring. This is crucial. If it is Amy then I'm going to need to see the body anyway.'

'Gut feeling isn't enough, Deano,' Savage rebutted.

'We have a couple of options, gents,' the DI interjected. 'We interview Groves, get a first account and allow the D and C boys and girls to do their thing. That way we lose nothing and potentially gain a talking Groves. Another seven or eight hours in our humble B&B and Groves may be less than congenial. Alternatively, we do it Deano's way.'

'Boss,' Deans persisted, 'so let's say we've interviewed Groves and we have an early account. We're potentially still waiting on D and C to feed us, and how hospitable do you suppose they'll be, dishing out fresh murder details to another force?'

The DI puckered his lips as Deans continued, 'So, what do we then do with Groves? The custody clock would be down to three, maybe four hours. We may not even get an extension because we'd have already secured his initial account and without some game-changing evidence coming to light from Devon we might be forced into a position of charge or bail. And I don't want my name anywhere near that if bail is our only option.'

The DI put his hand up to stop Deans. 'Okay. Okay, fine. We will stand more chance of the custody extension if Groves has yet to be interviewed, so long as we can show that our other enquiries have been diligent and expeditious. If we do too much, too soon this end, we may be forced to consider bailing him and I don't want my name on that either – if he's our man.'

'Fact is, Deano,' Savage said, 'I can't spare anyone else to buddy up with you. You'll have to fly solo.'

Deans understood. His problem was not a partner for the trip; it was going to be Maria's reaction.

'Leave the superintendent to me,' Savage said. 'Just make sure you keep me in the loop. Okay?'

'When I know, you'll know,' Deans replied.

The DI patted Deans on the shoulder with a firm hand. 'You'd better hit the road, Deano, time's a-ticking.'

CHAPTER NINETEEN

They had arranged to meet up directly at the scene. Deans dropped down over the familiar hill, revealing the same wide expanse of frothing water at which he had previously marvelled. He picked out a cluster of police vehicles in the distance, the alternating blocks of high visibility markings making them stand out against the dull greyness of the pebble ridge. A solitary white tent perched on the precipice of the mound and black dots scurried about its perimeter.

Deans approached via a long, pothole-strewn track and showed his warrant card to a forlorn-looking PCSO on point duty. He parked next to a marked van and could see plenty of activity going on around him. Forensic officers adorned in white paper cover suits huddled beside a CSI van, and Support Group officers in black overalls crawled in a tight line against the buffeting onshore wind, like some absurd-looking slug race.

The forensic shelter stood proud of the vast stone elevation, its pop-up joints straining hard against the wind; undoubtedly, every guy-rope employed to keep the tent from blowing away.

Deans looked around, taking in the scene: the long potted

entry road bisecting the large, green expanse of flatland. The steep pebble ridge, with millions of rounded boulders – some hand-sized, others clearly too heavy to lift. The makeshift slip-way, the lifeguard hut, the position of the forensic tent, the rough-surfaced car park, and to his dismay, two men inside the perimeter of the police vehicles – one in a suit, the other in jeans and an anorak clutching a scratch pad and camera. The press.

Deans went across and instantly recognised DC Mansfield in the suit.

'Can I have a private chat, please?' Deans insisted, and ushered Mansfield away with him.

'Who's that?' Deans barked.

'Nev, from the *Herald*,' Mansfield replied obstinately.

'What the hell's he doing here? Who authorised media contact at this stage?'

'Chill out, city boy. He's all right, I know him. He just wants first dibs.'

'Who's in charge here?' Deans demanded.

Mansfield looked Deans up and down. 'Sure as hell isn't you.'

'Where's the CSM?'

'In the pod, I guess, slick,' Mansfield said, gesturing towards the tent on the ridge.

Deans stomped away, headlong into the bitter gale force wind. He clambered up the steep embankment of boulders to the summit, losing his footing several times. Ranford was just the other side, decked out in a white paper cover suit. His normally well-trained jet-black hair fluttering like ribbons into his face.

'Hi, Andy,' he said, clearly happy to see Deans. 'She's still in there. We're just finishing off the final photographs.'

Deans pointed with a thumb. 'Why is Mansfield speaking to a reporter down there?'

'I didn't know he was. Christ. I'll go and have a word.'

'I already tried. What's his game?'

'Who knows? Mansfield's a chancer at the best of times.'

The tent flap opened from the inside and another officer in white coveralls emerged and fought against the pummelling wind to secure the entrance flap once more.

'Mike, this is DC Deans who I told you about,' Ranford said.

Although only his eyes were showing though the mask and tightly drawn hood, Deans could tell the officer was smiling. He lifted an index finger, creating a momentary interruption, and gently placed his camera into a metal carry case on the rocks. He turned back to Deans and removed his mask, exposing a magnificent grey handlebar moustache.

'Hello. I'm Mike Riley, Crime Scene Manager. Thank you for travelling down.' He nodded back to the tent. 'This is an interesting one,' he said enthusiastically.

'Any ID yet?' Deans asked impatiently. 'Is it Amy Poole?'

'I believe it could be, given the information we have,' the CSM replied. 'We'll have to go through the normal channels of identification, unless she has her passport with her.' He chortled and twisted his moustache through thin blue vinyl gloves.

Deans was not finding anything at that moment remotely humorous.

'We currently have her boyfriend in custody. What can you tell me?'

The CSM looked down briefly at his notebook. 'This appears to be more than a random, senseless killing.'

'How so?' Deans asked.

'Someone's been bothered enough to glue her eyes shut.' He looked sternly at Deans. 'And her face has been disfigured.'

Deans frowned. 'Anything else?'

'Well, yes, actually. There was a rather questionable attempt at concealing the body. I don't think this would be my first choice of locations.'

The CSM unzipped the entrance to the tent and held the wildly flapping material high on an outstretched arm, inviting Deans to venture inside.

Deans took three steps forwards ducking beneath the CSM's arm, and crossed the threshold of the tent. Another forensic officer was squatting beside the body, which was face-down and twisted into an unnatural position. The tent was much quieter inside, tranquil even. Deans nodded over to the CSI officer, who nodded back towards a box of clear-packaged forensics clothing, and returned to her work.

Deans gazed at the body. It was as if she had leapt from the top of the slope and belly-flopped into position. Of course, that was not the reason why she was there. Her head faced away and her right arm stood proud, forming a triangular shape at the elbow. Her left arm was flat – the forearm bent at a sickening angle of two hundred degrees or more. Deans winced. Her legs were together, feet folded one over the other. She was dressed as Ranford had stated, in a white and green top, and a denim skirt, just as Scotty had indicated. Deans needed to see her face.

He ripped open one of the packaged paper suits and donned a facemask and overshoes, becoming aware of his own shallow, urgent breathing. He rolled on a pair of forensic gloves and, fully kitted out, took tentative steps across the unstable pebble floor until he was facing the entrance of the tent, and the maimed corpse of Amy Poole.

A wave of sorrow overcame him. He could not explain why. He had seen dozens of dead bodies before and never reacted quite this way. He shook his head and blinked away the building wetness from his eyes. His stomach gurgled, his vision tunnelled and a blistering coldness shook him to the core, as if a super-cooled net of air had dropped over him.

He did not need to see her eyes to confirm her identity. Her mouth was ajar, the flesh of her cheeks shredded. Her grey lips framed the white teeth that seemed to be the only part of her to have retained original lustre. They would of course still need to follow procedure but Deans needed no further confirmation of who he was looking at.

He had not even realised the CSM was right beside him.

'Her underwear appears intact and undamaged,' he said, taking Deans by surprise. 'She does have significant bruising and damage to her face and body, but she was of course well covered by these blasted boulders when we first arrived. Only a full examination will indicate whether these injuries were inflicted pre- or post-mortem. Some joints are quite obviously displaced and again we should await any post-mortem findings before reaching premature conclusions.'

'Can I see the photographs of how Amy was found please?' Deans requested sombrely.

The CSM picked up another camera nearby and started flicking through the digital images. 'So, do you think this is your missing person?' he asked, handing Deans the camera.

Deans studied the small LCD screen, and his imagination created a lucid reconstruction of Amy being dragged across the boulders and dumped, as she now lay. If her final moments in life were treacherous, then equally so was her improvised tomb.

Deans nodded and handed the camera back. 'Can we get anything from these?' he asked, pointing to the rocks.

'Unlikely,' the CSM replied. 'The tide would've washed away and contaminated pretty much every contact trace, unless we were extraordinarily lucky and found the body between tides. But I would say from the rigor that she's been here days rather than hours.'

'Does the water cover the area we're on now?' Deans asked.

The CSM nodded. 'We have a six metre swing down here and I would venture she is well within that range. Talking of which, we're just a few hours short of high tide so we need to crack on.'

'One last thing,' Deans said. 'Have you seen that before?' He gestured towards Amy's face.

The CSM shook his head. 'No. That's a new one on me.'

Deans exited the tent, stepping back into the fierce squall. He hugged his North Face jacket close to his body and stared out at the rapidly approaching ocean that was already licking the lowest of the boulders. He looked back beyond the tent and saw the unmistakeable stripe of flotsam between Amy and the summit. A voice from behind intruded on his thoughts.

'Alright, Andy?' It was Ranford. 'He's good isn't he?'

'Where will she be taken for the PM?' Deans asked.

'The mortuary at the Royal Devon,' Ranford replied.

'Who'll go with the body?'

'I can,' Ranford said willingly. 'I just need to run it by the Hoff.'

'Thanks mate. I need to see the family.' Deans winked and began to walk off.

'But we don't yet know for sure who it is,' Ranford said, reaching for Deans' arm.

'I do,' Deans said ruefully and struggled his way back down the pebble slope towards his vehicle.

He sat silently in his car for a few moments, troubled by the scene. It just was not *right*. The body was no more than fifty metres from the public slipway, when there was probably two miles' worth of embankment to choose from and hundreds of thousands of tonnes of rock. And little effort had been expended to hide her, which was how she had been found so readily. Why did the killer not find a spot further along the bank where fewer people would go? And why wasn't the body buried far deeper? It was almost as if the killer wanted Amy to be found, but why?

CHAPTER TWENTY

Deans waited in his car outside the Poole residence, staring pensively towards the estuary.

Notifying family of bereavement was probably one of the most unpleasant and sometimes challenging aspects of the job. He had received no formal family liaison training, but he did the job adequately enough.

He had learnt over the years not to rehearse. There was no set routine to follow. Each time was different. Each time involved reacting to and managing the most undefiled emotion a human being would ever have to deal with – the unexpected death of their child.

He walked up the pathway as he had done previously, and straightened his tie at the doorstep. He sucked in a shaky breath and held it for a long moment, checked his mobile phone was off for the third time in as many minutes and then knocked on the large front door. Those seconds before the door opened, he would gladly swap with anyone. The waiting was probably the worst bit.

Mrs Poole opened the door with a smile. Deans lifted his

head and looked directly into her eyes, no greeting expression of his own.

She knew in an instant and began sliding down the edge of the doorframe as her legs failed to support her weight, and her face melted into misery. Her hands half-heartedly grabbed for the door but could not resist the downward momentum and she crumpled to the floor, wailing hideously, before Deans could reach her.

Deans quickly entered the house. 'Mrs Poole, please allow me to help you.' He thrust his hands beneath her armpits and took the deadweight in his arms. Her cries of anguish bellowed in his ear.

Mr Poole entered the hallway and on seeing his wife on the floor and Deans struggling to hold her, he stopped walking and crashed onto his knees, arms reaching out towards his wife.

'Please, no,' he appealed. 'No, no, no. Not Amy.' His voice fractured and he began to weep.

'Mr Poole,' Deans shouted sternly, 'please help me. We need to get your wife to a chair.'

Like a zombie, Mr Poole scraped himself from the floor and helped Deans drag his wife into the living room.

'Mr Poole, please sit down, sir. I have some regretful news that I must give you.'

Deans gathered up a chair, pulled it directly in front of them, and sat down so they were all on the same level. He hesitated, and asked himself how he would want to hear it.

'I'm very sorry to have to say that, this morning on Sandymere Bay, the body of a young woman was discovered.'

He paused, anticipating the next reaction. It did not come. He drew breath.

'I've been to the scene and viewed' – he coughed nervously – 'the body, and I believe that it may be Amy.' He stopped again. This time, Mr and Mrs Poole crumpled into one another's arms.

Deans remained silent, his eyes welled and he coughed away the makings of a whimper. He stood up. It did not go unnoticed by Mr Poole whose eyes, reddened and resigned, acknowledged Deans as he left the room.

He took a few steps away – far enough to be respectful; close enough for them to know he was with them. But right then, at that moment, he recognised he was both the henchman and the healer.

CHAPTER TWENTY-ONE

Denise Moon was coming to the end of a client session. She had not been efficient that day. She was feeling disturbed and exhausted and was hoping to have some time alone for reflection. It had been a long day.

She had been disappointed with the officer's reaction to her phone call and self-doubt had weighed her down since that time. She would not pass on information unless she believed it to be valid. It was true that the flow of communication was meagre; however, she had deciphered the necessary elements. There was no denying she needed more detail but somehow her attempts to achieve clarification had failed. She took a moment to block everything out and lay down on the treatment couch, slowly drifting into meditation.

Am I too close to Amy? She thought, breaking her transition. 'Was it the way she died?' she questioned aloud. She groaned, rolled off the couch and ambled through to the shop front where Ash was sitting behind the counter as usual. The waiting area was empty and the LEDs burned brightly in the display cabinets. Ash confirmed there had been no calls during the previous hour and no other appointments were planned for the day.

'Are you feeling okay today?' he asked.

'Yes, flower, I'm okay, thank you.' She rubbed a hand down the front of her face. 'I'm just experiencing a rather confusing connection. Struggling to extract clarity.'

'Can I help at all?'

'Not at the moment, darling, thank you.'

'Is it anything to do with that policeman?'

Denise whimpered. 'Well, yes. In a way, I suppose it is.'

'Why was he here? Are you treating him?'

Denise laughed at the irony. 'No. I can't imagine that one would ever drop his barriers enough for that to happen.'

'I know what you mean. They're a different breed, the police,' Ash said. 'I guess it's the way they have to work to all those rules and regulations. It's black or white, nothing in between, no stone left unturned and all that. I wouldn't want to do it for a job.'

'The saddest thing is, we could help them if only they'd allow themselves to open their minds,' Denise said dejectedly. 'Together we could help provide unspoken words, help mend broken bonds or reassure loved ones left behind.'

'That will never happen, Den. Don't get your hopes up. Our poles are too far apart. The police would never give any credence to the gift.' He touched her hand. 'I'm worried about you. Don't set yourself up for a fall.'

Denise broke into a resigned smile. 'I suppose you're right, but there was no harm in trying. I'm going to take a lie-down, close my eyes for twenty minutes. Be a sweetie and take care of anyone coming in.'

Denise shuffled away to the back room, slipped off her shoes, lowered the blinds and spent the next five minutes taking deep, controlled breaths.

. . .

Betrayal. Chameleon.

Denise immediately recognised Amy's voice. Two spoken words, but what was the meaning? She felt Amy's presence again. Denise had not searched for it. Amy had come to her. Amy needed salvation and she was showing Denise the way.

'Tell me, Amy,' Denise whispered. She was attuned, her senses acutely aligned.

'Use me,' she implored louder.

She tried to lift her head but a downward pressure pinned her to the couch. Her eyes were open but could no longer see daylight. A dull resonating sound confused her mind.

A pressure in her chest increased with every breath, a tightening band of fear began to take hold. She fought to bring her hands up to her face but they were unwilling. There was no feeling of movement in her legs. The crushing sensation grew stronger. Every cell of her body was now super-fuelled with the effects of surging adrenalin and she could sense a building panic in Amy, and within herself. Her own heart was now racing and she could feel the connection to Amy was slipping away as her own body prepared itself for self-preservation. Denise sensed the killer.

'Show me,' she pleaded. 'Show me, Amy,' she screamed, clawing at the material beneath her.

'Denise? Den? Den!' Ash had charged into the treatment room on hearing the disturbance. He grabbed her hand and held it tightly between his. Denise was breathing fast and shallow. Her skin had turned pale and clammy.

'Jesus, Denise. Come back,' Ash said, slapping the back of her hand, but she was unresponsive. He swiftly placed her into the recovery position and squatted beside her. 'Den, Den, come on. Break the contact,' he said, rocking her forcibly by the shoulders. Her eyes were open, but it was as if her soul had left her.

Ash snapped his fingers inches from her face and shook her more violently until finally, he saw a glimmer of recognition in her eyes.

'Christ, Den, are you okay?' he gasped, a bead of sweat forming on his own brow.

Denise blinked rapidly and attempted to raise herself.

'It's okay,' she panted, pushing herself up to a seated position. 'I'm all right, thank you.' She slumped forward, shaking life back into her arms.

'Let me grab you a drink,' Ash said in a dither, and rushed out of the room.

'Any chance of making it a stiff one?' Denise joked weakly, but Ash was gone.

The shop door opened, setting off the bell chimes in the reception. Ash was there and could deal with whoever it was, so Denise lay back down and pondered Amy's message. The words *betrayal* and *chameleon* repeated in her head. What did they refer to, and how was she supposed to decipher them?

The gift allowed a practitioner to connect between the here and now and the afterlife, and occasionally communication was effortless, but more frequently it was jumbled, almost coded, and that is when the skill of the medium is measured. Denise prided herself on her ability to untangle any web of words but this particular scenario was unique, as well as personally upsetting.

The door to the therapy room opened and Ash walked in.

'Den, I'm sorry. That policeman is back. He wants to speak to you. I told him you were otherwise occupied but he's rather insistent.'

Denise was relieved. Their last contact had left her feeling unusually downhearted.

'That's fine, flower, let him through. Would you be a darling and put the kettle on, please?'

Ash nodded, but his disapproval was evident for Denise to see as he left the room.

Deans knocked politely and poked his head around the door.

'Come in,' she said. 'Hello, Detective. I wasn't expecting to see you again.'

'Funnily enough, I wasn't expecting to be back,' he retorted with a smile, which was one of awkwardness rather than friendliness.

'How may I help?' Denise asked.

Deans' day-old stubble crackled beneath his fingertips, as he thought about her question. He could not fathom if he was anxious about what he was about to ask, or what he was about to hear.

'You said Amy had a lift from her killer, and then you said Amy was dead before I knew about it. Where were you getting your information from?'

Denise smiled knowingly and patted the sofa seat next to her as she sat down. Deans responded and noticed her studying his face.

'I told you already,' she said. 'Amy showed me.'

Deans shook his head. 'I don't understand. How's that possible? How are you receiving the communication, and what exactly did she say?'

He was asking multiple questions at the same time, a big no-no for any successful interrogation, but he would be happy with just one answer to any of them. It did not matter which at this stage. Deans felt a desperate need for understanding, and then perhaps he could start believing.

'She came to me again,' Denise said, 'just now.'

'Go on,' Deans prompted.

'She was in a dark, confined space.' Denise looked away vacantly. 'It was...' she shook her head. '...Cold and she couldn't move.'

Deans leant forward, elbows on his knees.

'She was terrified,' Denise continued. 'I felt her panic – pure, stricken fear.'

Deans had not moved. Denise focused on him.

'You've found her. Haven't you?' she said, more as a statement than a question.

'Tell me more,' he urged, avoiding the question. 'Please.'

Denise evaluated Deans with her eyes before she spoke again. 'Amy has mentioned two things that I don't yet understand.'

Deans nodded, opened out a hand.

'She said two words. Quite individual, but not in any context. *Betrayal* and *chameleon*.' Denise looked purposefully at Deans as if he would have an instant answer.

Deans slumped back firmly in the seat and the cool, comforting leather wrapped around his frame. He bobbed his head a little, and exhaled slowly.

'Amy's boyfriend is in custody as we speak,' he said. 'That could account for the betrayal.'

'Why has he been arrested?' Denise asked interestedly.

'I'm afraid I'm unable to divulge that at this time. I'm sorry.'

Denise let out a stifled laugh. 'Detective Deans, I understand the constraints you work under. Please don't think I'm trying to prise information from you. That was not my intention. I'm as determined to establish the facts as you.'

'I know,' Deans said. He could tell she was genuine, and in truth, he was becoming increasingly intrigued by Denise Moon. He stood up and as he did so, his forehead thumped with a surging pain. He waited silently for a second, clutching his head.

'Are you okay?' Denise asked.

'I need to go back to Bath,' he said, pinching the bridge of his nose.

She stared at him. 'Would you like some water?'

He shook his head. 'Do you mind?' he said apologetically. 'If it's okay, could you keep me updated with any other contact from Amy?'

'Of course, Detective.' She was watching him intently. 'Maybe we can work through this together?'

Deans' mouth twitched to a semi-smile, he removed a business card from his wallet, placed it on the arm of the sofa and patted it. As he opened the treatment room door it was clear that he had caught Ash off guard.

'Ah, there you are,' Ash improvised. 'I was about to knock on the door but I didn't want to interrupt anything.'

Deans was standing in his path. Ash tilted to the side and addressed Denise. 'One of your clients called for you. I told them you were busy. Didn't leave any messages.' As he turned back towards the reception, Ash gave Deans a wary peek.

He was very different to his employer. A willowy, wiry man. Deans could tell with no hesitation that Ash did not like him. It probably was not personal; after all, they'd only just met. Perhaps he had suffered a bad experience with the police. It did not bother Deans. He normally struggled to get along with people like Ash and thus far, nothing about the man was proving the contrary.

CHAPTER TWENTY-TWO

Deans finally got through to Savage and informed him that he was heading back. An ETA of three hours meant he would reach the office at around four thirty, give or take.

The custody extension had not yet been authorised, and minus travelling time, they had just about two hours left on the clock. *Nowhere near long enough*, Deans thought as he started the long journey home. He bolstered himself for the long drive ahead with a welcome sugar hit from a Snickers bar and put a CD into the music system. Driving alone was one of the few times when he could grasp a piece of normality in an otherwise surreal day, but as he forced a hummed tune, his thoughts turned to Amy's mangled body amongst the cold, dank boulders. He remembered the panic Denise had described, and cringed at the terror Amy must have experienced and the abject horror of it all. He did not register any more of the song and little more of the journey.

· · ·

He arrived back in the office not far off his original estimation. His colleagues were buzzing around. Something else was going on.

He caught the eye of Savage across the room.

'Deano, how are you doing? The extension is set. We got the full twelve, giving you until six fifty-three tomorrow morning.'

Deans looked at the clock on the wall as if he needed to check what 6.53 a.m. looked like. He was completely knackered and his mind was draining him of what energy he had left as it played out a variety of scenarios, none of them making much sense. He acknowledged Harper with a nod, who was deep into a pile of papers across the desk.

'What've you got, Dais?' Deans asked.

'Stranger rape beside the canal locks. Looks like a proper job.' She flashed him a knowing look and returned to her work.

Deans did not want to interrupt her unnecessarily, and he certainly did not need to become embroiled in that job, so he said no more, shut the room out and began to focus.

He took a red pen and drew a large square box on the right-hand side of his timeline. Inside he wrote *MISPER LOCATED – DECEASED – Sandymere Bay, Saturday 11th October, 07:20 hours.*

He stared intently at the sheet. All the noise around him faded out. There were still so many gaps to fill: when, how and why she was murdered? If the murderer was Groves, and how and why was she dumped at Sandymere Bay?

He removed his phone and checked for messages. He had not spoken to his wife since leaving home that morning and she had not made any attempt to contact him either. How could he try to make it up to her knowing that she probably wouldn't get to see him again until at least late tomorrow afternoon?

His prisoner had now been with them for almost twenty-four hours. Groves was apparently being a model detainee. No complaining, no banging on the cell door, no shouting or swearing and always polite when spoken to, however the cell staff were growing concerned at his lack of eating or drinking.

Deans had some time before the solicitor would be back at the station so he made a call to Ranford, who had been attending the post-mortem examination.

'What's the update?' Deans asked.

'I haven't done one of those before and that was bloody gruesome,' Ranford replied.

Deans chuckled and thought back to his first PM; the suspicious death of a homeless drunk following a drugs overdose. The question had been; who had administered the fatal dose? It was one of those first-time experiences indelibly ensconced in the mind. He had only been in CID for a couple of weeks when the job came in. The blasé way in which the pathologist and mortuary team dissected the body had been astonishing. Every organ and body part of interest examined and removed with such enthusiasm that it was a somewhat disturbing experience for a novice. Two things in particular stuck with him, the first being the appalling odour that was unlike anything else he had previously experienced and remained with him for several days after, and secondly the gruesome yet fascinating procedure of peeling the dead man's skin from his head to access the brain.

'They improve with practice,' Deans said.

'I don't want another for a while, thank you,' Ranford retorted.

'You'll see they're like buses. Anyway, give me the lowdown.'

'The pathologist was very interested with the glue in the eyes. Said it was cyanoacrylate adhesive, or superglue to you and me. He said there was no evidence that she attempted to remove it. Her ear canals were full of it too.'

'Really?' Deans said.

'There's more. Much more, they tidied up her face. Looks like letters carved into her cheeks.'

'What?' Deans uttered breathlessly.

'Left cheek appears to spell *SNE*, the right, *HNE*.'

Deans scribbled the initials in his book. 'Go on,' he said.

'The incisions were rough, jagged, different depths.'

'She was alive,' Deans said beneath his breath.

'Sorry?' Ranford said.

'Nothing. What else?'

'There was a large, well-established bruise to her right temple, which according to the pathologist indicates infliction before death, but was unlikely to have killed her. Asphyxiation is the likely cause of death, suffocation. There are some markings that might suggest attempted strangulation, and other deep tissue bruises around the body, probably from being buried while she still had a strong circulation of blood. In other words, it appears she was buried alive.'

Deans thought back to the pebble ridge. He viewed it distinctly in his mind's eye, but it was night-time, even though he had not visited the scene in the dark. The unrelenting barrage of waves created a din that clogged his mind. He jerked his head, but the vision remained.

'Is there any way to establish if she was conscious when she was buried?' he asked.

'Impossible to say. The mass of pebbles would have prevented any body movement. If she was conscious to start with, she soon wouldn't have been able to do anything about it.'

'Was she interfered with?'

'Almost categorically not. She was certainly no virgin but there was no trace of semen or evidence of any other kind of forced struggle. The only other unusual aspect the pathologist commented on was a broken nail on her right ring finger. Said it was recent, and that it looked nasty.'

Deans clasped his forehead with his free hand, and pressed his fingers into the temples.

'Any scope for DNA comparison?' he asked.

'We've taken fingernail cuttings and scrapings and swabbed around her eyes, mouth, hands and vagina, but given the location in which she was found the pathologist and CSM don't hold out a lot of hope due to water contamination.'

'Okay, thanks. Do yourself a favour and find some Vicks,' Deans said. 'It will help get rid of the smell. I'll be in touch.' Deans ended the conversation and rested his head in his hands. He was surprised that sexual contact had not been identified. Lust, desire or sexual hatred had been top of his motive stakes.

Time to rethink.

CHAPTER TWENTY-THREE

Interviewing was Deans' domain. It was the time when he could gain a degree of control in an otherwise spiralling investigation. So far, he had been playing catch-up, chasing shadows, scratching around for evidence. This interview would be his first opportunity to get answers directly from Groves.

Some prisoners had the mistaken belief that by saying 'no comment' they would throw the interviewing officer off-balance and gain the upper hand. Deans had lost count of the number of interviewees that smirked their way through a 'no comment' interview only to wish they'd put their point of view across when they were subsequently standing before the custody sergeant and being charged. Frequently they were positively encouraged to say nothing by their solicitor, through fear of implicating themselves or because the police did not have enough evidence to warrant an account by the defendant. And that was exactly what Deans predicted was about to happen with Groves, though he was not worried. He was well prepared regardless of the limited evidence to hand, and he had the advantage of that previous witness testimony, which had more holes in it than a colander.

When Deans was young in service, he was excited but inadequate at interviewing. He sometimes had all the answers before the interviews started and would try his utmost to trip the defendants up; to make them look silly or prove they were lying; to show how clever he was and complete it all as quickly as possible.

He used to keep tabs with a couple of colleagues as to who could get the quickest interview time. Four minutes was the record set by one of his response team colleagues, PC Gower: a four-minute 'no comment' interview; that was all. It was a joke, shameful. Gower thought it was clever until six months later when the case landed in court. He practically crapped himself at the thought of having to justify his inept interview to the magistrates.

It was rare to find an officer who genuinely enjoyed court. Maybe it was the waiting around, sometimes for days on end. Maybe it was being under the spotlight and scrutiny of others, or maybe it was because defence solicitors and barristers took a particular pleasure from making police officers squirm in the witness box. Whatever it was, Deans still did not relish court time and always viewed it as one of the more hostile environments of his job.

It had taken Deans a while to work out that it really did not matter what a defendant might say during an interview so long as his own preparation was thorough and his questions were valid and appropriate.

The brief, Johnson, had already been provided with disclosure up to the point that Deans was informed about the body. Johnson knew that CCTV suggested Groves was in Hemingsford on the date and time of Amy's disappearance. He had even viewed the orange Citroen Saxo on the laptop, but Johnson appeared, on the whole, unimpressed. It was obvious he would more than likely advise Groves to make no comment during the interview, and he would be quite right to do so. Johnson's job was to protect his client, not allow Groves to implicate himself. His ethos would be; let the police do the hard yards – get accurate facts, provide firm evidence and then, maybe, Groves might talk. This would be a tedious one-way interview. Not so much cat and mouse as cat and mute.

The thought of sitting in a room for a couple of hours with Johnson made Deans restless. It was not because he was a particularly clever solicitor who would test Deans' ability. It was simply because Johnson loved to make life as difficult as possible, even if it meant making his own life more problematic in the process. He was one of a kind; the only solicitor Deans knew who went out of his way to be an arse.

Johnson was probably in his mid-fifties, overweight with lank, dark hair combed back from his clammy grey forehead with Brylcreem, or perhaps cooking fat. His thick black square-rimmed glasses were frequently used as a prop during interviews to highlight an issue or augment an opinion, when he would remove them and literally poke them at the interviewing officer. His breath smelt stale. He had poor dental hygiene and generally looked like a bag of shit. He rarely managed to keep his shirt from flapping out over his belt and his tie knots always appeared to have been made by a toddler.

Deans' thoughts sometimes strayed during Johnson's interviews and he would imagine him being that person you'd notice in a traffic jam with a finger fully extended up one nostril, rooting around regardless of who else might be watching. He suspected that Johnson was a lonely man, even though he did not know anything about his personal life.

Deans was already occupying the stuffy interview room. His papers spread out in front of him, Maxpax coffee on the go. The room was small and hot, old and dirty. The sound-proofing tiles must have been thirty years old and they looked every day of it. Five people in the room was about the limit. The single desk was bolted to the floor, the floor tiles were well used to say the least, and the build-up of spilt coffee and tea made for an interesting visual effect. A window at the end of the room had opaque glass so that nothing outside was discernible, and the thick metal bars on the inside had been painted white so many times that the holding bolts were barely recognisable. The recording equipment was so out-of-date that cassette tapes were still used. Deans had used the same kind of cassettes as a kid to record music from the Radio 1 chart show each Sunday. He did not know if they were even still available in the shops. Probably not, but his station appeared to have them in abundance. Management had always argued that until a station revamp took place, officers would have to make do with the existing technology and just get on with it.

The soundproofed door to the interview room opened and Groves walked in, anxiously scanning between the four walls, his shoulders drooped, eyes wide open. He looked exhausted.

Johnson followed close behind. His voice arrived before Deans saw him. *The performance has already started*, Deans thought.

Johnson ushered Groves to the end chair opposite Deans, as he waffled on about what was about to happen and took his seat alongside his client. He should have already explained that guff during the consultation period, and Deans would repeat it anyway, but it was Johnson's way of trying to get the first break of serve.

Groves simply looked beleaguered, and Deans watched him with interest as Mitchell took the seat between himself and Johnson.

The DI had already decided not to arrest Groves for murder at this stage. A formal ID of the body still needed to take place and until the family confirmed that the corpse was Amy, Groves' status was not to change.

8:21 p.m.

Jesus, Deans thought. It was already getting on for a double shift and he was only just starting the interview.

Deans had not broken eye contact with Groves during the entire seventeen minutes it took for him to explain the interview process. This was not only a thorough and professional introduction, it was also a display of control and confidence and it showed Deans was not going to accept any messing from Groves, or Johnson. He could sense Groves wouldn't be any trouble for him but was less sure about his solicitor.

As he went through the introduction, he could see Groves glancing over at Johnson, who was smugly jotting something down on his scratch pad and occasionally bobbing his head or pursing his lips in a display of attention, purely for Groves' benefit. He had no reason to react to anything Deans was saying at this point. It was a standard introduction and one that Deans could do backwards and probably whilst sleep talking. Those glances only confirmed that he was waiting on Johnson to prompt him into 'no comment' responses.

As Deans watched Groves' timid and hesitant body language, he became less clear about his suspect. There was the false statement and the CCTV, both compelling, and not forgetting the discovery of the body. However, something about the man in front of him did not seem right. It was true he had not been completely honest in his statement, and Deans would suggest he was at Amy's hometown at the time of the murder, but was he a killer? Groves was a candidate for sure, but not a dead cert.

Standard interview practice was to invite the interviewee to provide their own detailed account prior to the interviewer explaining and describing the evidence against them. It would allow a suspect to be open and furnish an unprompted account. Deans could then dissect each part of the version in fine detail until he was satisfied every topic had been exhausted. That would have been how Johnson sold it to Groves during their consultation, and that was just how Deans intended to play it, until he saw Groves sitting opposite him, scared and shaking.

Deans delayed his opening question, said nothing and waited for Groves to engage eye contact.

Johnson stopped scribbling and looked up at Deans from over the top of his glasses. Deans could sense Johnson's anticipation, readying himself to interject.

Still saying nothing, Deans removed a buff-coloured A4 envelope from the papers in front of him and slid the package across the table towards Groves, who recoiled away from it.

Deans waited.

Groves flashed a glance in his direction. Game on.

'The body of a young woman was discovered at Sandymere Bay earlier today.' Deans gestured to the envelope. 'Take it. Have a look inside.'

Groves' hand hovered over the envelope, and he nervously looked at Johnson for guidance. This was Johnson's cue to interject.

'Officer, might I ask what this is? What are you giving my client to comment on?'

'An exhibit.'

Johnson removed his glasses and held them out in front of his face, prodding the air between himself and Deans.

'I don't believe my client and I have seen this material. Have you provided me with full disclosure, Officer? You know if I haven't been made privy—'

'Open it, Carl. Take a look inside.' Deans said, cutting Johnson short.

Johnson's voice was now the loudest in the room. 'Officer, before my client looks at the content of that envelope I wish to know if this material has been subject to primary disclosure. If this is evidence that I've not been made privy to then I must request that this interview be suspended in order that my client may fairly view all available material that he is being asked to comment on.'

Johnson had not taken a breath. His cheeks were red and his jowls were still vibrating.

Deans leant over the table and took the envelope back with a dry smile. Ignoring Johnson's rants, he peeled open the flap and slowly removed the six A4 colour photographs contained within. He laid them out, facedown, at arm's-length from Groves, so that all Groves could see was the white backing of each sheet. Still snubbing a now flapping Johnson, Deans increased the tension by slowly lining up the pages so they were neat and equally spaced.

Groves was now shifting uncomfortably in his seat, his face a mixture of bewilderment and alarm; every subtle movement interpreted by Deans.

Johnson now at thirty-eight thousand feet shouted, 'Officer, I really must object to this. I demand the interview be suspended and I demand to see the Superintendent at once.'

'I tell you what, Carl,' Deans said, shunning Johnson, 'we can come back to these a little later.'

Groves was rigidly mute. He had turned pale and had slumped forwards onto his forearms, staring bug-eyed at the sheets before him.

'Do you remember that statement you gave me, Carl?' Deans asked. 'You know the one you signed as being truthful?'

He paused just long enough to gain an impact. 'Not misleading or false in any way?'

Groves turned desperately to Johnson for guidance, who in turn nodded in such a ridiculous manner it must have been a pre-arranged signal to make a 'no comment' response.

Sure enough, Groves conformed to his reply: 'No comment.'

'Shall I refresh your memory?' Deans said, pulling out a copy of the statement from the pile of papers. 'This is the same statement, isn't it, Carl?' he said, dropping the pages beneath Groves' nose.

A quick look left and a nod from Johnson and Groves replied, 'No comment.'

Deans leant back in his chair and coupled his hands behind his head.

'The thing is, Carl, you said on the weekend Amy went missing you were at home; that you did not see Amy after the lift from university on Friday. And most importantly, that you had never been to Amy's hometown.'

'No comment,' Groves replied without hesitation. No need to involve Johnson this time.

'I didn't ask for your comments, Carl. I was refreshing your memory.'

The silent stare across the table shut out everyone else in the room.

Deans did not let up. 'So tell me. How can you account for the fact that your car was in Amy's hometown on the night she disappeared?'

'Well, I—' Groves started to respond before Johnson hastily interjected.

'Mr Groves, I've given you my advice regarding the lack of evidence against you at this present moment in time. Would you like to speak privately with me before we continue this interview any further?'

Johnson had an annoying trait of not looking at the person he was speaking to, closing his eyes and tilting his head backwards, as if he was addressing an auditorium.

'Um, no. I wouldn't,' Groves responded.

'I am merely reiterating to you my professional advice regarding your input during these proceedings,' Johnson persisted.

'Mr Johnson. He said no,' Deans said. 'We all heard it and I am sure the tape recorded it. Now please, allow me to continue with this interview.'

Deans was secretly delighted that Groves was already showing signs of discontent with Johnson. He turned back to Groves.

'Sorry, Carl. Please, you were saying?'

'Um. No comment.'

Johnson nodded smugly. Moral victory, for now.

That's enough foreplay, Deans thought.

'Tell me what time you met up with Amy in Devon.'

'I didn't,' Groves replied instinctively.

'Mr Groves, may I please reiterate—'.

'Tell me why not. You were clearly there,' Deans said, speaking over Johnson.

Groves began bouncing his left leg, knocking his knee against the table leg, causing Deans' coffee to ripple. It was clear he had something he wanted to say. He took a glance at Johnson, who with eyes closed, was shaking his head.

'No comment.'

Deans referred to Groves' original statement and read out the description of his car.

'So tell me, Carl, what happened to your bonnet?'

Groves frowned but did not reply.

'You see,' Deans said, reaching forwards, 'I took the liberty of checking the CCTV from the car park next door on the day that you attended the station to speak with me.' He picked up the A4 sheet closest to Johnson and flipped it over.

'There you are,' Deans said enthusiastically, 'getting into your car. And it appears to me that the bonnet is a different colour to the remainder of the vehicle. Would you agree?'

Groves turned anxiously to Johnson who was already tilting his head and closing his eyes.

'Officer, forgive me but I was under the impression we were talking about an offence that happened a number of days before this image was taken. Can you please explain the relevance so that my client can fully understand your line of questioning and therefore respond appropriately?'

'Well, there's not a lot of "we" in the talking so far as I see it and if you could refrain from interrupting the interview after every question I ask, perhaps your client would have an opportunity to understand the questions more clearly.'

Mitchell, for the first time, glanced over to Deans, who was already spinning over the next sheet.

'Look, Carl, there is that same vehicle in Hemingsford, on Saturday October the fourth, at eight fifty-seven p.m. How do you account for that if you've never been there before?'

'Officer,' Johnson interrupted with hostile tones, 'are you suggesting that there is no possibility a car of similar appearance exists? This image doesn't even show a clear registration number. My client will be making no comment to your question.'

Deans leant back in his chair and faced Johnson with an icy glower. 'Mr Johnson, have I missed something here? Are you no longer the legal advisor? At some point in the last half-hour, has Mr Groves become a juvenile? Or maybe he's suddenly developed learning difficulties, because you seem to be answering the question on his behalf.'

'I did nothing of the sort,' Johnson responded defensively.

Deans had the bit between his teeth. 'It sounded to me like you were not only prompting your client's answer, but giving it on his behalf. I'm now formally warning you that any further infringement of the codes of practice will force me to stop this interview and inform the duty inspector of your conduct.'

'And what about your underhand tactics, Officer? I want this interview stopped, right now.'

'It's continuing.'

'This is outrageous.'

'It's continuing and if you have something to say afterwards, fill your boots. I'm sure the inspector will be delighted to hear from you.'

Poor Groves did not have a clue what was going on and simply looked terrified.

A silence enveloped the room and seemed to last minutes, but in reality was probably only a matter of seconds.

Deans revealed the next image of the car. 'Take a look at the windscreen, Carl. Look at the two yellow stickers on either side. Now look at this photo.' He turned over another sheet. 'This is you in your car, having left the car park next door. This was taken by one of our ANPR cameras and look, it even shows your number plate.'

Deans glanced at Johnson, whose red cheeks were wobbling.

Deans continued. 'And if we look at the windscreen we can see two yellow stickers at either side.' Deans created ten seconds of imposed silence. 'Now, tell me exactly what you were doing in Devon on the night Amy disappeared.'

Groves hunched forward and emitted a hollow breath. The

nails of his left hand clawed at the tabletop. He did not look over to Johnson and his leg stopped bobbing beneath the table.

Here it comes, Deans thought.

'Can I stop the interview please? I need to speak to my solicitor.'

CHAPTER TWENTY-FOUR

Deans took the opportunity to call a thirty-minute comfort break and headed for the tiny kitchenette. Mitchell followed behind.

'That was fun, Deano,' Mitchell enthused. 'Johnson's gone running off to find the custody skipper.'

It was now 9:10 p.m. Deans had been working since eight a.m. and after six days on duty his tolerance threshold was starting to wobble.

'I'm sorry I lost it with Johnson,' he said softly.

'No worries, Deano. It's about time that old fart got something back in his face for all the shit he gives us. Good for you.'

'You know what? I feel a bit sorry for the kid,' Deans said.

Mitchell's jaw dropped 'What are you talking about? He's a bloody murderer, Deano. Don't feel sorry for him.'

'Is he, Mitch? Is he? Groves had no idea what was on those photographs, and the thought of seeing them genuinely shocked him. He was expecting to see his girlfriend in some dreadful state but when he saw his own car his relief was undeniable. I'm not so sure he's our killer.'

'What're you talking about, Deano? The fact he's going "no comment" shows he's hiding something.'

'I agree. He is hiding something, but the "no comment" is all about Johnson, not Groves. I can see the poor kid's conscience is playing out its own little battle in there. He wants to speak to us but feels he mustn't because of Johnson.'

Mitchell groaned and shook his head.

'I want to go it alone, Mitch.'

'What do you mean? You'll need backup for Johnson.'

'No. I'll be fine. I think we'll get more success of Groves talking with a less intimidating environment.'

Mitchell checked his watch, but Deans had already calculated it was almost the end of their shift and he was not anticipating too much resistance from Mitchell.

By 10:02 p.m. they were all back in the interview room bar Mitchell, who had scurried upstairs to the office without a second invitation.

Deans prodded the record button on the cassette machine and offered some lame excuse for Mitchell no longer being part of the interview. He then got straight to the point.

'Carl, I know you were in Devon. I know you went down to see Amy. I know you probably saw her before she got on the bus.'

Deans noted a change in Groves' expression; his eyes were intense and he was rocking his head, just enough for Deans to notice. Deans was getting close to the truth but something was wrong.

He dipped Groves a single slow nod. It was a silent acknowledgement – a moment of understanding between suspect and interviewer.

'Did you have some kind of argument with Amy before she went into town?'

Groves was now fixated on Deans, but did not respond.

Johnson was writing down Deans' questions verbatim and so his attention was on his scratch pad rather than on Groves and Deans.

'Describe your feelings towards Scott,' Deans continued.

Groves glared and Deans noticed a flicker of his eyelids.

Deans made a note in his book. Time for another reaction.

'Amy was your girlfriend of… what? About a year? How did it make you feel to know she was seeing her ex-boyfriend in Devon?'

Johnson leant forwards and glanced at his client. Deans knew he was getting somewhere. Johnson looked confused. This was obviously news to him.

Deans continued. 'Did you know Amy was seeing Scott that Saturday night?'

Groves' cheeks reddened, his jaw muscles rippled and his hands interlocked so tightly that Deans could see the crimson red and blood-drained white of each finger.

It's time, Deans thought.

'Carl, I believe Amy is dead.'

The eyes of his interviewee flickered and faltered, but Deans did not soften.

'A woman's body was found this morning buried beneath a pile of rock on a beach not far from Amy's home. She was brutally murdered. I saw the remains with my own eyes.' Deans sat back and watched Groves squirm and redden as the young man struggled to process the news.

Johnson for once did not try to intervene. He could also see the impact of the last thirty seconds.

It was time for Deans to follow his instinct.

'Carl, if you want to tell me something about last Saturday night, this would be a good time, buddy.'

Groves was quaking as he fought back tears and rage and possibly guilt.

'Go on, Carl. Help me find Amy's killer.'

There it was, on the table. Deans was making it official. He no longer viewed Carl as the killer.

Johnson looked over at Deans quizzically, but before he could say anything Carl spoke as tears streamed down his cheeks.

'She got a lift from the bus stop.'

'Go on.'

'Scotty pulled up in a car. Amy got in. I didn't speak to her. I didn't even get near her.' Groves threw his head into his hands.

Scotty? Deans thought. *Why would he lie about picking her up from the bus stop if he was happy to describe being with her later on that night?* It did not make sense.

'Are you sure it was Scotty?'

'Yeah,' Groves said, wiping his face. 'Almost a hundred percent.'

'How do you know?'

'They hugged and kissed. It could only be Scotty.'

This time it was Johnson and Groves waiting for Deans to speak. He gently nodded. Needed a change of direction.

'Carl, thank you for talking to me. It's the right thing to do, I assure you.'

Deans checked out the now-redundant Johnson, who had just slapped his pen loudly onto his pad.

'Carl, I want you to know that I believe you.'

Groves collapsed into his arms, and flopped in a heap on the table.

'I really need to know about the man with the car,' Deans said. He stopped talking and waited for Groves to engage.

'This is real, isn't it?' Groves spluttered, lifting his head. 'Amy is really dead?'

Deans nodded. 'You can really help me, son, and you can help yourself and Amy. I need you to relax as much as possible and put yourself back to last Saturday.' Deans needed him to not only think about the night, but also relive it. That was the only way the fine detail could come out, and that could make all the difference. Under the circumstances Deans was chancing his luck, but he needed Carl now. It was some irony.

Deans would have much preferred Johnson not to be in the room with them. He was more than capable of screwing things up. Deans crossed his fingers beneath the desk and took a deep breath.

'Carl, I need you to clear your mind of everything that has just gone before and I want you to concentrate on my questions and nothing else. I promise this will help you and in turn it might help Amy. Do you agree to try?'

Groves nodded tentatively. 'Am I still under arrest?'

'Yes, but what goes on between now and the end of the interview could significantly improve your situation if you cooperate.'

Deans looked at Johnson, who had now folded his arms and legs in a closed, defensive pose. He just hoped the man could shut up long enough to allow Groves to concentrate.

Deans began slowly feeding Groves with prompts, kickstarting his recall. His voice was calm, unrushed and reassuring, akin to a hypnotherapist.

'You're in a perfectly safe environment, Carl. I want you to take yourself back to Saturday night. To the moment, you saw Amy. Close your eyes if it helps. Think about where you are for a moment. Look at what is around you. Listen to the noises and sounds, or tunes playing in the background.' Music had a strong cognitive quality that could take an individual back to a very specific time in their life. Deans continued. 'Look at the clothes you're wearing. In your mind, starting from the top, describe each item in as much detail as you can, as if someone on the end of a phone has to draw each piece of clothing accurately based on your description alone.' He paused.

'Remember how the material feels against your skin.'

He waited again.

'Now. You can see Amy at the bus stop. Just concentrate on her and nothing else. Focus on Amy. Take in as much detail as you can, no matter how small.'

He was asking a lot of Groves and it would be a hard task for a completely willing volunteer, let alone someone who'd been stuffed in a cell for over twenty-four hours.

'Keep concentrating on Amy,' Deans softly prompted. 'Don't miss a single detail.'

He let a few more soundless seconds calmly slip by.

'Describe what you see, Carl.'

'Amy's alone,' Groves replied. 'She's looking gorgeous.' He was answering in the present tense.

Deans inwardly smiled. 'Describe what happens next, Carl.'

'The car's arrived.'

Deans readied his pen. 'Look at the car. Take it all in… notice the colour… and see the shape.' Deans' pen hung over a fresh page of his daybook.

'It's seven fifty-two.'

'How do you know that, Carl?'

'The clock on my dash.'

'Very good. Now bring into your sight the moment the car pulls up at just before seven fifty-two. Look at it. Concentrate on the front of the car and when you're ready, slowly move towards the back, taking in as much detail as you can.'

Groves' eyes were closed and his head was bobbing.

'Tell me about the car.'

Groves cleared his throat. 'It's a mark five Golf.'

'A VW Golf,' Deans said, reinstating the image. 'Good, Carl, excellent. How certain are you about the make?'

'I'm sure. A mate's got one back home.'

'Stay with the car, Carl. Look at it in even more detail. Explore the design of the wheels. The windows. The bodywork. And concentrate on the colour.' Deans paused and watched Groves' face twitching. 'Now, if you had to point this particular car out to me in the street from any other mark five VW Golf, how would you do it?'

Groves frowned and his knee began to bounce once more.

'Take your time,' Deans reassured him, almost whispering.

Johnson was saying nothing. He seemed happy that the longer his client was cooperating with Deans, the less time he had to answer about being a potential killer.

'A tow bar,' Groves announced and stared forcefully at Deans.

'Good, Carl. Is there anything else about the car? Think again about the colour.'

Groves shook his head. 'It was dark. Possibly dark blue or black.' His responses had changed to past tense. He had come out of the cognitive zone.

'Okay, Carl. You have done really well, but there is still a lot of hard work for us to do. I need you to take yourself back again, but now I want you to concentrate on the man. To when he first arrives. Start by looking at the top of his head and slowly take in every detail.'

Deans slid his book onto his lap and sat back in his chair. 'Tell me about his head and face.'

'He's wearing a beanie... but I can't see his face.'

'Describe the beanie hat, Carl. Close your eyes again if you feel that'll help.'

Groves shook his head. 'It's quite baggy. Covering his head.' Groves was now rocking in his chair.

'Go on,' Deans said softly.

'It's a kind of purple, with some sort of black pattern.'

'Describe the material.'

'It's knitted,' Groves said quickly.

'How do you know?'

'It's got a bobble on the top.'

Now that Groves was seeing this so clearly, Deans had a great chance of getting a description of the man.

'Look to where the beanie is pulled over the ears. Now tell me what you can see.'

Groves was still rocking back and forth, but even more exaggerated than before.

'Carl, look at the bottom of the beanie and describe any hair you can see.'

'I can't really see.'

Deans squinted. Groves needed prompting.

'Is the hair tucked under the beanie or is the hair short?'

Groves shook his head, his face tightening. He was becoming frustrated.

'It's not tucked under. It's short. It's definitely short and light-coloured.'

Deans jotted the details in his book. He was now looking for a fair-haired man who possessed a knitted purple and black bobbled beanie hat, and who drove a dark-coloured Golf with a tow bar.

Groves then gawped at Deans, his face pained. 'It's not Scotty.' he said. 'He's too old.'

CHAPTER TWENTY-FIVE

At the end of the interview, Deans left the room, shattered. Cognitive interviewing was mentally draining at the best of times, but this had been something else.

After Groves had cooperated further, Deans managed to extract from him why he had been in Devon that night. Johnson had tried to interject but it was Groves who ended up telling Johnson to shut up, which brought momentary light relief to an otherwise demanding day.

Groves went on to describe how he had gone to Devon, not to meet Amy, but to catch her out with Scotty. How he had battled with extreme bouts of jealousy since becoming involved with her, how men took her bubbly personality the wrong way – even when he was with her, and how he no longer trusted the validity of their relationship. Amy had told him about Scotty several months before; said he was an ex, said they were still close friends. From that time on, Scotty had become his adversary. Groves described how he found Amy's house; sat up watching, did not know if he would see her, but was prepared to wait for as long as was necessary. When he saw her affection towards Scotty at the bus stop, he fell apart. It was the sorry confirmation he had been looking for, but it was also proof that their relationship was terminal. Since that night, he had struggled with insecurity and the mistaken belief, until now, that she was still in Devon with Scotty.

Deans did not have the heart to tell Groves that Amy did meet up with Scotty after the lift. It would probably tip the young lad over the edge. He was fragile enough as it was, but the biggest puzzle remained; who was the other man?

Groves had done well and managed to hold it together for the most part. Now it was over, the emotion of the interview and exposing his inner demons had reduced him to a whimpering mess. To make matters worse, he would have to return to the cell until a decision was made regarding his release.

11:16 p.m.

Deans leant back against the wall of the custody corridor, his head soothed by the cool paintwork.

'Andrew, can we have a chat please?'

It was a familiar voice coming from further along the corridor.

Deans struggled to focus through his bleary eyes and saw Detective Chief Inspector Bellamy dressed in casual clothing, standing with the custody sergeant. Saturday night in the custody suite at just before midnight was not the normal place for the boss to be. Deans stood tall and tucked a flap of shirt back into his trousers.

'Good evening, sir,' he said, and wondered what event had happened during the time he had been interviewing Groves to prompt this visit.

Deans felt awful. His eyes were gritty, he was starving hungry having eaten nothing since breakfast, and he had a day's growth on his chin, not to mention a humour deficiency – not ideal circumstances to be chatting with the boss.

Deans walked through to a side room that the boss had just entered. He knocked on the door and hesitated, seeing Bellamy facing into the room from the far corner, like a prize-fighter waiting for the opening round.

'Andy, I hear you've been doing a fine job on this missing person case.'

'Thank you, sir,' Deans replied. He knew Bellamy had not bothered to come into work at this time just to tell him that.

Bellamy pointed to a chair, already positioned to face in his direction.

Deans cleared his throat, and gently lowered himself down. 'Thank you,' he said uneasily.

'Andy,' the boss said, taking two casual steps forwards, 'there's a delicate divide building with this investigation that I realise might now be a Devon murder enquiry.'

Deans nodded. 'Sir.'

'I understand you've been interviewing the suspect here tonight.'

'That's right, sir, Carl Groves.'

'Yes.' The boss walked over to the door and gently closed it. 'Let's get the bollocks out of the way first, shall we – Mr Johnson's put in a complaint against you.'

'You're kidding—'

'Don't fret, I've heard all about Mr Johnson, but I do need copies of those interview tapes.'

'Yes, sir.' Deans said reluctantly.

'Fine. That's that part done. Now... your man Groves; we have pumped a lot of resources into this job and a week has already slipped by. The time and effort we have put in and continue to put in will count for nothing without a positive outcome. The significance of this job hasn't been missed by the

Chief, who wants an early Somerset result. The press are likely to be all over this and DI Feather will be facing the music, so I need to ensure we are portrayed in a positive light. Being a Devon murder it is highly irregular to have someone of your skill mix, shall we say, seconded to assist when they are sure to have competent officers available.' He paused. 'Are we at a stage where we can go to the CPS tonight for a charging decision?'

Deans did not respond at first and he wondered if the boss had practised, or if that shite just came naturally to him. He found it unbelievable to be having this political conversation on a Saturday night with the DCI. The scowl he had been wearing since the end of the interview was not fading.

'Sir, thank you for coming in tonight to keep me appraised of the management thoughts on this case. I am acutely aware of the cross-border issues; however, there is still a very long way to go with this investigation. We are not at a stage where we can get a charging decision tonight because I don't believe Carl Groves is our man.'

The boss frowned, but Deans continued unhindered. 'I suspect that a third party, as yet unidentified, may have some valuable information for us.' Deans then stunned himself by what next came out of his mouth. 'I have to be honest, sir, I don't give a shit whether this job belongs in Devon or Somerset. The fact is I've been working on it flat out since Monday. My wife hasn't seen me and I've been living between two counties throughout the week. I've seen the body and spent crucial time with the family. They trust me and we have a rapport. I'm the only person, be it here or in Devon, who has the faintest idea of what has happened. Groves did not kill Amy Poole. He may even have seen the killer, but a lot of work still needs to be done before we know that for sure and I'm the best person to do that. Sir.'

The DCI glowered ominously. He was a man highly regarded in the station, but he also came with a fierce reputation.

'Andy, have you been getting enough rest? You seem, shall we say, on edge.'

'No, sir, in a word. I'm completely knackered but crime won't crack itself and in the absence of anyone else giving a damn about this case, up until now it seems; I've had little choice in the matter.'

'Well, now I'm giving you that choice. I have discussed it with DS Savage this evening and we have agreed to release you on secondment, for one month only, or alternatively, I can pull you out of the investigation with immediate effect and you can resume normal duties. So, what's it to be?'

It was an easy professional decision to make, but unbelievably tough from a personal perspective. It would undoubtedly mean living away from home. Maria would freak out.

Deans looked away; his pounding forehead reminded him how tired he was, but his thoughts turned to Janet and Ian Poole.

'I want to stay on the case, boss. It's reached a significant stage.'

'Fine. Your dedication hasn't gone unnoticed, Andy.'

Before leaving, Deans updated Bellamy with the content of the interview. The boss agreed with Deans; Groves was to be bailed, having spent the last thirty hours in custody, but on the proviso that he adhered to strict bail conditions. The last thing they needed was for Groves to be the most compelling storyteller the station had known.

Deans returned to the office. All the lights were out apart from one solitary strip of fluorescence above his desk. It was a stark image confirming that this investigation was beginning to dominate his life.

A note was Blu-Tacked to his computer monitor. He tore it off and held it beneath the light.

Deano, we are off on rest days now. I am sure you will have already seen the boss. I bet that was a pleasant surprise! If you choose to continue with the job, your overtime and cancelled rest days for this week will be authorised on Monday; just let Admin know what you need. I hope you opt to spend a few days at home with your wife. You deserve it – you both do. Mick

CHAPTER TWENTY-SIX

Amy was very happy to accept the lift into town. She was surprised to see him but thought well of everyone and appreciated his generosity. She also felt unusually stimulated to be in his presence – could not quite put her finger on it. He was enigmatic – precise and wise, yet fragile. He gave her a feeling of security, like an uncle or aunt would, after all, he must have been twice her age.

She chatted happily about her coursework and he showed a genuine interest and understanding about the subject. They discussed how unusually warm it had been for the time of year, and about where she was planning to go that night.

They arrived at Torworthy in good time, and Amy said she would see him soon. He wished her a fun-packed night, pulled away, and Amy strolled towards the bus stop where she then heard a shrill whistle from across the road. It was Scotty.

Jumping Joe's was just around the corner and was about the best place in town. She guessed that was from where Scotty had emerged. It sold cheap booze in plastic containers and the oldest person there would be Liz behind the bar, who was probably in her mid-thirties but lived life like she was desperate to remain ever-young. The floors and furniture were sticky, drink-soaked timber and the bar was long and narrow with enough spirits lined up behind to encourage over-indulgence for the most discerning of drinkers. Joe's was open until two a.m. and most weekends it was busy right to the end.

Amy ran across the road and flung her arms around Scotty, squeezing him firmly.

'Hey, you,' she said.

'Hello, gorgeous,' he replied, and they kissed and remained that way for a number of pleasurable seconds.

He took her hand and they walked the short distance to Jumping Joe's where they met with three other friends. They chatted, laughed and joked, and Amy danced to her favourite tunes. And after a few glasses of wine, Scotty encouraged Amy to join him in drinking flaming sambucas. She was not overly keen on the taste, or the thought of burning her lips, but being with Scotty, how they used to be, was feeling good.

They danced together with intoxicated eagerness but by about half past midnight, Amy was feeling the effects of the booze.

'I'm going to head off,' she said to Scotty, in a quiet area away from the others.

'Why? Come on, Ames, we're just getting going,' Scotty said, pulling at her arm.

'I'm not feeling too good.'

'Ames, come on. Stay. Just a bit longer. I'm not ready to go.'

'Who's inviting you anyway, cheeky?' she said playfully.

He reached for her hand. 'You know what I mean.' He was looking serious for the first time that night. 'When will I see you again?'

'Maybe next week. I need to chat to my parents, and see what's happening, but I'm definitely down the weekend after, so we can do something then if you like?'

Scotty ducked his head close to hers. 'Are you really going to finish it with sport billy?'

She smiled and kissed him gently on the cheek. 'Definitely.'

Amy slipped out through the front door as an expectant queue of young revellers hugged the building line to enter. She made her way to Diamonds burger bar, which was a van that always parked on the quayside at weekends, and as she queued to get a bottle of water she realised she was tipsier than she wanted to be and giggled at her recklessness. All she could think about was her luxurious bed and soft pillow back home, but the taxi queue was thirty deep.

Being a small town the taxis were in scarce supply compared to when she was at university, and she knew from bitter, cold experience that she could be waiting for at least half an hour before she could plop herself into a ride home. At least it was dry and her alcohol cloak was keeping the chill away, so she sat on a nearby bench and steadied her wobbles.

A couple of younger guys approached and began asking where her boyfriend was and where she was going next. It did not matter that she was quite drunk; Amy was used to being chatted up. That happened a lot at university, much to Carl's distaste. She did her usual routine and humoured the guys in a friendly yet unmistakably hands-off fashion, and it worked. They got the message and directed their attention elsewhere.

Amy wondered what Carl would be up to and guessed he was out with his rugby crowd getting as drunk as he could and chatting up pretty girls. She looked at her phone to see if he had left any messages. He had not, and she could not help but feel disappointment.

He was probably no more than forty metres away from the taxi rank and had been watching Amy since she came out of

Jumping Joe's. In fact, he had hardly moved from the time he dropped her off, and could still make out the faint, lingering trace of her perfume.

He was parked within one of the busier police loops, and had seen the same squad car cruising for the last couple of hours. Sometimes it stopped for ten to fifteen minutes in a prominent position opposite the taxi rank and the rest of the time, it drifted, looking for flash points, or more likely at the partying girls. A riot van had joined the others for a short time but then sped off to the jeers of the loutish youths that were kicking empty beer cans around the quayside. For all he knew the squad car he kept seeing was the only police presence left in the town. He was unconcerned; his story was sound. If asked, he would say he was waiting to collect his daughter, and who would think otherwise? Besides, nobody had bothered him up to now.

Amy was clearly quite drunk. He had taken particular notice as she bumbled her way down the street and had sniggered at his fortune, though he was increasingly concerned that she would be taking a taxi.

He had to intercept Amy before she joined the rank, but the one-way system meant that she would be out of view until he could drive back along the quay – where he hoped she would still be sitting on the bench. He did not want to get out of the car, could not risk one of the cameras identifying him. It would have to be swift, smooth, and of course, Amy would have to agree to come with him.

He saw her readying to move, and he swiftly started the engine. His eyes lingered on her one final time and he headed off along the one-way system, taking him on a loop around the outside of the bars and pedestrian areas that closed to traffic during the day. It should take no more than three to four minutes to return to the quay, but that would be enough time for Amy to get away.

A glance at the speed dial showed he was doing thirty-eight. If the cops were out there, he would be stopped for sure.

Anxiety was beginning to bite as he approached the final right turn. Amy was out of his view, but he needed to be patient and wait before re-joining the main road, because a procession of boy racers was passing in front of his junction. He slapped the top of the dashboard. Sod's law; they were slow cruising. He gripped the wheel tightly and inched out slowly into the road, anticipating the final boy racer's passage. The rear lime green Honda, with its unsocial barking exhaust caused him more than a fleeting distraction.

He strained to focus ahead through the bright glare of brake lights. The rear Honda was now but a crawl. *Do your posing else-where*, he thought, irritation growing. He could now see the row of benches, and searched frantically for Amy. She was still there.

He slammed the wheel. *Would you believe it?* They were taking turns to show off their cars to Amy, in some kind of urban courting gesture. He had no choice; he would have to stay tucked in behind and bring up the rear. His car most certainly could not be mistaken for a boy racer's, and she might even find it amusing. He just needed her to get in.

The front passenger window buzzed down and he leant across the gap until she could see him.

'Amy, Amy,' he called out, waving to grab her attention, which appeared to be on the lads that were now stopped to her left. He did not have a strong voice and had to shout as loud as he could until she noticed him, and gestured for her to come across to the car. Without hesitation, she complied.

'Hello, Amy. What are you doing here?' he asked with an air of surprise.

'I'm just waiting to go home,' she said in an unconvincing effort not to sound drunk.

'Come on, jump in. I'll get you home in no time.'

'Oh, I couldn't,' she slurred, flapping her arms in an animated fashion. 'But thanks, you're so sweet.'

'Now come on. You shouldn't be alone out here at this time of night. You never know who might be around.'

'I'll be fine. I'll get a taxi now,' she waffled, and began to move from the car.

'I won't take no for an answer,' he persisted, and unlatched the handle so the passenger door swung open. 'Come on. In you get,' he said with more assertion.

'Okay, if you're sure' she said with a beaming smile, and dropped into the passenger seat.

'It must be your lucky night that I saw you here. Pop your belt on and let's get going.'

He watched her pull at the seat belt, exposing more of her right thigh, and as she turned back in his direction, he quickly smiled.

'I really do appreciate the lift, thank you. I promise I won't be sick in your lovely car,' she babbled.

'It's not a problem at all,' he said, lingering on her face with an insincere smile. 'Where to?' he asked, as if he did not know.

'Hemingsford, please, if that's okay? I don't want to put you out though,' she said.

He shook his head and reached over, touching the skin of her leg above her knee.

'You're my angel tonight,' she said, snuggling into the seat.

Bless her, he thought. *Angels won't help you now.*

CHAPTER TWENTY-SEVEN

Amy woke up with a thunderous head and a searing pain above her right eye. The light in the room was intense and penetrating. She drew breath and winced as she touched a tender spot on her forehead.

Several moments passed before she realised she was not lying down. Her head was hanging forward and the bottom half of her body was numb. She fought with the pain to open her eyes but each time she tried light jabbed at her retinas like shards of glass.

She groaned as she lifted her head. Had she had a seizure? She patted the small pocket at the front of her denim skirt feeling for her mobile phone, but it felt empty. She moaned loudly and grabbed her forehead. The pain was splitting. *Shouldn't have mixed my drinks*, she thought, and forced her eyes open and took in the four feet of space in front of her. She was sitting on a white wooden chair with tall arm supports and it felt firm and unforgiving beneath her. She frowned, could not remember Mum and Dad having a chair like this?

As her eyes continued to adjust, she saw that she was inside a brightly lit box room. Her attention then fixed on a tripod and camera immediately before her and she tracked a thick grey cable to a flash umbrella at the side. She bunched her eyes and swayed her body, her discomfort increasing with each passing second.

How long had she been asleep? Her stomach lurched and the taste of acid came to her throat in a burning instant. She put a hand to her mouth but there was no stopping the upward surge of vomit and she spewed uncontrollably onto her lap and the floor. The taste of aniseed returned to her lips and a steady, flowing slick between her thighs brought unwelcome warmth to her legs.

Her eyes were now streaming and any focus she had briefly gained was lost once more. She blindly reached out for something to wipe herself clean, but there was nothing. Nothing at all. Just the camera, the equipment, the chair and herself.

Where the hell am I? she thought and tried hard to compartmentalize the night: Scotty, Jumping Joe's, sambucas, the lift… the lift.

'Fuck.' A wave of panic gripped her senses. She looked down anxiously through watery eyes; she was fully clothed.

The right side of her head was pulsing with pain, as if the veins were at bursting point. How did she injure herself?

Amy gently touched her right temple with the tip of her index finger. A pronounced dome dominated the space between her eye socket and the hairline. Perhaps she was in a hospital somewhere. That would account for not recognising her surroundings, the bright lights and maybe the camera.

'Where are the nurses?' she whispered gently.

She leant forward and took some weight through her legs, just as another powerful rush of pain overcame her. She blindly stumbled forwards onto her knees with a loud echoing thud.

The floor was hard, smooth and cold, like wood or laminate. She felt behind, took hold of the chair leg and hauled herself back to her feet in a crouching position as another torrent of vomit escaped her control. The smell of fear was disgusting.

Steadying herself with the chair, she stood tall and performed a three hundred and sixty degree sweep. There was nothing. Bare white walls and nothing else.

She shuffled gingerly over to the camera using the tripod to steady her progress and looked down at the viewfinder. As expected, the chair from which she had just woken up was front and centre.

She looked towards the closed door and back at the camera. It was on standby, good to go, ready to view. She looked behind again and stared intently at the door handle, then the rest of the room. She gagged from the pit of her stomach. This was no hospital. 'Oh my God!'

Amy edged closer to the small LCD screen, her mouth slack, saliva trickling down her chin. She needed to know. Another glance over her shoulder and a flick of a button, the silence of the room evaporating in electronic resonance as the equipment came to life.

She turned sharply towards the door and held her breath, her watering eyes fixed on the handle. *Please don't move, please don't move*, she willed.

Shallow breath and heart pounding, Amy stared down at the screen, and saw herself, sitting in the chair – asleep, head back and rolled to one side, her hair swept away from her face. She looked at the injury to her head, and instinctively touched the tender spot and immediately regretted it.

She flicked the images backwards through the camera and saw more shots of her slumped in the same chair. Some were close-ups and others full-length, and all fully clothed. She paused on another shot. This time it was a surveillance-type shot, taken somewhere on the High Street.

She studied the image, noticing the clothes she was wearing at the time, working out from the shops in view where the photo had been taken. She searched further back. There were more shots of her, but also other women in similar circumstances.

The door burst open, Amy spun around, her heart in her mouth. She was once again face-to-face with her captor, who this time was gripping a white pillow between both hands.

Amy was stood beside the camera; hadn't been given the opportunity to turn it off. Her captor squinted at the display, sneered menacingly and gave a Mediterranean-style shrug of the shoulders.

Amy reached out with her hands. 'I promise, I won't say anything to anyone,' she pleaded.

Her captor smirked and replied simply, 'I know.'

CHAPTER TWENTY-EIGHT

Deans made it home in the early hours of the morning. A cab had cost him eight quid and twenty minutes of his time queuing in front of the abbey with the piss-heads. He had hoped to bum a lift from the night shift but they were all committed with various jobs.

The bedroom door was closed. That was a statement of intent on Maria's part; the door was never closed. He grabbed a blanket hanging over the banister, took up an uncomfortable foetal pose on the sofa and did his best to relax.

As he stared at the walls, grinding his teeth, he contemplated the situation he was now facing. Truth was, the only time he had managed a work/home balance was when he had been a single man and could work hard and play harder. These days he was all played out and it was a case of work hard, work harder. Back in the day, the only person he could let down was himself, and he had been disappointed plenty of times, but always managed to make up for it. These days he disappointed Maria far too frequently and rarely managed to make amends.

Over the years, he had watched colleagues' good relationships go down the pan. Strong couples, simply caved in, could not make it work any longer. The job was a relationship grave-yard but Deans was not ready to commend his to the depths just yet. He swore that this would be the last time he would sacrifice himself for the cause. After this investigation, he would find a way to harmonise his life once again, even if it meant taking some boring desk job.

Deans awoke to the sound of Maria coughing in the bedroom above. He rolled over onto his side, pressing his face firmly into the upright of the sofa. His head was banging from yet another night of inadequate rest and repeated dreams of Amy dumped on the rocks. Daylight was streaming into the living room through a gap in the white drapes, but Deans was completely unaware of the time. The house was silent apart from Maria's sporadic dry cough.

He cursed his timing. He was going to spend the day at home and at some point, he would have to inform Maria that he would be working in Devon for a month, starting tomor-row. Worse than that: he was not going to be around for the scan.

He stumbled through to the kitchen and sank two parac-etamol with a tall glass of water, flicked the switch on his coffee machine and stared emptily out of the window.

As the coffee machine warmed up, he looked for messages on his mobile phone. Only a handful of hours had elapsed since he last checked his phone at the office, but the result was the same. No messages.

It was 9:13 a.m. Deans made a tactical decision – make a drink, or two, then call Ranford, and then find the courage to face Maria.

The coffee part was the easiest and most fulfilling, and

probably the only stable aspect of his life right then. He spoke to Ranford just over half an hour later to be informed that the murder squad from County HQ had taken the investigative lead, but were expecting Deans on Monday morning for a full detailed briefing. He was already earmarked to make up an enquiry team with Ranford, which suited him fine. It was a given that he would have to relinquish any hopes of becoming the OIC because of the boundary politics, but at least he would still be hands-on and able to influence proceedings.

He arranged to meet up with Ranford mid-morning, allowing time to sort accommodation and settle in before the murder squad picked his brains apart. He ended the call and moved on to the third task of the day. The one he was dreading most.

CHAPTER TWENTY-NINE

Deans arrived in Devon by eight thirty, Monday morning. It was an early start. Maria had barely spoken a word to him the previous night and he felt distance was probably the best, for both of them. He was wise when helping others in times of extreme circumstances, but less apt at dealing with his own strife.

He found a B&B that would be his home until Friday and threw his kit bag onto the floor beneath a lamp table in the corner of the room. He had packed light: a clean shirt for each day, the same suit, enough clean underwear, his work shoes and a small bag of toiletries. If he needed anything else, he would buy it in town.

The room was small, with a single bed up against one wall and the lamp table in the opposite corner. A thick mesh curtain masked what view there may have been, although he was on ground level so did not feel a desperate need to check. Looking at the end of the bed, he hoped his feet would fall short of the stud wall. The en suite was a basic affair: budget shower cubicle, sink and toilet, and just enough room between them to be practical. The Bellagio it most certainly was not, but clean and functional it was, along with cheap. This was coming out of his own pocket until he could claim back expenses, so it just had to do.

He sat on the edge of the bed. A small shelf was screwed to the side of the wardrobe, housing a white mini plastic kettle and long-life beverage facilities. Deans unplugged the kettle and filled it under the bathroom sink, thinking that there must be some place that did a roaring trade in supplying miniature kettles to guesthouses. Then thought, as he plugged the kettle back in, that somewhere else should supply longer leads, as he battled to reconnect the male and female connectors.

After waiting several minutes for the world's loudest kettle to finish boiling, he made a drink and rummaged through his work folders. He was not sure what reception to expect from the County HQ Murder Squad as every department was different. Even his own CID office did not always see eye-to-eye with their uniformed brothers. There was often an underlying 'them and us' atmosphere that only really came to the surface when blame needed to find an owner. It was then the labels would be tagged: lazy, clock-watching woodentops, or dough-nut-dunking tea-drinkers on the pleasure deck. Of course, none of it was true. Most detectives he knew drank coffee.

Deans headed out and almost straight away found a small café where he took his obligatory seat in the corner of the room. Soon he was into a seven, maybe even eight-out-of-ten Americano with a slice of yoghurt-coated flapjack. One of life's great breakfast combinations – fully loaded with caffeine, carbs and sugar, he was ready to begin the day.

He figured he had roughly two hours until he would head to the nick, so in the meantime he would revisit Rayon Vert.

He opened the door and saw Denise standing at the counter.

'Detective, what a pleasant surprise.'

Deans closed the door and scanned the room. They were alone. 'Hello, Denise. How are you?'

'Fine, thank you.' She tilted her head and gave a wary smile. 'I take it this is for business?'

'Of course. Is there somewhere we can talk, please?'

'I'm free all morning as it happens. Come on through to the back. I can close the shop for a bit if you'd prefer?'

'You really don't need to do that,' Deans, hoping Denise was not putting too much emphasis on his visit.

'I'm the only one in today. If I don't close the shop you'll never get me to yourself,' she said, flicking the lock and turning the shop sign in one smooth motion. 'There,' she said, and walked towards the treatment room.

Deans followed tentatively a few steps behind.

Denise sat on the single chair and gestured Deans towards the sofa.

'Detective. How may I help today?' she said almost knowingly.

Deans scratched at the back of his head. 'You said Amy needed me for the investigation. Why did you say that?'

'Amy requested it. I merely passed it on to you.'

Deans pulled a face and squirmed in his seat.

'What's troubling you, Detective?'

'Please, call me Andy. Nothing is troubling me as such. I'm just curious I suppose...' he hesitated, '...about your contact with Amy.'

'Okay,' she said, and then nothing more.

They both studied each other. Who was going to make the next move? It was Deans.

'Well, can you tell me any more?' he asked.

'Are you asking me if I've connected to Amy since we last spoke? Well, yes, I have.'

Deans leant forwards. 'Go on.'

'Amy is in a bad place and is between destinations. She has moved on from the life as we know it, but the manner in which she's been taken from us has placed her in a type of purgatory, and she can't move on until certain factors are resolved.'

'Her killer?' Deans prompted.

'Inevitably that is one such factor.'

'Why me? Did she name me?'

Denise shook her head. 'She said, "He mustn't lose faith in me." And she referred to "the detective" several times.'

'So it may not even be me? It could be any number of the detectives working on this now.'

'But it was you who worked on it first, and who worked on it when Amy needed to be heard.'

'But how could I lose faith when I don't understand what the hell is happening? That suggests I had some kind of belief in the first place.'

'I know it's a lot to comprehend, Andy. But the very fact you're here now means we are already halfway there.'

'Argh,' Deans grumbled.

'Andy. I have spent the vast majority of my life as a pupil to the gift. I don't expect you to understand it in one week. I can't have all the answers for you at this time, but I can guide you, based on my contact with Amy. Remember, she can't pass over until our job is done.'

'No pressure then,' Deans quipped, more out of nerves than anything else.

'Indeed,' Denise said with a resolute expression etched into her features. 'Look, we can do this a number of ways but maybe we should meet up regularly and exchange notes. I'm not expecting confidential information. I just need to know if my interpretations are aligned to your enquiries.'

'Okay,' Dean said with a shrug. 'Well, what can you tell me today?'

Denise huffed. 'It's a little confusing. She told me, "Don't let her do it again."'

'Her?' Deans said quickly. 'What do you mean, "Her"? Are we looking for a female killer?'

'I can only convey the messages, Andy. I haven't yet seen with enough clarity to enable me to make judgements.'

'Well, when will you know?'

'I don't know,' she said. 'It's unusual not to have more by now. Something's affecting my connection, but what, I don't know.'

Deans pinched at the bridge of his nose as if staunching a nosebleed and stared back at Denise through the gaps of his fingers as he spoke. 'Have you chatted to any other police officers about this?'

'No. You're the only one.'

'Good. I need your absolute honesty. If this is real, then we could probably help each other. If it's not, then I'm not prepared to jeopardise the investigation.'

'I understand,' she said, and then hesitated, concentrating on his face. 'Andy, do you mind if I say something about you?'

'About me personally?'

Denise nodded.

'Okay,' he said with a shrug.

'Maria needs you more than ever right now. You'll find a time very soon that will test both your emotions and dedication to each other.'

'What?' Deans recoiled. 'How do you know about Maria?'

'I'm sorry. Please don't think I'm trying to interfere.'

'What, in my bloody private life?'

'You have difficult times ahead and all I want to do is give you warning,' she said calmly.

'Are you reading me or something?' Deans said angrily.

'Not exactly.'

'Well, whatever it is you're doing, don't. Okay?'

'I'm sorry if I've offended you. That certainly wasn't my intention. I just thought you should know.'

'I already bloody know,' Deans shouted. 'My relationship is heading for the shitter, and this job isn't exactly helping. So the sooner we crack it, the better all round, okay?'

Denise did not flinch.

Deans shot to his feet. 'I'd better go. Got things to do.'

Denise led the way back to the entrance with Deans panting and foaming close behind. She unlatched the door and watched as Deans marched silently away from the shop.

CHAPTER THIRTY

Deans made his way to the station, arriving earlier than he had planned, and was greeted at the front desk by Ranford who accompanied him upstairs to the CID office.

Mansfield was at his desk having an animated conversation over the phone and it sounded like he was holding his own. Two other suits were at Ranford's desk perusing a pile of papers and Ranford introduced them to Deans as DS Jackson and DC Gold from HQ, Major Crime Investigation Unit.

DS Jackson was an old sweat, complete with knurled forehead. He wore his police service like a seasoned leather. Gold was young, petite, blonde and fresh-faced. They all shook hands and Jackson informed Deans that Gold was the new OIC.

Deans was instantly aware that Jackson was protective of Gold from the way he stood close by her, on the verge of occupying her personal space. As they continued chatting, he also noticed Jackson sneaking extended glances her way, even if she was not talking. Could there be something going on between them? Or was Jackson living in a fantasy land, using his rank to give favours that he hoped could lead to favours?

'So you ladies are one action team,' Jackson said snidely. 'Do you think you can manage to stay out of mischief? Or do you need me to hold your hands?'

Deans looked at Jackson with measured disdain.

'I imagine we'll be just fine,' Ranford chipped in. 'Thank you, Sarge.'

'Good. Get on with it then,' Jackson sneered, the trenches of his forehead deepening. He turned and headed back over towards Gold.

'I take it he wants us out of the way?' Deans said quietly to Ranford, who nodded his answer. 'Come on, let's grab some actions and find somewhere else,' Deans suggested.

They gathered up their things and stopped at the action allocation tray. Operation Bejewel was printed in bold black letters on an A4 sheet and Sellotaped to the wall. Much like naming a hurricane, the operation name wouldn't have specific meaning, but the first letter would normally be associated to the police district where the offence took place, in this case 'B' district. The rest of the word was randomly generated.

Deans collected a bunch of tasks and looked back to Jackson, who was watching their every step to the door.

'What's the story with Jackson?' Deans asked as they walked down the stairs into the blustery and cold outdoors.

'What, old Hasselhoff? He's got a bit of a rep for being a ladies' man,' Ranford replied.

'You've got to be kidding me? Really?'

'Seriously. He's seeing a WPC, twenty-six years his junior.'

Deans was staggered. It looked more a case of hassle than the Hoff from what he could tell so far.

'She's a bit of a babe by all accounts,' Ranford continued, 'but I haven't seen her personally. He's divorced twice over with two of his kids not much younger than his new woman.'

'Difficult,' Deans commented, not really giving a damn.

'You're telling me. And he can kiss his pension goodbye with the two previous marriages.'

'Don't tell me,' Deans said. 'I bet he pulls as many OTs as he can and is always the first to volunteer for bank holidays and Christmas.'

'In one.' Ranford chuckled.

It was an all too familiar scenario: cops with failed marriages working their butts off to lessen the deficit of their passed-over pensions.

'So, what was all that about with Gold? Is he giving her one as well?' Deans asked after a few moments.

'I don't know. If he isn't then he probably wants to, and who could blame him?'

Deans raised his brow but did not reply. They kept on walking to the small café just a few minutes from the station. They took a round table in the back corner of the room and looked through the bundle of actions Deans had picked up.

First up would be a revisit to the scene and a check for all potential CCTV and house-to-house opportunities. Deans was pleased. He had hoped to check over the scene again with fresh eyes. The other actions were general TIs – trace and interviews. They would be people named during other enquiries who had not yet been spoken to. These often proved fruitless but they had to be done. The HOLMES (Home Office Large Major Enquiry System) database would collate, generate, and continue to do so until all actions were complete or signed off.

They finished their coffees and used one of Ranford's pool cars for transport. It was a very tired Vauxhall Astra, complete with customary war wounds. From the rusted scratch that ran from the driver door all the way back to the rear wheel arch, Deans surmised that just like his own pool car, this was also easily identifiable as a police vehicle. He had previously known whole windscreens put through, so a few scratches were comparatively nothing to get excited about and not worth the cost of repair.

After ten minutes enduring Ranford's unique style of driving, they were back on the bumpy approach road to the spot where Amy had been found. The car bounced and scraped along the potholes and craters as Ranford rode the terrain in carefree fashion, and Deans let out the occasional profanity as the floor banged into the road surface.

There was nothing around. No houses, no shops, no bus stops, no trees, no lampposts, absolutely naught. It was a wasteland with meandering waterways cutting through the perfectly flat grassy landscape. The pebble ridge dominated the horizon between them and the ocean. This area was named, *The Burrows*, according to Ranford.

It was agreed that they would start at the burial scene and work the radius back to the main road. In reality, it was a half-moon shaped piece of open land consisting of at least several hundred acres. The rest of it was rock, water or sand depending on the tide. Although there was a lot of land to scope, the reality was far simpler. There was one road in and the same road out. A small cluster of farm buildings at the northern edge wouldn't take long to assess and other than that, it was grass, small waterways and a whole lot of sheep. An hour at most should do them; Support Group had already completed the nose to ground search, the hard part.

They stood on the peak of the grey boulders, the crashing ocean behind and the green expanse before them. Deans felt strangely unsettled; his stomach tight and his shoulders knotted. The spot where the body had been located was just feet below them. The heap of pebbles created by the forensic team stood proud like a miniature cairn. A spray of flowers and a small white teddy had been wedged between rocks at the summit and a label of some description was flailing in the breeze. Deans stepped over and read it: *Forever a Princess. You are never out of our hearts XXXXXX.*

It was unsigned but Deans did not need a signature to know it was from Mum and Dad. He gazed out to the ocean and watched the white frothing leading edge. The sky was battleship grey and blended a soft contrast to the horizon. This is where Mrs Poole said Amy had spent much of her youth. It was some irony, if not coincidence, that the killer chose this place for Amy's life to ebb away.

'So we know access was via the road,' Ranford said, breaking Deans' distant thoughts. 'He would've used a car and parked at this far end in order to carry her up and over the rocks to where we are standing now.'

'How do we know it was a he?' Deans asked.

'What?' Ranford laughed. 'You think a woman could lift the girl over these rocks by herself? I struggled to carry myself up here.'

'Fact is, at the moment we don't know much about anything at all. I just think we need to keep an open mind.'

Ranford laughed again. 'Or maybe we should keep an eye open for an Olympic weightlifting midget with a bad attitude.' They both chuckled and struggled back down the slope to the car.

The farm buildings drew a blank, and they headed back towards the village.

'Where do you think the closest CCTV is located?' Deans asked.

'Probably the Seven-Eleven. Which isn't much use, unless we know one or both of them went inside, at a time we don't yet know, and on a day we don't know either.'

'No council cameras outside in the street?'

'Nah. Nothing ever goes on here.'

They both looked at each other, probably thinking the same thought.

'Would you mind if I drop away a little early today?' Deans asked. 'I've got a few things to sort out, like unpacking my bags.'

'I can do better than that. Give me the tasks for today and I'll drop you at the B&B now if you like? There's nothing here that I can't do alone and I'll cover for you if anyone asks.'

Deans accepted and soon he was back at his humble accommodation. Ranford had agreed to call Deans in an emergency, but other than that, he would see him again in the morning.

Deans threw his daybook on the lamp table and stretched out on the bed fully clothed, and drifted off in an instant. He was totally worn out from the long hours and travelling, not to mention the unique stresses the case was presenting him.

He awoke with a start, not in the slightest bit refreshed, and now with a banging headache. He quickly checked his phone – no messages or missed calls from Maria – but there was still time to get to Rayon Vert.

CHAPTER THIRTY-ONE

Less than an hour later Deans had showered and was making his way towards Rayon Vert. He had a discernible trepidation about going back. It was hard to explain, but if Denise was correct in her disclosures about Amy then she was probably also correct regarding Maria. He had not told Denise anything about his wife, their relationship or the current problems, so the very fact Denise mentioned it indicated a precursor of foresight, unless she had other sources.

The door chimes signalled his arrival. Denise was at the counter.

'Hi,' he said gingerly and glanced around. The room was empty. It was just the two of them.

'Detective,' she replied curtly.

'Look, I'm sorry about earlier,' he said. 'I was rude to you and I want to apologise.'

'I'm sorry about earlier too. I suppose it was my way of showing you that I am for real, that *this* is real.'

Deans nodded and made a point of looking around the room once again.

'It's okay, we're alone,' she said.

'Um—'

'Yes,'

Deans stumbled over his words, 'What... what did you mean about me and Maria?'

'I can't answer that at the moment. Only time will make that clearer to the both of you.'

'So why say it in the first place?'

Denise sighed. 'I don't predict the future but I do interpret the present.'

'How did you know Maria's name?'

'Through the spirit world.' Denise broke eye contact and looked down to the floor. 'Have you spoken to your wife yet?' she asked quickly.

'No. I haven't.'

'Give her a call now. Use my treatment room if you like. There's no one in there.'

'Why are you so bothered about Maria?'

'Just take the opportunity to do it. I can see you are worn out and you may not get a better chance again today.'

'You're not going to let this lie are you?'

Denise flared her eyelids. 'You know the way to the back room.'

Deans smiled. 'Fine. You win.'

He paced around the room a few times, phone in hand, and then settled on the edge of the treatment couch. He tapped the call button and the ring tone sounded in his ear. It was strange; he did not know what he was going to say.

'Hello,' Maria answered neutrally.

'Hi, babe,' Deans said cagily. 'How's it all going?'

'Okay, I suppose. I'm home again today.'

'Oh, babe! Are you still feeling poorly?'

Maria did not answer the question. 'When are you coming home, Andrew?'

'I'm going to be here all week. I already told you that.' He winced, recognising that he could have been a lot less antagonistic.

Maria spoke after a painful hush. 'The hospital wants us... me in at nine thirty tomorrow for the scan.'

Deans imagined Maria struggling alone with the hospital appointment and all of the associated stress and his heart plummeted.

'That's great, babe,' he said, doing his best not to come across as unsupportive. 'I'll speak to my DS down here and see if he will allow me to take the day off.'

Maria was silent for a moment. 'No. You made it clear that your work was more important to you than the progress of our treatment.'

'Oh, come on, Maria. That's not fair.'

'Well, where are you now, here or there?'

Deans groaned. He could not argue the facts. 'Look, I'm going to speak to my skipper, see what I can do. I want to be there, Maria.'

'No. You'd better not let your work colleagues down. Mum and Dad are coming to the hospital with me.'

Deans bit down tightly, and the silence that followed spoke more words than either of them could say. Deans eventually broke the deadlock. 'I'm really pleased about tomorrow, Maria. You'll be great, and everything will be fine.'

'Andrew, we need to talk – properly.'

His whole body fell saggy. 'I know,' he said softly. 'I'll let you know what the skipper says.'

'I won't hold my breath,' Maria said.

Neither will I, he thought.

They said their goodbyes like two strangers and Deans

ended the call. The phone screensaver reappeared and he stared at the image of the two of them on their Greek holiday looking healthy and contented. Those days were like living someone else's life. A life that he craved for.

He leafed through his papers, found Jackson's contact number, and dialled.

'Yes,' came the curt reply.

'Hi, Sarge, it's Andy Deans.'

'Yes.'

'I was wondering if I could take tomorrow off? My—'

'No.'

'My wife is having a scan at the hospital in Bath.'

'And you're working on a murder enquiry.'

'It's very important to us both.'

'Is she dying?'

'I'm sorry?'

'Is she dying?' Jackson asked impatiently.

'No, she's not bloody dying.'

'Then this conversation is over.' With that, Jackson ended the call.

'Wanker,' Deans shouted and clenched in a tight, knotted rage.

Denise did not make a big deal about his arrival, just continued with her work. Deans liked Denise. Her presence was relaxing in a strange kind of way. He would never understand her vocation but he did not need to in order to feel comfortable around her. He checked his watch: 4:46 p.m. He wondered how Ranford was getting on and contemplated heading back to the nick, though he did not trust himself around Jackson. What he really needed was to head back to the B&B for a power nap.

'Andy, can I make an observation?'

'So long as it's not about Maria,' he said with a twinkle in his eye. They both chuckled.

'You're a sensitive man.'

Deans snorted, unsure if this was intended as a compliment or a criticism.

He noticed her looking at him with a strange curiosity.

'Um, thanks?' he said.

She raised a smile. 'That's okay. That's really okay.'

'Well, I'm glad we sorted that out then.'

Denise laughed. 'What are you doing tonight, Andy?'

He sucked in deeply and shook his head.

'If you have no plans then come over to my place. I can cook you some proper food. I think it will do us both good to have some company.'

'Okay,' he said after considering everything. 'But only if it doesn't put you out.'

'Not for a moment. I enjoy cooking and rarely get the chance to have stimulating company.'

He laughed. 'I can't necessarily promise the stimulation, but I'd be delighted to come over. Thank you.'

They agreed to meet up at seven, and clutching her home address on a scrap of Rayon Vert headed notepaper, Deans set off back to the B&B, picking up a bottle of red wine en route, and taking the opportunity to break the news about Jackson to Maria.

He arrived at his compact accommodation and checked his phone: no messages. He set the alarm for 6:30 p.m., drew the blinds, removed his suit jacket and loosened his shirt and tie. Within moments, he was sleeping.

CHAPTER THIRTY-TWO

The alarm woke him with a startling abruptness, as planned. Deans sat upright and wiped his puffy eyes. He was beginning to ache from sustained sleep deprivation.

He flicked on the small TV at the end of the bed, bolted to the wall on a crude-looking cradle, and he fiddled with the controls until he reached the local news. Increasing the volume, he went to the bathroom.

He considered cancelling Denise. The snooze appeared to have had a detrimental effect on his general wellbeing and he felt significantly more jaded than before, similar to jet lag, but much worse. Sadly, there was no hot and sunny destination waiting for him to take the edge off the tiredness and he had no idea where the endpoint of this journey was taking him.

From the TV Deans heard: 'Today the parents of murdered local woman Amy Poole were speaking to the cameras.'

He rushed back into the room and stared intently at the fourteen-inch screen as the news reporter relayed details of Amy's disappearance and subsequent discovery.

Janet and Ian were sitting behind a desk housing numerous microphones and recording devices. Their faces stared absently into the room and told the observing world of the extreme agony in which they were now living. The camera closed in mercilessly to track down every last nuance of their grief. Two senior officers whom he did not recognise were either side of them and they were all in front of a bright blue felt board adorned with the constabulary crest.

The officer in the suit spoke and gave a short statement on behalf of the family. She delivered it respectfully and accurately. She was a good public speaker. Deans was glad, he had seen too many ranking officers fumble and stutter their way through televised interviews or statements, but he certainly wouldn't fancy the job himself.

The segment changed to a reporter speaking live from the pebble ridge, the now sodden and greying teddy the focus of their shot. The reporter emphasised that the killer was still at large and the police were working tirelessly to piece together the horrific events that led to Amy's death. A photograph of Amy then filled the screen before the programme returned to the studio and a news report about a fire at a farm building somewhere Deans had never heard of.

He wondered if the killer was watching the same thing and his thoughts drifted back to the comments made by the outside broadcaster – *horrific events* – and he wondered just how much the press knew. A vision of Mansfield cheerfully wagging with the news reporter at the scene came into his head.

He caught himself daydreaming and fumbled with the controller to switch the box off.

Denise lived in a very old-looking small stone cottage at the end of a private road, in a small village not far from Torworthy. It was a warm house, both in temperature and atmosphere.

Denise ushered Deans through to the kitchen area where the unmistakable smell of Bolognese filled the air.

'Thanks for inviting me,' he said politely.

'You're most welcome. I hope spag-bol is up your street?'

'One of my favourites, thank you.'

Denise filled a glass with Merlot and handed it to Deans with a clink of her glass, and they both sat at the table. Deans did not feel uncomfortable about being with Denise in her home. There were no pangs of guilt associated with being with another woman. This was different, this was purely platonic, and a very kind gesture.

'Amy's gone national,' Denise said. 'Leading headline on the six o'clock news.'

'Really?' Deans said. 'I saw the local report, but hadn't expected wider interest.'

'Her poor parents. They looked dreadful,' she said.

Deans nodded. Every murder was tragic, and brutal, and unfair in its own right. Some had desperate circumstances while others linked to loved ones, or involved persons in the public eye, and something was making Amy's case particularly attractive to the newshounds.

'The reporters already seem to have the daggers out for the lack of police results,' Denise said.

Deans shrugged a noncommittal shoulder.

'What's your take on it, Andy? What do you think happened?'

He pulled a face. 'We don't really know.'

'Not we. You. What do you think?'

He hesitated. 'I honestly don't know. I thought I was getting somewhere a couple of days back, but that scenario has gone. I guess time will tell, and how much time we have before this whole thing turns into a circus is anyone's guess.'

Denise scowled and lifted her glass in symbolic cheers and

Deans followed suit. He savoured the smooth, velvet taste and held it in his mouth longer than he normally would. He usually liked to drink in the evenings, but the way the shifts had been recently this felt like his first drink in a year, and it was one to relish.

'We'll need to be cautious about the press,' he said.

'We?'

'They'll have their own investigators sniffing about, trying to speak to witnesses, attempting to bag the next breakthrough.'

'Why should I be concerned by that?'

'I'm not saying be concerned, just be careful who you speak to about Amy.'

'I already am.'

Deans took another large mouthful of wine but this time it went straight down. 'So how did you get into this medium thing?' he asked.

Denise chortled and took a sip of her own. 'It kind of chose me,' she replied nonchalantly.

'Well, it seems I have all evening,' Deans said, 'so please, I'm seriously interested to know.'

Denise pulled gently at a strand of hair trapped in the corner of her mouth and smiled. 'I had an alternative upbringing. My father moved away before I had any memory of him and so I ended up alone with my mother, who was into all sorts of things from tarot card reading to clairvoyance services. So, I guess, from a very young age I was surrounded by the alternative lifestyle. And as I grew older, Mother introduced different techniques for me to learn and practise. I kept it quiet from my friends at school and Mother was good at not making a big deal out of it. I wasn't embarrassed by her; I just didn't want her to be branded a witch by the other kids.'

Denise paused for a moment, and looked to the floor. Deans waited.

'When she passed away I was already quite skilled in many aspects but decided to progress the gift further.' She tittered. 'You could call it an homage, I suppose.'

Deans smiled, took a sip of wine.

'Therefore, I read up on specific facets that interested me and I travelled the world to meet some of the practising legends, who in turn gave me one-to-one tuition, guidance and foresight. You see, everyone has the ability within them to do what I do. The human brain is underutilised with daily life and all I've done is unlock a gateway and opened a flow of communication.'

'Wow,' Deans said. 'And the shop name, does that have some meaning?'

'*Rayon Vert* – the green flash. Next time you see a sunset over the ocean, particularly here at Sandymere Bay, look closely for the final second before the sun drops away and you may well witness the green flash. The significance is that the sun sets every single day of our lives but some days our view is shrouded by cloud and on others its magnificence burns bright to the very end. Yet, either way, there are individuals that have never seen the rayon vert. It's not simply looking but *seeing*.'

'So when did you decide to make a living from it?'

'I wouldn't say it makes me a living but it's enough to pay the bills. You see, only a relatively small percentage of the population open themselves up enough to embrace the gift and so, unless there becomes an influx of believers or the greater powers dictate another direction, I will be satisfied following this path in life.'

'What brought Amy to you?'

'Dear Amy,' Denise said, staring thoughtfully into her

glass. 'She was studying law and was interested in the ways in which psychic ability could complement criminal investigations.' She tutted. 'Isn't that some irony?'

Deans nodded.

'Because she was brought up in these parts she probably felt more comfortable speaking with me rather than someone else closer to her university. Maybe she felt she had to distance herself from her peers to avoid potential ridicule.'

'It's sad that she would have to do that,' Deans said.

'Be honest, Andy. Before you got to know me a little better, you must admit your own opinion would have been prejudiced.'

'Fair comment.'

'There you go, and how many of your colleagues have you told about your enquiries with me?'

'None.'

'And why would that be?'

Deans sighed. 'Because they'd probably think I'd lost the plot.'

'So why do you keep coming back, Andy?'

He smiled dryly. She was good. 'Because maybe Amy was right… let's just leave it there.'

'Well, that's good enough for me. Come on, let's eat.'

Deans enjoyed the meal and Denise's company, and they chatted about each other's former years, and how Deans became a police officer. Denise opened a second bottle of wine, and as she topped up his glass she said, 'I can help you.'

'Help me, or help my investigation?'

'Both.'

'Do I need help?'

'We all need help from time to time, Andy, even me.'

'So who helps you?'

'The guardians. They show me when I'm going astray and redirect my energy.'

'The guardians?'

She nodded, did not expand.

Deans did not push his luck. 'I must admit you've said some things about the case that have me interested.'

'Such as?'

'You mentioned a lift.' Perhaps the wine had softened him up. 'Amy did get a lift, or at least one that we know of, on her way out that night. But we haven't identified the car or the driver yet.'

'Why don't we attempt to connect with Amy about it tomorrow?' Denise suggested enthusiastically.

Deans was curious about the process and rapped his fingertips against the side of his glass. 'Okay. I'll need to work it around my enquiries, but that should be fine.'

Denise watched Deans with a fixed grin.

'What?' he asked. 'What've I said?'

'You've got it, you know.'

'What? What have I got?'

She leaned towards him, her eyes flitting around his face. 'The gift.'

Deans spluttered. 'Don't be daft. You've had too much vino.'

'No… I haven't.'

'You serious? Come on.'

Denise was unblinking.

Deans sniggered nervously. 'Why? Why do you say that?'

Her face turned more serious. 'Have you ever had a tune in your head, turned on the radio, and there it was, perfectly in-sync? Or have you been thinking about someone and the next thing you know they're contacting you on the phone?'

Deans shrugged. 'That's coincidence.'

'Is it?' Denise put her glass down. 'I'm sure you've seen condensation shadows on your car windscreen from stickers long since removed?'

Deans frowned and nodded.

She smiled. 'That's what I do. I perceive the shadows of spirits. I see their outline and hear their voices. And so could you.'

Deans sat motionless.

'You just have to tune-in.'

Denise fell silent for a minute, still focusing on Deans.

'Have you found yourself driving along, and for no apparent reason you shudder at the thought of impending jeopardy, despite the road conditions being perfect?' she said.

He bobbed his head.

'That's your gift,' she whispered.

'But nothing happens.'

'No. It has *already* happened.'

Deans stared at her, slack-jawed, his eyes demanding an explanation.

'You're experiencing the spirit forces attempting to connect with you,' she said.

'What?'

'Embrace it. It's okay.' She touched his hand. 'You can manage the signals. I can help you.'

He looked away and pinched his bottom lip between his teeth.

'Go on,' she encouraged.

'Argh!' he growled, and partially covered his face with a hand.

'Come on, Andy. You won't find a safer environment to open up.'

He closed his eyes and kept them tight. 'I can...' he paused and rubbed behind his ear. 'I can read people. Haven't always. Only since…' He shook his head.

'Something happened to you.'

He opened his eyes and stared at Denise.

'Do you want to tell me about it?'

He raised a brow. 'Well, it's no secret. Half of my blood belongs to someone else.' He chuckled and turned away.

'You had a near death experience?'

'I wouldn't go that far.'

'And since that time you've had an ability to read people, as you put it.'

He nodded.

She beamed a wide smile. 'Yes, that's it.'

'Well,' he said following an awkward silence, 'maybe I'd better be making tracks.'

'Nonsense. You can stay the night here. I have a spare room already set up for guests, and I promise we'll speak no more of this tonight.'

Deans checked his watch and puffed out his cheeks. 'Well, I suppose I've already drunk too much to drive, and we do still have the rest of the bottle to finish. All right, thank you. I'll have to leave first thing in the morning though.'

CHAPTER THIRTY-THREE

Deans woke at six fifteen, fresher and more alert than at any time during the previous few days. Maybe it was the two bottles of wine, or perhaps it was the crisp cotton sheets and comfortable bed. Either way, he felt a whole lot more human than before, if a little preoccupied.

He had sent Maria a text during the night telling her that he loved her and wished her luck for the morning. Her reply was more pragmatic, but at least they were communicating.

He quietly dressed and slipped out of the front door, making as little noise as possible.

He arrived at his B&B and ran the shower hot as he selected his shirt and tie combo for the day. He wanted to be at the office as early as possible and was feeling more than a degree of guilt for leaving Ranford to get on with the previous day's enquiries alone.

A rapid rinse, scrub and brush later, he was standing in the empty CID office. A note on Ranford's desk from DS Jackson informed him there would be a briefing in the conference room at eight thirty. He would need to collar Ranford before it got underway so that he would have something meaningful to contribute.

The action tray was stacked, so he gathered up a bundle and perched himself at Ranford's desk and started reading through.

Gold was next into the office and gave Deans an unenthusiastic 'Hello', before taking herself over to an additional table placed at the end of Mansfield's desk.

'How's it going?' Deans asked.

'Not bad, thanks,' she replied and then pretty much ignored him.

His chatter was not intended as a chat-up, but he guessed she was plagued by blokes cracking on to her, Jackson being a prime case in point.

'Any progress?' he asked.

'No. It was a slow day,' she replied without looking his way.

A few deathly moments went by and then she spoke again. 'How did you get on?'

Deans thought about his response. 'Pretty much the same really. So, how did you get this gig then?' he asked, diverting attention back to her.

Her face softened. 'I was offered it by the sarge and thought it'd be good for my personal development, so I agreed to take it on.'

'Have you been involved in many murder cases before?'

'No, this is my first.'

Deans had yet to become OIC on a homicide even though he had previously worked six murder cases. It was a big ask, the ultimate ask, and a huge professional compliment.

'So, how long have you been a DC?' he asked.

'Couple of years now.'

'Wow, you've done well to land this job.'

Her big brown eyes lingered on Deans' face, and then Ranford walked in.

'Hi, Andy,' he said and beamed a 'Hi' at Gold, who turned back to her work with a disinterested nod.

'Hi, Paul,' Deans responded. 'How did you get on with those other enquiries?' He flared his lids, gesticulating in Gold's direction.

'Not much joy, I'm afraid. The witness Granger did not offer anything we didn't already know. She only saw Amy inside the bar with the others, and unfortunately, I couldn't get hold of Warner. How did your enquiries go?'

'Much the same.' Deans winked thanks to Ranford.

At precisely eight thirty a.m., they all funnelled through to the Conference Room, which was not exactly a room of splendour. It was narrow and dark with a small window that allowed a token amount of natural light into the room, and two fluorescent strips took up the shortfall. Two tables were butted together end on end with eight chairs set around them. Surely there were more detectives working this case? Deans noticed the blue felt Constabulary board leaning against the end wall and imagined the claustrophobic scene of the press conference.

He sat down next to Ranford facing the window, with Gold, Jackson and two other new detectives taking the remaining seats opposite. Deans tossed Jackson a curled lip, but he did not respond. He appeared only interested in Gold.

Two suits then entered the room, one male, and one female and took their places at the top of the table. The female officer was the first to speak, introducing herself as Detective Chief Inspector Fowler from Police Headquarters, and then introduced the man on her left as Detective Inspector Crow, also from HQ. DCI Fowler had given the televised press conference.

Clearly a no-nonsense individual, probably in her late forties, she was a shade overweight and exuded extreme confidence. She looked at each officer individually as she addressed the room. For once Jackson had taken his eyes away from Gold.

The DCI stopped on Deans.

'Here's a face I don't recognise,' she said.

'DC Deans, Ma'am,' he said.

'Ah yes. Our A and S colleague. Well, it's good to see you, and thank you for your help. I do hope the distance isn't putting any pressure on your home life.'

Deans flicked a glance at Jackson and saw the corners of his mouth lift. *Wanker*.

'Thank you, Ma'am,' Deans replied. 'In fact my wife is probably glad to have me out of the way for a while.' His polite smile masked the rising hostility he felt towards Jackson.

At the end of the meeting, Deans had learnt two things; firstly, that there were only six full-time officers working the murder including himself and secondly, no one had any significant information to progress the case. He hoped his meeting later with Denise would change all that.

CHAPTER THIRTY-FOUR

Back at the office, Deans checked his mobile phone and saw that he had received a text message from Maria during the meeting.

Call me. Urgently.

He made his excuses to Ranford and slipped out to the corridor. Maria picked up after only two rings.

'Where've you been? I've been trying to reach you for ages,' she said frantically.

'In a briefing. What's up?'

'I've had a bloody crank call, Andy.'

'What?'

'A weirdo has called me.'

'When?'

'This morning. I ignored the first call because it was early and I thought it was you, but then the calls kept coming until I answered. He knows my name, Andy. He called me Maria Deans.'

'Who did? What the hell did he say?'

'He knew my name,' Maria repeated.

'Okay, but what did he say?'

'I assumed it was someone you must know, but he sounded too young. He kept going on about my beautiful eyes.'

'What?' Deans said sharply, and pressed the phone closer to his ear.

'He mentioned you as well. A message I had to give you.'

'What message?' Deans was now searching the corridor for an unoccupied room.

'He said I had to tell you that eyes don't always see the truth, or something bloody odd like that. Look, it's really freaked me out, Andy.'

Deans' mind flashed to Amy as she lay amongst the boulders. A shiver shook him to the core.

'Where are you now?' he asked, backing into a darkened room, full of desks and computers.

'Why, what's wrong, Andy?'

'Nothing's wrong,' he said quickly. 'What time are you due at the hospital?'

'I'm there now. We've been sitting in the car waiting for you to get back to me.'

'I'm sorry, babe. I'm glad your parents are with you.'

'Who the hell was it, Andy?'

'I don't know who it was, Maria.' He was not strictly lying. 'What time are you expecting to be out from the hospital, honey?'

'About midday... Andy, you never call me honey. If you need to tell me something you'd better start now.'

'Honestly, Maria, I've no idea who it was. It was probably some kids messing around. Don't give it any more thought, okay?'

'Not good enough, Andy. Tell me how he knew my name.'

'I don't know. Look, did he call on your mobile or the landline?'

'Landline.'

'Okay, let me make some calls and I'll see what I can do. Just, don't worry about it anymore. It's over. I take it you did 1471?'

'Of course I did 1471. The number was withheld.'

'Do you know what time the call was made?'

'The one I answered was around eight forty-five but the calls started at least two hours before that.'

'Okay, leave it with me. Now, get yourself settled and relaxed for the scan.'

'Will you call me later?' she asked firmly.

'Yeah, course I will. I want to hear how it all went. We'll speak later. Good luck, babe. Love you.'

He waited until Maria cut the connection, and then launched a metal bin across the room, crashing it against the far wall. *Who the fuck was it?* They were ex-directory. Deans had to wise up to protect Maria, and quickly.

He called Savage immediately and requested a marked unit keep a high profile near to his house throughout the day.

'What shall I tell the guys to look out for?' Savage asked.

'Wish I knew, Mick,' Deans said. 'It's possible he's got a dark-coloured Golf. Other than that, we're looking for a white male.'

'Age?'

'Young adult?'

'Well that really narrows it down,' Savage said sarcastically.

'That's all I have. I'll call you again once I've done some digging.'

He did not tell Savage that Maria was at the hospital. She had already requested against work colleagues knowing anything about the treatment. They were under enough pressure as it was.

· · ·

Ranford stopped working at his computer the moment he saw Deans enter the room. 'You okay, mate?' he asked.

'Yeah, fine.' Deans cut him off and slumped down in his chair. *Why would anyone want to get to me, or Maria?* he brooded, chewing the lid of his Bic pen, and then it struck him; someone he had met during the previous ten days was the killer, or closely connected. He bundled up his papers, and stuffed them swiftly into his go-bag and headed out of the door without saying another word.

He took a bunch of steps into the brisk breeze, and then stopped. Could the killer be watching him right then? He looked around. He certainly hoped so. That way they couldn't also be watching Maria.

His car was parked on the quayside. 10:42 a.m. showed on the dash. It was time to make some forthright decisions: drive back home and wait, maybe for nothing to happen and certainly freak Maria out even more, or stick around, and trust in Savage and the station to keep Maria safe.

He sat playing it over in his mind – the people he had met, those who knew his name, the people that knew Maria's name – she said it was a young man on the phone. *Why contact Maria? I'm not even the OIC.*

Within seconds, he was back on the phone to Savage.

'It's someone from our own patch, Mick. Why else would they be interested in contacting Maria? They think I'm still the main threat.'

'It has to be Groves, Deano,' Savage said bluntly.

'No. It's not.'

'I disagree. We should keep close tabs on him.'

'Mick, don't waste time and energy on Groves. It's someone else.'

'Deano, you're too close to the action. You're not thinking straight.'

'Argh,' Deans groaned. 'Do whatever, Mick, but either way, do me a big favour and keep it low key.'

'Of course, Deano, I understand.'

CHAPTER THIRTY-FIVE

Deans drove to the car park overlooking the bay where Amy had been found. He could see the attraction of living by the coast, especially here. It made him realise that there was no corner back home where he went for solace – there was always someone around, or something to be done.

He watched the surfers with envy and after a few minutes, sent Maria a text. *Hope everything went well. Let me know what they've said. Love you loads, speak soon xxx*

He waited, clutching the phone, willing it to vibrate with her reply.

The phone rang.

'Hello?' He answered without looking at the screen.

'Deans, this is Sergeant Jackson. I need to see you when you can break away from your current commitment.'

'No problem,' Deans said. 'I can be back at the office in about thirty.'

'Make it ten. This is important.' Jackson did not sound as if he was ready to negotiate.

'Fine,' Deans replied. 'Ten it is.'

Jackson had already ended the call. Deans suddenly felt

buoyed by the urgency in Jackson's voice. He must have some news. Progress at last.

Deans trotted up the stairwell to the CID office and saw Jackson standing in the middle of the room. Gold was at Ranford's desk and Mansfield was opposite. They both looked at Deans, and then quickly turned away. Nobody acknowledged him, including Jackson whose expression was ferocious.

'Follow me,' he barked, walking towards the door.

Gold and Mansfield were now looking over at Deans. Mansfield gave him a wink and a loud *chlick* with the sidewall of his mouth.

Deans scowled, turned, followed Jackson and found him pointing into a room with an outstretched arm as if he was directing traffic. Deans had not been to this room before but adhered to Jackson's silent instruction.

It was a small box room with a single table and two chairs, one opposite the other – similar in appearance to an interview room.

'Sit down,' Jackson demanded.

Deans deliberately took the chair facing the door to dominate the room and therefore exert a degree of control in whatever this was turning out to be. He did not need his astute body language skills to realise this was not a good situation.

'What's up, Sarge?' Deans asked.

Jackson stepped into the room and slammed the door, backing into it with his bony arse. He stood facing Deans, arms folded; probably annoyed that Deans had taken the primary seat. Jackson was biting his bottom lip, his cold grey eyes narrowing. He was not a pleasant-looking man.

Deans had not been this close to him before and was

getting a waft of bad breath. He suddenly felt pity for all the female officers Jackson latched onto.

'You're off the case with immediate effect,' Jackson snarled.

'What?' Deans gasped.

'You heard.'

'Why?'

'It has come to my attention that you've been carrying on with a witness.'

'Carrying on?' Deans repeated. 'What the hell are you talking about?'

Jackson closed Deans out. 'I'm not at liberty at this time to disclose the full details. This may yet take a disciplinary route. All you need to know is that you are no longer welcome here.'

'This is bullshit,' Deans shouted.

'You should've thought of that before playing away from home, son.'

'But I haven't fucking-well played away. This is crazy. I want to see the DI.' Deans demanded.

'As far as you are concerned, I am the DI. I'm acting on his behalf.'

Deans slammed both hands loudly onto the table. 'I can't believe this bollocks. You lot need me on this case more than you realise. You lot haven't got a clue who killed Amy.'

'And I suppose you do?' Jackson said, more as a statement than a question.

It was time to close up shop. Deans had no idea what was going on but it was clear he could trust no one.

'I've already contacted your superiors and they're expecting you back today. No doubt they'll want to know what's been going on, and I'll personally complete an incident report.'

'Very kind,' Deans snapped, pushing his chair away from

the table with a piercing screech, and walked out of the door before Jackson had a chance to say anything else.

Deans stormed back into the office and directly over to Mansfield, who was still at his desk.

'I want a word, Mansfield,' Deans said, baring his teeth.

'I'm busy,' Mansfield said without looking away from the computer screen.

Deans leant over and turned it off. 'Now, fucker.'

Mansfield looked Deans up and down. 'What about?'

'Outside.'

'How about a nice coffee then?' Mansfield suggested calmly. 'I could do with a posh coffee. You buying?'

'Let's go.' Deans stomped out of the room and waited at the top of the stairs.

Mansfield followed shortly after, sporting a smug expression. 'You know if you have anger issues there are people who can help you.'

'Put a lid on it, Mansfield, I'm not in the mood.'

Outside, Mansfield approached Deans with jaunty steps. 'Well, this is an unexpected pleasure.'

'What do you know?' Deans demanded, his eyes blazing.

'About what?'

Deans stepped in, crowding Mansfield's space. 'Why did you wink at me as I left the room with Jackson?'

Mansfield shrugged. 'Just being friendly.'

'Give it a rest, Mansfield. I sussed you out the moment I arrived. You're a sneaky, untrustworthy bastard.'

'Ouch, Andrew. Be very careful what you say.' Mansfield smirked and made a point of looking up at a CCTV camera positioned nearby.

'Are you setting me up?' Deans asked through gritted teeth.

'Setting you up for what exactly, Andrew?'

'You tell me.'

'I honestly don't know what you're talking about.'

Although Deans was seething, he was still observing Mansfield closely, and he appeared to be telling the truth.

'Tell me what you know about Jackson and the complaint against me.'

'A complaint?' He was lying now.

'Enough of the bollocks, Mansfield. This is my fucking career someone's trying to ruin.'

Mansfield broke into a salesman-like grin and shuffled his feet. 'Before you got back to the office, Jackson was with his little shadow and I overheard them gossiping.'

'Gossiping?'

'About you. Jackson said you'd been watched, shacked-up with a witness.'

'Watched? By who?'

'I don't know. I just overheard it. I wasn't included in their little tête-à-tête.'

'But Jackson was loud enough to make sure you heard.'

Mansfield nodded. 'Yeah. Was like I wasn't there.'

'What do you know about Jackson?' Deans asked.

'What? Apart from fungal breath and an eye for the crumpet. Not much. He's HQ. I try to stay way clear of that corporate crowd.'

'Why would he have it in for me?'

Mansfield shrugged. 'Perhaps you're some kind of threat.'

Deans turned away. *A threat.*

'What did you talk to the reporter about at the scene?'

'Reporter?'

'At the ridge, where the body was found.'

'Oh, Nev, he's okay, we're mates. He's a photographer, not a reporter. I didn't tell him anything I shouldn't. And I didn't know anything anyway.'

'Did you mention who I was?'

'He did ask, obviously hadn't seen you before and you didn't exactly blend into the background.'

'What did you say?'

'Something like "city-slick come to show us hicks how to do it", you know – something complimentary like that.' Mansfield grinned.

'Has Ranford given you any of my contact numbers?'

'No, don't think so. Why?'

'It doesn't matter.' Deans looked away, sucked in a lungful of briny air. 'Who else knows how to contact me?'

'How should I know?'

'Look, I'm being stitched up. God knows why, but someone wants me out.'

Mansfield shrugged again. 'Makes no difference to me either way.'

CHAPTER THIRTY-SIX

Within minutes Deans was at Rayon Vert and the shop front was empty.

'Denise, are you here?' he called out impatiently.

She appeared from the rear corridor. 'Yes, of course I'm here. What on earth's wrong?'

'I need to know who this is Denise. Right now. The bastard's made it personal.'

'Oh my God! What's happened?'

'Maria had a crank call this morning.'

Denise looked nonplussed. 'I'm sorry, Andy, what's the significance of that?'

'Some bloke called my wife saying weird stuff about her eyes not seeing the truth.'

Denise shook her head.

Deans had no choice, if he wanted her help he would need to divulge details of the case. 'Amy's eyelids were glued together. It has to be the same man.'

Denise gasped and covered her mouth. 'My God! Why would someone do that?' The colour drained from her face in an instant and she broke into rapid-fire blinking.

'What is it?' Deans asked.

'Tell me again about the phone call. What did the man say about the eyes?'

'I don't know it wasn't word for word. Maria wasn't exactly with it when she told me.'

Denise pressed her hands to her cheeks and turned away.

'What is it?' Deans asked impatiently.

She shook her head, still masking her face.

'Denise?' Deans said firmly.

He waited for what seemed like an age. She was visibly trembling.

She then asked softly, 'Could it have been "The eyes show you what you want them to believe?"'

'Possibly.' Deans scowled. 'Why?'

She shook her head again.

'Tell me,' Deans commanded.

She covered her face once more.

'Denise. He knows where I live. He knows my wife's name. He's already contacted her—'

'Okay, okay.' Denise held her hands up to stop Deans talking, reached for a glass of water on the counter, and took a purposeful sip.

'Did anyone see what car it was? The lift, I mean?' she asked.

'VW Golf. Dark. Tow bar.'

'Do you still have Amy's diary on you?' she asked, holding out a hand.

Deans sifted through his bag, keeping an eye on Denise. He knew what was coming. He handed the diary over and watched closely as she flicked through the pages as if looking for a specific date. She slowed and stopped with the pages open.

'Excuse me a moment,' she said glumly and began skimming through her own desk diary before again stopping on an open page. She viewed Amy's diary a second time and then back to her own.

Deans noticed wrinkles on her face for the first time.

Denise gestured for Deans to go through to the back room as she flipped the shop sign closed.

She joined him in the treatment room and sat down. Deans remained standing. She held Amy's diary delicately in her palms, and for a moment, did not move.

'Amy has several dates in her diary that don't match mine,' she eventually said. 'Sundays are my one day off.'

Half a minute of silence slipped by.

'Where is he?' Deans said sternly.

'I don't know,' she said quietly, and looked up at Deans through misted eyes. 'He was here this morning but then left. He was agitated. Angry.' She paused, shook her head. 'How could I miss it?'

Deans observed her anguish in silence.

'Ash must have met up with Amy on those Sundays.' Denise's voice wavered. 'He... he has a saying.' She coughed behind her hand, and hesitated.

'Go on,' Deans demanded.

'…Your eyes show you what you want them to believe.'

'Meaning?'

'Meaning all is not as it might appear.' She rubbed a hand across her face.

'And?'

Denise sighed, hesitated. '…And …he drives a dark blue Golf.'

Deans scrunched his fists; finally, he had something to

work with. It was minimal but for the first time in over a week, he had reason for optimism.

'Where does he live?' he asked eagerly.

'I've never been there in all the fifteen years that I've known him.'

'You've known him fifteen years and never been to his house?'

Denise snapped back, 'Have you been to everyone's house that you've worked with?

'I'm sorry. I didn't mean that to sound like a criticism.'

She glanced at the closed door. 'I have his personal file.' She spoke in secretive tones.

'Great,' Deans said, moving a rolled white towel away from the treatment couch, clearing a space for the documents. His pulse was racing, and his energy levels revitalised. He looked over at Denise bent double in the chair. 'Any chance of a brew, Denise? I'm gagging for caffeine.'

Denise nodded, rose to her feet and slowly stepped out of the room.

With Denise out of the way, Deans turned to the diaries. The most recent Sunday appointment was four weeks before Amy went missing. *Why would Amy meet Ash without Denise knowing?* He pondered it a while and then frowned. *Why contact Maria?*

Denise came back into the room with two steaming mugs and colour back in her cheeks. She handed Deans his drink and clutched hers as if she had heat-resistant palms. She took a seat on the couch and Deans followed suit.

This was a potential game-changer. Deans sympathised with her situation; not only had she lost someone she clearly cared about, the killer was likely to be her protege.

Denise spoke first. 'Amy doesn't deserve to be where she is right now. I will do all I can to help you.' She turned to face

Deans. 'And if that means Ash is found responsible, then I'll support you all I can.'

'Thank you, Denise. I'm sure this is difficult for you.'

She nodded, and crumpled into floods of tears.

Deans wrapped his arms around her, placing her head on his shoulder, and that was how they remained for the next few minutes until she spoke again.

'If it's okay with you, I will try to contact Amy now.'

'Okay,' Deans said with uncertainty, and released his arms.

Denise stood up, walked to the window and pulled the blinds. Deans searched her face; she was already somewhere else.

'Would you like me to communicate out loud or in my head?' she asked, pinching the inner corners of her red puffy eyes.

Deans shrugged. 'Whatever works for you? Will I hear any of the responses?' He scratched his nose nervously.

'No,' Denise said. 'Only I receive the answers.'

'I'm in your hands.' A wave of anxiety flushed through him, and his stomach erupted into a loud rumble. 'I'm sorry,' he said, pressing a hand against his belly. 'I must be hungry.'

'No,' she replied, surprise evident on her face. 'That's a good sign. Your body is tuning-in.'

Denise pulled the single seat over, sat down immediately in front of Deans, and gazed directly into his eyes.

An icy blast of energy surged downwards through his core in a juddering split-second.

'She's here,' Denise said simultaneously, and then studied Deans' face. 'You felt that, didn't you?' She leant forward, gently touched his knee and closed her eyes. Her fingertips still pressed lightly through his trousers. 'I can feel your energy.'

Deans coughed. 'Can I... speak through this?'

'Yes. Amy knows you are with me. She's pleased you're helping her.'

'Um, thanks. I'll do my best.'

'She knows that already.'

Denise took a series of deep breaths, and then spoke. 'Amy, do you know your killer?'

Her eyes widened. 'Did you get that?' she said breathlessly.

'No. I didn't pick up—'

Denise gasped and turned abruptly towards the door.

'What is it?' Deans said, rising instinctively to his feet.

'I'm not safe,' she said, curling herself into the chair.

Deans was now standing between Denise and the door, his body taut with anticipation. Half a minute raced by.

'Are you okay?' he asked.

Denise slowly raised her head, revealing a wounded grimace.

'Don't trust her,' she said, her voice fading.

'Don't trust who?'

Denise did not reply.

'Don't trust who, Denise?'

'I don't know.'

'Is he married? Who is she talking about? Is there someone else we need to find?' Deans was growing impatient.

Denise dropped back into the chair.

'What? What is it?'

'She's gone.'

'Gone where? Get her back.'

'I can't. She's gone.'

'Well, how long for?'

'I don't know.'

'Argh,' Deans growled and tight-lipped mouthed an expletive.

'Amy will make contact again when she needs to,' Denise

said. 'This is how it works. I can't dictate the flow of communication. Amy has told us enough for now.'

'Enough?' Deans said sharply, 'We have nothing. No evidence whatsoever.'

Denise glared at him, her eyes cloudy and red. 'We know it was Ash.'

Deans paced the room, wrought with frustration and conflict. Had he really witnessed some paranormal event or was Denise having him on?

Several minutes went by with neither of them speaking. Each of them deep in their own thoughts.

'Will you go and arrest Ash now?' Denise finally asked, her vulnerability increasingly evident through her fragile voice.

Deans shook his head slowly. 'We need more evidence.'

'Surely there's something you can do?'

Deans walked to the window, lifted the blind and stared distantly out. 'Yep. Good old-fashioned policing.' He turned and smiled insincerely. 'One small problem.'

'What?'

'I'm off the case.'

CHAPTER THIRTY-SEVEN

Neither of them spoke. Deans did not know what to think. Just how much could he rely on Denise? How could he verify the information she had just given him? And what the hell was he meant to think about his supposed untapped potential? His mind was galloping, yet he had little option but to trust Denise if he wanted to find Amy's killer and safeguard Maria.

He desperately needed to find Babbage and his car, and certainly a whole lot more evidence than a series of dates in a diary to link him to Amy's death. Above all, he wanted a lot more luck.

Denise had been flaky about the quality of the information. Was that because everything she had alluded to was pure fiction and she had struck lucky with a few comments to hook his interest? Again, validation was in scarce supply. How could he tell his Devon colleagues how he came by the Babbage information? They would laugh him all the way back up the motorway to Somerset.

Deans was disillusioned, frustrated to be kicked off the case, to be falsely accused of having an affair, let down by the reaction of his Devon colleagues, but overriding all of this, bitter regret for Janet and Ian Poole.

He wondered how they were coping and if their FLO – Family Liaison Officer – was doing a decent job. It was no longer his responsibility to be concerned by it, but he was. That was his way. That was what made him good at what he did. That was what made him so angry about what was happening. It was not just the effect on him – he was letting them down too.

Somebody had gone out of their way to ensure he was off the case. He thought about the people he had recently met, and silently questioned if there was more to Jackson than simply being an arsehole with stripes.

Deans was on the precipice of exhaustion. It had been far too long since he had a suitable rest. He knew he should be at home, spending a few uninterrupted days with Maria, forgetting everything else, but this case... it was absorbing.

The door chime sounded, making both of them turn.

Denise leapt towards Deans. 'It's him,' she whispered breathlessly, desperately grabbing Deans' arm.

'It's alright,' Deans said. 'It could be a customer.'

Denise dived behind him, still clinging on tightly.

'Do you want me to take a look?' Deans asked.

'Yes.' Her voice was timorous.

'Don't worry,' Deans said, patting her hand. 'I'll sort out whoever it is.'

As he walked towards the shop front, his pulse rate quickened. Even if Ash was there, he could do nothing – officially.

He paused at the door, pulled down softly on the handle and took a tentative step into reception. Ash was rummaging beneath the counter, just feet away. Blood rushed to Deans' cheeks and Ash stood upright in apparent surprise. For several seconds they faced off with their finest death stares, and then Ash broke into a wolfish smirk.

'Denise out back?'

Deans nodded. His stance was solid and unyielding, and he was blocking the exit from behind the counter.

'You two playing *detective* again, Detective?'

'Perhaps you'll find out someday.'

Ash snorted loudly. His eyes narrowed and his crow's feet lengthened. Deans noticed a small ring-bound notepad in Ash's hand.

'Got what you need?' Deans said.

'Ha ha,' Ash tittered. 'Oh, I've *almost* got everything I need, Detective.'

Ash scrutinised Deans with a purpose as tiny ridges appeared on his brow. He peered over the top of his glasses. 'Huh,' he murmured, and for a fleeting moment, displayed outward concern. 'Well, I'll be off now, Detective.' He chuckled and grinned. 'I'll see you again… someday.'

'You'd better count on it,' Deans said, taking half a step to the side allowing Ash to brush past.

'It's actually you that can count on it,' Ash said as he reached the door. 'Cheery-bye for now.'

Deans heaved a sigh once Ash was gone and toyed with the idea of following, but what would that achieve, except frittering away valuable time later with Maria, and chasing fantasy evidence that was no longer his problem.

He returned to the back room. Denise was curled up on the sofa, her knees tight to her chest.

'Was it him?' she asked.

Deans nodded. 'It's okay. He's gone.'

'What if he returns?'

Deans was in no position to offer protection, and had no magic answer.

'Act normal and pray that we're wrong.'

The pitiful look on her face highlighted his inadequacy.

'He took something from under the counter – a small notepad or something?' Deans said.

Denise shrugged. 'Don't know.'

'Can you shut up shop for a few days, until the guys find something solid on Ash?'

'I don't know. I have appointments.'

'Tell them you're going on holiday. Take some time out. Visit friends, go somewhere.'

'He would have sensed your abilities.'

'What do you mean?'

'An intuitive can identify the gift in others.'

'He's psychic too?'

'His methods are different to mine, but he's extremely gifted.'

'Look,' Deans said, helping Denise to her feet, 'take care of yourself, and don't be scared to call on the nines if you need to, okay?'

She nodded.

'I'm sorry. I can't do any more.'

She reached out and hugged him, and as he held her tightly in his arms, he felt as helpless as at any time in his career. Jackson had forced him into an untenable position.

Outside on the quay, Deans observed a squabble of seagulls battling for the remains of a dropped bag of chips. A salted breeze clung to his face. He checked his phone – missed call from Maria. He called her back, but Maria did not answer, must have been busy, so he left a voicemail informing her he would be back by seven and was no longer needed in Devon.

There was one last thing he had to do, and soon he was on the doorstep of Tradewinds.

Mrs Poole answered the door. Deans saw through the facade of *normality* – the makeup, subtle fragrance, faux smile.

'Have I come at a convenient time?' he asked.

'You are welcome here, any time,' she said, her twitching mouth exposing the inner strain.

Deans nodded courteously and followed her through to the living room. Mr Poole was sitting in his cane armchair, staring out through the large panoramic window. Mrs Poole smiled apologetically, invited Deans to sit down, and called over to her husband.

'Ian. Ian, dear. Detective Deans has come to see us.'

Mr Poole turned partially and acknowledged his wife with a solemn dip of the head.

'How have you both been holding up? I saw the press conference,' Deans said to Mrs Poole who was mouthing *I'm sorry* as she lowered herself onto the sofa.

Deans shook his head and held out a hand. Mrs Poole reached forward and took a firm grip.

'We are managing. Thank you,' she said and encased his hand in hers.

Mr Poole's anguish was obvious, as it had been from day one, but Mrs Poole remained spirited, at least to the outside world. Deans wanted to hold her close and not let go until her emotions spilled out. He was concerned that she had not acknowledged Amy's death. She did not need to understand it, but for her own good, she should give up the battle against it. There was no escape from grief. The further you run, the harder it hits. Thoughts turned to his own unborn child. He looked at Mrs Poole and struggled to imagine the enormity of her sorrow.

'I just wanted to see you in person before I leave,' he said.

'Leave? Where are you going?'

Deans broke eye contact. 'Something has come up back home, so I'm afraid I have to return. My colleagues here are doing all they can.'

The firmness of her grasp highlighted her despair.

'How are you finding your liaison officer?' Deans said, shifting focus.

'Fine. He's fine,' she said, still clinging onto his hand.

Deans did not try to pull away. When they first met, he wanted Mr and Mrs Poole to count on him and trust in all he did. Now he was abandoning them.

Deans cleared his throat. 'His job is to be someone from the police that you can talk openly with and deal with any questions or issues that may arise. Someone you can rely upon.'

Mrs Poole loosened her grip. 'Why couldn't that be you?'

'I wish that it could. I sincerely do.' He gave a gentle squeeze and Mrs Poole slowly released her hands. 'I hope you and your husband find resolution soon. My thoughts are with you both.'

Mrs Poole began to weep. It was incredible to think she had any tears left to spare. What must it take to find the courage to start each day, let alone survive it? Deans hoped he would never in his lifetime need to find out, and made his way to the door.

'Thank you for coming over, Andy. It was a lovely gesture,' Mrs Poole said, dabbing her face with a tissue.

'I shouldn't do this,' Deans said, removing a business card from his wallet. 'But if you feel that you need to chat, about anything, anything at all, please call me.'

Mrs Poole touched the side of his face. 'Thank you.' She

smiled painfully as a tear meandered down her cheek. 'You know, Amy would have loved you.'

Deans gulped down his building emotion, nodded respectfully, turned and walked away.

CHAPTER THIRTY-EIGHT

The journey back up the M5 was a blur and before he knew it, he was turning off the M4 at Junction 18. He had been on autopilot, and now he was only a few miles from home. He was relieved to be returning to normality, but had to accept that he was unusually frazzled. The endless shifts, restless nights, staying away from home and the developments of the final twenty-four hours had taken him to the limit, unlike any investigation before.

He decided he would spend the evening with Maria, and then drop the pool car back to the office in the morning and he hoped Mick would grant him a few days off for some quality Maria time. He had worked far beyond the norm and if the European directive of working hours was normally a pain in the arse, this time he could use it to his advantage.

It was early evening and the sky was low when he pulled up outside his home, and as he walked up the pathway, he expected the front door to open before he reached it. Not this time.

Fumbling at the doorstep, he removed the house keys from deep inside his rucksack, which only emphasised how long it had been since he had needed to use them. He pushed the door open and stepped inside.

'Hello,' he called out, but heard nothing.

'Hello, Maria,' he said louder. 'I'm back.'

The hallway was dark and cold. He frowned. *Unusual*, he thought and moved to the bottom of the stairs. The landing was in darkness.

'Hello, Maria?' Again, there was no reply. He dropped his bag where he stood and entered the lounge. The curtains were open, the TV was off and the room was clean and tidy. He walked through to the kitchen. There was no trace of leftover washing-up or the smell of cooking. He touched the outside of the kettle; it was cold. Maria drank herbal tea like it was going out of fashion.

He crept upstairs as the silence of the house intensified and found the bedroom door closed. His frown was now a concerned scowl. He carefully offered his ear to the wood, gently twisted the handle with a metallic moan from the constricting spring, and quietly pushed the door.

The room was empty, the bed made and everything was in its rightful place. He puffed out his cheeks and scratched at the scar behind his ear. *Where is she?*

He checked the other two bedrooms and bathroom. Leaning over the edge of the bath, he touched the luxury soap she loved so much. It was dry and waxy and the flannel was crisp. He gripped his chin, his mouth wide open. *Where the bloody hell is she?*

Taking the stairs two at a time, he ran into the kitchen, directly over to the fridge. Maria's IVF calendar took prominence on the door; her daily injections, the nasal sprays, the weekly routines she observed with unyielding dedication. He pulled at the handle and leaned in; the milk was out of date.

'Bollocks,' he yelled. *Maria never lets that happen.*

He whipped out his phone and called her number with trembling fingers. The dialling tone changed as she answered, and he breathed out a sigh of relief. 'Babe, where—'

'You fucking bastard,' she snivelled.

'What?' Deans took a backwards step.

'You – fucking – bastard.'

'Maria, what's happening?'

'How could you?'

'How could I what?'

'This was the happiest day of my life—'

'Maria, what the hell are you going on about?'

'Don't you dare…'

'Maria,' Deans' voice was now raised. 'I don't fucking know what you're talking about. Where are you for Christ's sake?' Deans could hear Maria bawling and the sound of a male in the background – her father.

'Maria, talk to me,' Deans pleaded.

The phone went dead.

Deans did not move for at least a minute.

'Shit,' he blurted, flopped down on the sofa and gripped his head. 'What the fuck's going on?' he said to himself.

He leapt to his feet as the landline rang. 'Hello, Maria?' he said urgently.

'Andrew, this is Graham.' It was Maria's father.

'What's going on, Graham?' Deans' voice was full of hostility.

'Maria doesn't want to talk right now, Andrew. You are best giving her some space. A day or two to come to terms—'

'With what, exactly? I'm sorry, Graham, but I seem to be the only one who hasn't got a fucking clue what's going on here.'

'Maria had a call, Andrew. Regarding you and your… antics in Devon.'

'Fucking antics? Hold-on a minute pal. There were no *fucking antics*. I'm being right royally shafted here.'

'Andrew, do yourself a favour and keep out of Maria's way. She's got a lot to contend with at the moment—'

'A lot to contend with? Jesus, Graham… try filling my fucking boots if you want a lot to contend with.'

Graham went quiet for a moment, and then spoke calmly, 'The scan was successful, in case you were wondering.'

Deans gasped, felt a bleed of tears pool in his eyes, and an uncontrollable tremor of his bottom lip. He waited, wiped his streaming nose, and turned towards the large canvas print of them both above the fireplace.

'That's great, Graham…' his voice fluttered. 'Thank…thank you.'

'We will take care of Maria. You… well; you do whatever you need to do. Just let Maria make the next move.'

CHAPTER THIRTY-NINE

Deans confined himself to the house for the next two days. He barely ate, and his stomach sloshed with caffeine during the day and cheap bourbon by night.

Savage was aware that Deans had returned. He had paid him an impromptu visit and taken back the pool car on Deans' behalf. Of course, they chatted about the reason why he was back, and the Maria situation, including the IVF treatment. Savage did not patronise him – the rumours were already rife in the station. Someone had gobbed off. If cops were outstanding at one thing, it was gossiping. Deans was not especially worried; he knew that within a week the next hot topic would be whispered in the corridors or debated during the small hours of night shift. Nonetheless, he was not looking forward to making those first steps back into the office.

Deans may have been out of the work environment but his mind had not stopped churning. His resolve was in free-fall, and he was beginning to question his own sanity in going along with Denise and her absurd suggestion that he had some sort of otherworldly power.

Savage had handed Deans a 'come back when you're

ready' voucher, said he would cover for him until Deans was ready to return. It was fair to say that he probably did need a couple of days to haul himself up out of the cesspit that he now found himself wading through.

Deans took a half-an-hour stroll into town headlong into the lashing rain. He had no purpose anymore and he barely acknowledged the downpour. He wandered the streets as thoughts ricocheted inside his skull. The city centre was better on miserable days like these – fewer people, even with Christmas beckoning. PC Rain, as it was affectionately known in the station, was doing a good job of keeping the masses away.

He eventually stepped out of the weather and into his favourite coffee house on George Street. Sitting at the farthest corner of the window, he rested his forehead in his hand, sipped from the strongest roast of the house, and watched people scuttling by, defiantly hunched beneath their umbrellas. A melancholy tune played in the background – music to slit your wrists to. Deans peered over to the waiting staff; they must have known he was coming.

He rotated his cup on its saucer, back and forth, back and forth, a grinding noise, oddly soothing. The foam art intended as a heart might just as well have been an onion. It was a fitting metaphor.

Did Maria really think he was capable of doing such a thing? Her response sadly suggested that she did. He had given her no reason to doubt him over the years, so why now? The timing was unbelievable. He was longing to see her, to kiss her, touch her, smell her, and place his hand on her stomach and tell her how proud he was. He closed out the room. Had he been so short-sighted that he could not see how the job was jeopardising his home life? Of course not, he had chosen to put the job before his home life.

He wiped his nose with the serviette. No matter how low he was feeling right then, Janet and Ian Poole's suffering was on a completely different scale. And that was why he did his job, and why he made his own personal sacrifices.

Deans slid a hand into the damp side pocket of his jacket, removed the object contained within, placed it gently onto the table in front of him, and for a long moment focused on nothing else. It was Maria's private treatment journal.

He'd discovered it on the kitchen worktop – didn't usually live there – must have been misplaced, in her hurry to get out. He took several considered sips of his drink, and then opened the cover.

Immediately inside, on the front page he saw Maria's handwriting, a dedication: *For you my baby.* Deans turned the pages, absorbing every word, hearing Maria's voice;

I can't describe the emotions I'm feeling, they change so often. At times I feel selfish for wanting you, needing you, craving you. Should I be happy with my lot, or should I chase my heart's desire? That is you my love – only you. Yes, I already love you, more than you could possibly imagine, and I know Andy does too.

The treatment so far has been bearable. I won't lie, I'm more tired now than at any time in my life. Andy says wait until you come along and then we will know tiredness. He is always so full of joy!

I pray every night that you will come. I promise Andy and I are ready to be parents. Please don't be put off by Andy's night-terrors. I know you will be the best therapy he could wish for. Andy is still working long, late hours, but that doesn't mean he doesn't want you, or love you.

Deans looked up from the page with misted vision. He scanned the room. Nobody else was paying him any attention.

He wiped his eyes with the knuckle of his forefinger and returned to the diary.

Thank you, thank you, thank you! I saw five eggs – how amazing – I so wish Andy could have seen you too, but he couldn't get away from the office. He knows already, I sent him a text. He'll be home later and so excited. I love him more now than ever before. Our incredible journey together as a family has begun.

Deans no longer heard the music in the background, or the chatter at the table near to him. He was inside the diary, just him and the sound of Maria. He devoured the pages to the latest entry.

You spoke to me last night in my dreams. You said, "Mummy, stop being silly, of course it will be positive", and it was! I saw two blue lines – can you believe it? I'm pregnant!! Daddy has been jumping around the room – he's ridiculously excited. Please stay, please, please, please. I promise I will take care of you, I won't do any more running and I'll look after myself.

I had to inform the clinic about the result. I can't believe I have to wait another four weeks before they will scan me. How on earth will I last? I want to sleep and wake up on the day of the scan. I just can't wait to see you.

This is torture, the waiting. I think my next entry will be when I have more news. I have to stop this torment somehow.

Deans drained the dregs from his cup, pulled on his sodden jacket, acknowledged the staff and left.

CHAPTER FORTY

He had been home for ten minutes when he received a with-held number on his mobile phone.

The office, he thought. 'Not this time,' he muttered, and slid the phone back into his pocket.

He busied himself as much as possible, but curiosity forced him to make the call; after all, it was likely to be Savage, and he did not want to alienate one of the few allies he seemed to have left.

DC Glover from Team 1 answered the call.

'Hi, Gloves, it's Deano. Did someone call for me?'

'Hi, Deano, yeah, I did,' Glover replied. 'I've had North Devon on the blower for you. They want you to call some custody suite, urgently. Have you got a pen?'

Dumbfounded at the request, Deans took down the details and without delay, dialled the number.

'North Devon Custody Centre. Sergeant Jarvis speaking.'

'Hello, Sarge. This is Detective Deans from Bath. I understand someone wanted to speak to me about something?'

'Do they ever! Thanks for calling back, mate. Hopefully you can put an end to all this bloody craziness.'

'Okay,' Deans said warily. 'But I'm not sure what this is about.'

'We've got this fella, brought in earlier today. Been a right pain in the arse ever since he came through the door. He assaulted one of my traffic officers, which is why he is here, but he's been bleating non-stop about getting hold of you. I did not want to bother you with this crap, but he's doing all of our heads in. So maybe you can do us all a favour?'

'Well, I don't know many people in North Devon. Who is it?'

'Hold on...' The line went quiet for a second or two. 'Hello?'

'Yeah,' Deans said disinterestedly. 'Go on.'

'Babbage. Ash Babbage.'

Deans went rigid. 'Sorry? Ash Babbage is with you now?'

'Wish he wasn't,' the sergeant replied.

'How long has he been in?' Deans asked, processing a myriad of thoughts.

'Came in about three thirty, give or take.'

'What are we on now?' Deans had not worn a watch since he returned home from Devon.

'Just gone five forty-five. I've only been on since four and he's already done my bloody nut in.'

'What's going to happen with him?'

'Well, because he's... how can I put it delicately? ...stark raving bonkers, we are waiting to get him assessed. Once we're covered there, he'll get charged and kicked out the door for court.'

'Charged with what?'

'Assaulting one of my finest.'

'What's he actually said with regard to me?'

The custody sergeant groaned. 'A lot of it is shouting and screaming – "Get me Detective Deans" and stuff like that. He is just relentless with it, won't say much else. We haven't managed any fingerprints or DNA yet because he's been such an obstreperous prick. It's taken us almost two hours to work out who you were.'

Deans' jaw was on his knees. What was Babbage doing? He had caught himself.

'Has he said what he wants to speak to me about?'

'Oh, just ramblings. Says it's something you are really going to want to hear, but he won't tell anyone else. Like I said, I'm sorry to call you but at least I can stick something on the log to say that I made contact with you.'

'Did he have a designated phone call?'

'Yeah. You.'

'What? No family or friend?'

'I take it you don't know what he's on about then?'

Deans did not answer; he was too busy trying to work out what the hell was happening.

'Hello?' the custody skipper said after a moment's silence.

'Sorry,' Deans said, shaking sense back into his head. 'Okay, thanks for the update. Can you do me a favour? Don't let him go just yet.'

'Why?' The skipper's voice had changed suspiciously.

'I need to make some phone calls.'

'Just who exactly do I have in my cells, Detective?'

Deans chewed for a beat on his response. 'He could be a crucial witness to the Amy Poole murder.'

'Witness or suspect?'

'That's what we'll have to find out.'

'Why didn't I know anything about this until now?' the skipper asked spikily.

Deans bypassed the question with one of his own. 'Where's his car? The one he was stopped in?'

'I assume it's where the stop-check took place. Hold on...'

There was a long pause and then the sergeant came back on the line. 'There's nothing from the arresting officer to suggest it's been moved.'

Excellent, Deans thought. *At last, we could be getting somewhere.* 'Do you happen to know the vehicle details?' he asked.

'VW Golf. Dark blue. Five-Five plate.'

'Thanks, Sarge. I need to make some enquiries. I'll be in touch again soon.'

'Make it quick. I don't want this one in my unit any longer than needs be.'

Deans checked the time on the cooker display. If he pushed it, he could be in Devon by eight, all things going his way. There was no time to arrange a job-car from the office so he bundled up his papers, jumped in the shower, threw some spare clothes into a bag, grabbed his suit and set off in his own car. So long as Babbage continued to play up he had a chance of reaching Devon in time. His main problem now was bringing others into the loop, and that was going to take some doing.

He decided he would call Ranford and Denise Moon whilst en route. Savage could wait. This was Deans' one chance to grill Babbage, but the more he thought about it, the more unbelievable the circumstances appeared to be.

CHAPTER FORTY-ONE

Deans waited until he was beyond the M4/M5 interchange, and then dialled Ranford.

'Tell me again,' Ranford said. 'Some prisoner is asking to speak to you about the Op Bejewel murder?'

'Yep. Ash Babbage. He was nicked earlier today for assaulting a traffic cop. I strongly believe that he's our suspect.'

'Hold up, Andy. Who is this Babbage? I haven't heard him mentioned before.'

'It's a long story. I just need you to trust me, the same way I trust you right now.'

'Who else knows you are on your way down?'

'No one. I was kind of hoping the bosses wouldn't be around at this time of night.'

'Well, you're right, they're not. Jackson has been floating about, but I expect he will get off soon. I have to be honest; I don't think you'll get a rousing reception. Jackson's made a point of making you a hot topic of conversation.'

'Don't worry about that. There's too much at stake to fuss about that bollocks.'

'What do you need me to do?' Ranford asked.

'Find the log that relates to the arrest. Find out where the car is. Then work on the inspector to get a full forensic lift.'

'I can't request a full lift without grounds, Andy.'

'I know, I know. The crux of it is, we needed a break and this could be it. Tell the inspector I was working a line of enquiry relating to Babbage; it was thin, but now he's banged up and making unsolicited comments about the murder. Run the registration details through PNC and ask someone from Intel to put the plate through ANPR for the night Amy went missing. I also need you to get hold of the custody centre – make sure Babbage isn't released before I get there.'

'I can't promise anything,' Ranford said. 'You're asking a lot. What shall I tell Jackson?'

'Absolutely nothing. Do your best. I'm just passing Weston-Super-Mare, so see you in a bit.'

'I've got to ask, Andy. Why are you still getting involved with this case?'

'I just have to. Let's leave it at that for now.'

Deans next contacted Savage, explained the phone call from Sergeant Jarvis and opened up about Denise Moon.

'Bloody hell, Deano, what are you playing at?'

'I know what I am doing, Mick.'

'You could seriously drop in the shit, Deano. You've got enough on your plate without chasing the evidence of a fantasist.'

'Well what else have we got?'

'There is no "we". You are no longer on the case and it is time you acknowledged that. Come on. Come back home.'

'I'm right, Mick. I know I am. I can't let this opportunity pass by.'

'Deano. You are going to make yourself look a prize twat, and how do you suppose it's going to reflect on the rest of us?'

'I don't care.'

'You might not, but I do.'

Deans did not answer.

'What are your intentions, Deano?'

'Get the vehicle examined, search his home address.'

'Bloody hell, Deano. He's only belted a traffic cop, that's almost no offence. How do you propose obtaining authority for all of that?'

'Leave that to me.'

'What about Groves?'

'What about him?' Deans had not even considered Carl Groves.

'Well, didn't he see the Golf and the driver?'

'You beauty,' Deans shouted excitedly. 'That's why you're a bloody skipper. Can you sort out an ID procedure for me, please?'

'You would owe me big time, Deano. What system do they use down there?'

'I don't know. Can you speak to the on-call ID officer up there and see if the systems are compatible, and find out if Groves is willing to play ball?'

'You're missing one big thing, Deano. Groves is on bail for murder. You cannot have the suspected murderer doing an ID procedure for a possible witness. It's the wrong way around.'

'Well then I guess someone with big *cojones* has to start making decisions about Groves' bail status.'

'He'll be on bail for months, until we can verify his account.'

'And this is one way.'

'No, it's not, Deano. It's fishing.'

'Do you trust me, Mick?'

243

'I do. But I also think that you're going through a tough time and maybe you need to back off and let Devon run with it alone.'

'Mick, we have a car. We have a different suspect. Groves could confirm both of them. No one else can.'

'If Groves is telling the truth, Deano. It could still be a bunch of bullshit.'

'It's not. Tap up the ID guys, please.'

Savage grunted. 'Let me mull it over, Deano.'

There were huge risks, not least treating Groves as a witness rather than a suspect. If he picked Babbage out, great. It would be another legitimate route to pursue. However, if they ran the ID and Groves failed to pick out Babbage, how would that look at any future court trial? It could seriously damage the prosecution case if Groves was indeed the killer. Any half-decent defence team would jump on the inconsistency and put enough uncertainty in the jury's mind to find reasonable doubt, and Groves would walk. Then again, the prosecution could argue a fair and transparent investigation – innocent until proven guilty and all that. It was a tough judgement call and one Deans was glad he did not have to make himself.

The phone remained silent for the remainder of the journey. He did not know if that was a good or a bad thing.

On arrival, Deans made his way into the police station and asked to speak with Ranford. The receptionist made a short call and returned to say Ranford was out, but handed Deans the phone.

'Hello,' Deans said.

'Sergeant Jackson speaking, how may I help?'

Of all the people it could have been.

'Hi, Sarge, it's Andy Deans. Has DC Ranford spoken to you about anything in the last couple of hours?'

'Are you in my reception?'

'Well, I'm downstairs in the public area, if that's your reception.'

'What are you doing here, Deans?'

'Perhaps I could come up to the office and discuss that?'

'No. There is nothing for us to talk about. Go home, where you belong.'

'I beg to differ,' Deans said. 'There's a prisoner in one of your cells requesting to speak to me personally. Someone who wants to discuss the Amy Poole murder, with me. Now, we could argue the toss about whether I've been stitched up or whether you think I should or shouldn't have anything to do with this investigation, but as I see it right now, that prisoner and I are your two best bets to progressing this case.'

'Which cell? What prisoner?' Jackson asked sharply.

'Well, there we go. It seems that we do have something to discuss after all.'

'Five minutes, starting from now.'

Deans heard the dead tone and handed the receiver back to the receptionist. 'DS Jackson has asked me to go upstairs.'

Moments later, he was in the CID office facing an angry-looking Jackson. Behind him sat Gold and Ranford. Deans glared at Ranford and suddenly doubted his own trust and judgement.

Jackson took two steps towards him. 'This way.'

The corridors were dark – cost-cutting in full effect. Jackson walked as if he had night vision and found the door handle to the little interview room with ease. Deans wondered if he had taken Gold down to this room yet, but in slightly different circumstances.

'Who's this prisoner?' Jackson asked with a spiteful tone.

'Ash Babbage.'

'Where?'

'North Devon Custody Unit.'

'Why should he ask for you?'

'That's what we should all be trying to find out.'

'Who told you?'

'Custody Sergeant Jarvis.'

'Never heard of him.'

'You should arrest a few more people then.'

'Stay here,' Jackson stormed, leaving Deans in the brightly lit shoebox of a room alone.

After several minutes, Ranford poked his head around the door.

'Where were you earlier, buddy?' Deans said angrily.

'It was Jackson. He told me not to have anything more to do with you or I'd be off the case as well.'

'What a tosser,' Deans said just as Jackson came back into the room.

'Follow me,' he said to Deans, and cast a ferocious glare at Ranford.

Jackson headed them back to the CID office.

'Shut the door,' Jackson told Ranford.

Deans found the corner of a desk, perched his weight on the edge and sat on his hands as Jackson paced back and forth menacingly.

Then it began.

'Just who the hell do you think you are, eh?' Jackson said, bearing down on Deans. 'Tell me when you started to call the shots in my jurisdiction, Constable?'

Deans did not speak, refrained from catching eye contact.

'Well?' Jackson roared. 'I am asking you a question, son.'

Deans shrugged, but before he could say anything Jackson was on him, inches from his face.

'Since when do you start arranging forensic recovery?' Jackson's spittle was wetting Deans' lips. He knew Jackson was baiting him for a reaction and he was not about to feed the man's anger or ego.

'I'm told that CID requested a full lift and forensic examination of a suspect vehicle. Am I missing something here?' Jackson was now involving the rest of the room. 'Well?' he shouted.

Gold then showed her inexperience. 'I didn't.'

'I know that,' Jackson said still facing Deans. 'Apparently someone else has been making these supervisory requests.' He then turned to Ranford, who took a step backwards and bumped into a chair. 'It seems Detective Ranford has been in liaison with the Duty Inspector.'

Deans had heard enough. 'I asked him to.'

'You,' Jackson snarled, now practically nose-to-nose with Deans. 'You asked him to? Got your own budgets, have you?'

Deans stood upright from the desk and flexed blood back into his numbed fingers. He was altogether larger than Jackson was, not to mention ten or more years younger, and now they were standing toe to toe.

'Get out of my face, Sergeant,' Deans said with quiet determination.

Jackson, whose nose was now level with Deans' chin, pivoted sideways. 'What are you going to do, Constable... strike a superior officer? I don't think that would be a wise career move now, do you?'

'I've no intention of striking anyone,' Deans replied calmly, as Jackson crabbed a couple more half steps away. 'Do you know what I find most disappointing? You are here flexing your stripes, arguing about who organised the forensics, when all that matters is, it was done. We can bicker all night long but one thing hasn't changed: a young girl is dead and we're here to investigate how and why, and that's exactly what I intend doing. Now, we have someone locked up who knows something about it, and wants to talk to me. If everything goes tits up, then direct the blame my way, but until then, let's try to work this sodding case together.'

'Don't think you can come down here with your city ways, son. There are procedures, there is policy, and there is *respect*,' Jackson boomed.

Deans looked to the others, who quickly turned away.

'Respect?' Deans repeated through gritted teeth. 'Let me tell you what respect is. Respect is doing everything we can for the families of our dead victims. Respect is allowing highly trained officers to get on and do their jobs without making them feel like children—'

'Get out of my fucking office,' Jackson screamed, his face deep crimson red.

Deans looked again at the others. They clearly did not want to know. He nodded knowingly at Jackson, who was now practically melting with rage, turned and walked away.

CHAPTER FORTY-TWO

Deans returned to his car. The air was cold and miserable. He stared fixedly through the windscreen until his eyes glazed dry. Since discovering Maria had left home, he had managed to keep his emotions pretty much in check but it had taken a lot to remain composed in the face of Jackson's outburst.

A tap on the driver window disturbed his moment. He blinked moisture back into his eyes and focused on the silhouette beside his door, and realised it was Gold.

'Hold on a moment,' he said, wiping a hand down his face. 'Hi,' he said, buzzing the window down.

Gold was wearing her rain jacket and holding two document bags.

'I've been told to hook up with you,' she said.

'Really? Hook up or watch?'

She laughed. 'Can I get in, please? It's cold.'

Deans nodded over to the passenger seat beside him, and as she opened the door, he caught sight of his bloodshot eyes in the rear view mirror.

Gold stepped in, smiled awkwardly, closed the door and

pulled on her seatbelt before the cabin light once again dimmed to darkness.

'We all think he's a twat, you know,' she said, looking directly ahead.

Deans nodded thanks at her attempts to ease the situation.

'He's told me to go with you to the custody unit,' she said.

Deans turned to face her. 'You're kidding! I was expecting to have to storm it, like entering Fort Knox.'

'Well, no need now. I'm your little key into Pandora's box.' She grinned.

Maybe his straight talking had cracked Jackson's granite casing, or maybe Jackson knew Deans had no intention of walking away and it was better to keep him under a watchful eye.

'Okay. What else has he told you to do?' Deans asked.

'Report to him everything you do.'

'And will you?'

'Maybe,' she said, with a mischievous smile.

She was a sweet-looking girl. Fragile, like a china doll. A completely inappropriate OIC for the monster they were investigating.

They headed off with Gold giving directions, and arrived at the custody centre about half an hour later. The unit was a four-storey complex with a spiked, ten-foot perimeter fence surrounding the entire site. It was the modern way; ensuring people stayed on the inside and protected from the outside.

Gold swiped her proximity card and the gates motored slowly apart.

'We need to park near there,' Gold said, pointing over to a one-storey annex, the size of a trading estate unit. *The custody drop-off*, Deans thought.

Gold led the way in through a secure side door. A narrow, straight corridor with sparkling grey non-slip flooring took them to another door, but this time Gold had to press a buzzer and wait. Seconds later the door latch clicked and she pushed through into a spacious custody reception area. A raised staff base loomed over them and blocks of CCTV screens beamed cell and corridor images from the wall behind.

Deans noticed the profile of the front desk was angled forwards like the bow of a ship. He figured that was to make life difficult for any disgruntled shits, who might have an adverse reaction to the custody staff. His eyes followed a yellow line taped to the floor, three feet in front of the desk, until he lost sight of it deeper into the dim corridor, where Babbage would no doubt be waiting.

These modern, purpose-built custody units worked well. Designed with practicality in mind. They were clinical in appearance, but effective. Deans' own custody unit dated back to the sixties with only nine cells in total. Each year something else needed repairing or replacing, but it had character oozing from the pores.

Deans caught the three male staff behind the counter all gaping towards them – correction: towards Gold.

'How may we help?' the custody sergeant asked her.

'Hi, Sarge,' Gold said buoyantly. 'We're from the Op Bejewel team. You have someone in the cells asking to speak to my colleague DC Deans.' She waved a hand in Deans' direction.

'Ah yes, thanks for coming,' the custody sergeant replied, now acknowledging Deans' presence.

'Sarge,' Deans said, dipping a nod.

'Come back around here,' the custody sergeant said. 'You've certainly picked a strange one, I can tell you.' He turned to the bank of monitors and pointed to the top row, third screen in from the left.

'There's your man.'

Deans immediately recognised Babbage. He was perched on the edge of a low-level bench, sitting bolt upright with his hands on his knees. He was an intriguing sight.

'He's hardly moved,' the custody sergeant said. 'A very odd individual indeed. All he does is sit there demanding to see you.'

'Any development with the mental health assessment?' Deans asked.

The sergeant shook his head. 'Been assessed. Perfectly normal according to the doc.' He pulled a face. 'But we all know they've got to believe they're Elvis or Mickey Mouse before much else happens.'

'So, he's in play?' Deans asked.

'Be my guest. The sooner he is out of here the better as far as I am concerned. I still have him on constant observations for now, just to be safe. We will resort to DNA by force if we have to, but I would rather you speak to him first. Maybe you can convince him to cooperate.'

Constant observations varied between units and custody sergeants. Sometimes the detention officers did it and other times the police officers drew the short straw. Generally used for high-risk subjects to keep them from self-harming or to prevent loss of evidence; in Babbage's case, it was because he presented as unpredictable. Deans had spent many long hours sitting, or standing outside cell doors on constant obs and never forgot what a soul-destroying task it was. Whoever it was watching Babbage now, they had Deans' sympathy.

He thanked the custody sergeant and found a quiet office to speak with Gold.

'What has Jackson asked you to do now that we're here?' Deans asked.

'Not much. Just keep him updated about you.'

'Well someone needs to arrest Babbage on suspicion of murder. Was anything discussed about that?'

'No.'

'Did he not listen to anything I said?'

Gold shrugged, shook her head.

'Call him. Tell him we are good to go but we need his authority to make the arrest. Make him feel like he's calling the shots.'

'What grounds do we have for the arrest?'

'Amy was seen getting into Babbage's vehicle on the night she went missing.'

'Really?'

'That's what I think. The CCTV still needs some going over, but we also have…' Deans hesitated, '…a witness account.'

'We do?'

Deans nodded. 'All we need is for Jackson to green light the arrest and for the custody sergeant to buy it and Babbage is all ours. I'll give you some privacy,' Deans said, left Gold in the room, and headed back out to the bank of CCTV monitors.

Babbage had not moved. The custody sergeant was in the back office with the detention officer and had not seen him return. Deans looked around: the reception area was empty. All that was between him and Babbage at that moment was the cop on constant obs.

He quickly moved behind the custody desk, stepped in close to the bank of monitors and concentrated on the two screens that required his attention. Satisfied with his preparation, he soundlessly made his way down the cell corridor, and flashed his warrant card to the forlorn-looking PC sitting outside of Babbage's cell.

'Hey, buddy,' Deans said. 'I'm happy to give you five minutes, if you need a slash or something.'

'Thanks,' the PC said, looking slightly puzzled.

'No worries,' Deans said. 'Why not grab a coffee while you have the chance? I'm good here until you get back.'

'Okay, cool.' The PC replied and placed a well-thumbed copy of *Hello!* onto the floor and beamed broadly as he passed Deans, who watched until the PC was out of sight.

The cell door was open, but Deans had made a point of not showing himself to Babbage, yet. He could feel his heart quickening and slowly stepped forward until he was at the threshold of the cell. He had already established the camera blind spot and carefully positioned his body so that he was leaning against the left side of the door frame. From here, only his feet would be in shot, so long as he did not lean forwards. Babbage was still sitting on the low-level bench, his head in his hands, and had not noticed Deans' arrival.

As the seconds approached a minute, Deans became more anxious.

'Babbage,' he called out.

Deans was not permitted to interview Babbage there and then, or ask any questions relating to the investigation, but he needed Babbage to know he was there, accepting the challenge, and in control of whatever Babbage was up to.

Babbage looked up from behind his willowy fingers.

'Detective Deans,' he responded after a second or two of indecision, and rose excitedly to his feet.

'No.' Deans glowered and dipped his index finger. Babbage acknowledged the gesture with a grin and gently returned to his seated position, hands upon his knees in a display of total compliance.

'Oh, you and me...' Babbage said enthusiastically. 'This is going to be so much fun.'

Deans folded his arms and propped a shoulder against the doorframe.

'I'll bet you are just very slightly fed up with me. Am I right?' Babbage said.

Deans did not respond, but excitement was clearly building within Babbage.

'Oh, come on. Enter into the spirit, Detective.'

'This isn't a game.'

'Ooh,' Babbage said, cupping his hands loudly with delight. 'This *is* a game. And you are playing very well.'

The echoes of approaching footsteps intruded on Deans' building hatred. It was the PC.

'Cheers,' the PC said. 'Really appreciate that.' He stopped and noticeably registered Deans at the doorway. 'Sorry, has he been giving you any trouble?'

Deans turned to face a grinning Babbage. 'No trouble whatsoever.' He patted the PC on the shoulder and headed back along the corridor.

When he returned to the charge desk, Gold was waiting for him.

'What were you doing down there?' she asked.

'Just giving that poor sod a comfort break. What's the answer?'

Gold was looking Deans over with prying eyes.

'Jackson,' Deans said. 'What did he say?'

'He says we can go ahead with the arrest but you're not to have any contact with the prisoner.'

'Fine.'

Gold tilted her head. 'He also said you would take the hit if the evidence doesn't stack up.'

Deans shrugged. 'Fine.'

The custody sergeant was busy talking to a detention officer behind the charge desk, but Deans had the perception of Gold staring at him, and so made his way across to the skipper and interrupted their conversation.

'Sorry, Sarge. DC Gold here has just received authority to arrest Babbage on suspicion of murdering Amy Poole.'

'By whom?' the sergeant asked.

'DS Jackson,' Deans said.

The sergeant pulled a face. 'DS Jackson?'

'He doesn't get out of the office much,' Deans quipped.

'He's my sergeant,' Gold said, elbowing Deans in the ribs, 'from Major Crime in Exeter. He's the deputy senior investigating officer.'

'Well somebody had better convince me why Babbage needs to remain in my custody unit.'

They funnelled through to a back office, and Deans explained the circumstances and flowered up the evidence enough to secure a detention. The sergeant was less than ecstatic, but agreed to the arrest, once he had also spoken to Jackson on the phone.

The sergeant steered the way along the yellow line into the void of the cell corridor with Gold and Deans in his wake.

Gold acknowledged the PC waiting outside of the open cell door and Deans gave him a wink, but remained out of Babbage's view.

The sergeant entered the cell and his voice resonated throughout the corridor. 'Listen up,' he said. 'This officer is going to say something to you. It's important that you listen and understand what's going on.'

Gold hovered in the doorway, neither inside, nor out. She looked uncomfortable; holding her daybook tightly to her chest like it was body armour. She cleared her throat. 'Ash Babbage, I am arresting you on suspicion of murdering Amy

Poole between Saturday the fourth of October and Saturday the eleventh of October this year—' She coughed, and snatched a glance towards Deans.

'Is he out there?' Deans heard Babbage ask.

'Listen to what is being said to you,' the custody sergeant said loudly over Babbage's voice.

Gold continued, 'You do not have to say anything. but it may harm your defence if you do not mention when questioned something that you later rely on in court, and anything you do say may be given in evidence.'

The sergeant cut in. 'Do you understand what has just happened? I must remind you of your right to free and independent legal advice. Do you wish to have a legal representative notified of your arrest?'

There was silence.

The sergeant ushered everyone away from the cell apart from the PC whom he told to stay put, much to his obvious displeasure.

They returned to the charge desk where a uniformed inspector was already waiting for an update. They greeted one another and the inspector asked Gold to justify the grounds for her arrest.

Realising the inspector was not buying into the story, Deans interjected.

'Sir, I've been involved with this investigation from the outset when the victim was a MISPER in Somerset. Early enquiries led me to this area and when the body was located we had very little to go on. However, extensive enquiries have identified what I believe to be reasonable grounds to detain Mr Babbage for interview. Firstly, witnesses and CCTV would suggest that on the night Miss Poole went missing, she accepted an unexpected lift by an unidentified male driving a dark-coloured VW Golf. Although she later met up with friends, no one appears to know why she got the lift or from whom. A key witness watching this pick-up may be able to identify the driver through an ID procedure, although that line of enquiry is currently being pursued. As we understand it, Miss Poole left the club alone but did not make it back home. There is no evidence to suggest that she got a taxi, so our starting point for the disappearance must be on leaving the club. The driver of the Golf is vital to our investigation, and Mr Babbage owns a dark blue VW Golf that he was driving at the time of his arrest by your traffic officers.'

'Yes, I granted the recovery of that vehicle earlier today.'

'Thank you, sir, I'm very much obliged,' Deans said, currying favour. 'On being stopped by your officers, Mr Babbage apparently requested to speak personally with me in relation to the Amy Poole murder. This was completely unsolicited and I don't believe in coincidence, sir.'

The inspector peered at Deans, his features unyielding.

'Sir, I further request that we conduct a search at his home address for any evidence relating to the victim or the crime, and seek his cooperation in an ID procedure. Only then may we prove or disprove any involvement he might have in this murder.'

'Forensics?' the inspector asked.

'Well, sir, who knows what we may uncover at the home address, or from the vehicle, come to that.'

The inspector scrutinised Deans for an uneasy second, then nodded. 'I think, given the serious nature of the offence under investigation and the embryonic stage we still sadly find ourselves at, I'm willing to authorise a Section Eighteen search of his home address, and if he won't agree to an ID procedure then we can still go ahead using his custody image. Which we have, yes?'

Deans and the custody sergeant shook their heads in tandem.

'That's in hand I take it?' the inspector said to the custody sergeant.

The skipper nodded. 'He's been a difficult prisoner, sir, but we'll press on with that immediately.'

'Don't think I've come across a willing one yet,' the inspector said dryly.

That could be about to change, Deans thought.

'Good,' the inspector continued. 'And I think we'd be justi-fied in obtaining fingernail scrapings, clippings and hand swabs.'

'Sir,' Deans acknowledged.

'But we don't have any evidence of a sexual assault, so we'd be hard pushed to obtain intimate samples. Am I right?'

'Yes, sir,' Deans said.

'Thank you, sir,' Gold said.

'Thank you for that concise review of the case, uh… Deans. I did speak to Sergeant Jackson earlier regarding the vehicle lift, but he rather waffled.'

'Thank you, sir. To be fair to Sergeant Jackson, we haven't had much opportunity to exchange updates today.'

Gold concealed a knowing look to Deans.

'Keep me informed,' the inspector said, and waved the desk sergeant towards a computer screen, which they both then crouched over.

Gold sidled up beside Deans. 'How did you get away with that?' she whispered.

Deans chuckled. 'You just need to hit the buzzwords and hope the BS sounds good.' He noticed Gold had become subdued. 'Hey, are you alright?'

'Yeah, I'm fine.'

'Why not call Jackson, keep him sweet? We are going to need some extra staff for all this work I have just created us.'

'Okay,' she said and lightly brushed against him. 'I'm glad you're here.'

'Thanks,' Deans said somewhat surprised. 'It's sad your sergeant doesn't see it the same way.'

Gold laughed and wandered off to a side room to make the call.

Deans had taken a gamble with the inspector and now the result was on the flip of a coin. He was relying on something somewhere coming good, but he could never have predicted the events that were to follow.

CHAPTER FORTY-THREE

With a plan of attack laid out less than an hour later, Deans was heading off to Babbage's home address along with two uniformed PCs from the late shift, roped in to assist with the Section Eighteen search. Gold was back at the station, tasked by Jackson to interview Babbage along with DC Travaskis from her HQ unit.

Deans had nothing specific to search for at the address as so little information about the murder was known. Perhaps they would find the victim's missing mobile phone, a tube of recently opened superglue or a signed confession. Fat chance. Despite this, he felt a palpable excitement the closer they got to their destination. He had already seen the intelligence reports on Babbage and the address. Both were spectacularly void. He was entering the unknown, and cops never liked to do that.

They arrived on the housing estate shortly before ten and parked directly outside the address. Deans saw both late turn officers checking their watches anxiously. Their team was due off at eleven and the night shift would be arriving at the station for their ten until seven stint. That final hour of changeover was often the only chance officers had to complete any accrued paperwork during the shift, but Deans had used the drive over to good effect and had hatched a plan that would ideally work in everyone's favour.

The estate was modern, predominantly laid out with semi-detached properties and no apparent symmetrical basis of planning. As with most estates, there was a degree of claustro-phobia from the neighbouring properties but he had certainly seen much worse. These had decent-sized driveways and a patch of lawn at the front, and some had their own integrated garage. All the properties appeared to have the same red brick and white UPVC windows and doors. Toy town, Maria would call it.

Babbage's property was set in complete darkness on the left-hand side of the road. Deans could see the silvery number thirty-four on the front door, reflecting brightly in the street-lights. His anticipation grew as he gathered up his go-bag and a raid box from the boot of the car and pulled on a pair of blue vinyl gloves.

Deans directed one of the PCs to the rear of the property as he fiddled with a bunch of keys taken from Babbage whilst he was in custody. The other PC was shining a powerful dragon lamp directly at the door lock, causing the million times candle light to bounce back off the glossy surface directly into Deans' face. He gestured to the PC to kill the light so that a) he could see again and b) the entire neighbourhood wouldn't wake up to their arrival.

Once Deans confirmed the PC at the rear was set, he then unlocked the door, gently forcing it inwards. He did not know if he was about to trigger a house alarm, if a dog was waiting on the other side, or even if someone else might be there ready to greet him.

Darkness and silence were all that he found.

He pulled on a pair of elasticated shoe covers and entered the hallway, noticing an unset entry alarm box on the wall.

He's confident, Deans thought.

'This is the police,' Deans shouted, and listened for signs of movement or response. There was none.

He turned to the PC. 'You stay out here.'

'Shouldn't I come in with you?' The PC said, looking disappointed.

'No. I need you to deal with anyone paying too much attention to our arrival.'

'But what if you need help?'

'Well, then I will shout for it,' Deans said, and shoved the door closed from the inside.

He flicked a light switch, illuminating the narrow hallway. Closed doors were to his left and right. A stairway at the end of the hallway kinked out of view. He huffed and turned back to the front door. He was being bone-headed and should really have someone else with him, just in case.

He stewed for a moment and then opened the front door, to find the PC carving the illuminated dragon lamp through the air, as if it was some kind of giant lightsaber. He killed the light the moment he saw Deans.

'When you've finished battling Darth Vader, perhaps you'd like to come inside,' Deans said, holding the door wide open, already regretting his decision.

The PC immediately made towards Deans with a broad grin.

'Not that,' Deans said, pointing to the lamp. 'You'll need forensic gloves and shoe covers.'

'I've already got some,' the PC replied eagerly, rummaging through a pouch on his utility belt that was bursting with paraphernalia for every eventuality.

Fuck me, it's Bear Grylls in uniform, Deans thought, and

waited patiently while the PC slipped the covers over his brilliantly polished Magnums and carefully rolled on his gloves with surgical precision.

What have I done? 'Ready?' Deans asked.

The PC nodded enthusiastically.

'Do not touch anything. Do not open any doors. Do not go inside any rooms – unless I say you can. Understood?'

'Affirmative.'

Deans did not know whether to laugh or cry. Instead, he turned back to the hallway. His instinct directed him to the door on the right. The living room. It was unoccupied and sparsely decorated. A warm breeze brushed against his neck from behind. The PC was right behind him, straining to look into the room over his left shoulder.

'Tell you what,' Deans said, with a backwards swat of his hand. 'Just sit tight here for now. Okay?'

'Okay,' the PC replied dejectedly.

'Been in long?' Deans asked.

The PC pulled a face.

'The job. Been in the job long?'

'Oh, this is my first month without a tutor-constable.'

Figures, Deans thought. 'Well, take in all you can, but most importantly, do not cross-contaminate anything. Okay?'

'Affirmative.'

Deans turned his attention to the room on the left, the kitchen. He walked in hugging the wall line so as not to disturb any potential footprints or markings on the vinyl floor.

The room was fridge-cold, as if a window had been left open, yet they were closed. Deans stooped forward, and pulled his coat tight over his shoulders, becoming strangely lightheaded. He reached the far side of the room and discovered another narrow galley-way leading to a doorway that probably led to the rear of the property, and the second bobby.

He backtracked to the hallway and saw the PC was standing exactly as he had left him.

'Relax,' Deans said. 'I'm just going upstairs. Stay put, unless I call for you.'

The PC nodded, and Deans edged his way up the stairs. As he approached the top, the already-uncomfortable air temperature took a noticeable dive and his scalp felt like it was separating from his head. He zipped up his North Face jacket and stood on the landing.

Four white doors faced him, three closed and one, at the end of the short hallway, left open. He opened the first door on the right, being careful not to disturb any potential fingerprints on the handle. It was the bathroom. Standard three-piece and tiled floor to ceiling in a nautical theme. It was spotlessly clean and tidy. He worked anti-clockwise and next entered the room with the open door. Meagre furniture made the room look larger than it actually was, and he could not help but notice the vibrant pink, flower-patterned wallpaper lining the wall behind the bed.

He scoured the room. The bed was single, neatly made and smoothed down with new-looking white sheets. A single shabby-chic bedside table matched the wardrobe, and a full sized vanity mirror took the space opposite the bed.

The room was immaculate and starkly feminine. Denise's words *don't trust her* sprang to the forefront of his mind.

He moved on to the study. An altogether different room; deep red walls, black glass desk and modern computer equipment. A small red dot in the corner of the screen and a glowing cordless mouse revealed that the system was on. More reason to believe that Babbage had not expected his arrest.

Pine shelving took up the majority of one wall. On the upper shelves, numbered box files stood on end and reading material filled the remaining space. Stephen King was clearly popular, and then he noticed, one, then two, then several other books on witchcraft and the dark arts.

Deans' extremities were stiffening from the chilled air and he was glad there was only one room left to check, but as he stretched out for the handle, his entire body broke into a tremor and each hair on his body reached for the sky.

'Jesus, this place is cold,' he muttered, and rubbed his arms vigorously, and then noticed the vapour from his breath, drifting in an eerie and unnatural direction towards the fourth door. Mesmerised, he watched until the haze dissipated against the wood.

He shook his head and gently pushed down on the handle, to reveal a small, square room of complete emptiness.

Instantly, Deans experienced an intense burning sensation shoot from his eyes into the crown of his head. He dropped to his knees and he clamped his head.

'Everything alright up there?' came a voice from downstairs.

'Yep,' Deans called out as the pain intensified. Maria's smiling face flashed into his mind, followed by Amy's limp corpse lying on the pebble ridge.

'Argh,' Deans moaned through a tightly-clenched jaw, as he pressed his hands firmly into his face in a futile attempt to relieve the agony.

'Fuck's happening,' he squealed.

A voice in his right ear stunned him to a complete halt. *Don't stop.*

Deans snatched at his breath and looked over his shoulder. No one was there. He leapt to his feet and scanned the landing. It was empty. He crept back to each of the other rooms and cautiously looked inside. There was no one else around, other than PC Skywalker downstairs.

Deans bunched his eyes – there was no mistake – he heard

the words, as clear as if someone had been stood next to him, someone who was female.

His mind accelerated. *This is it*, he thought. *This is what Denise was trying to tell me. My sign. My connection.*

He walked to the very edge of the top stair and looked down. The PC was not in sight, but the intermittent radio chatter from his radio confirmed he had not moved from the hallway. A waft of familiar-smelling scent drew Deans back to the landing. It was the same brand that Maria used, he could not recall the name, but it was shaped like an apple. He sniffed the air, following the trail and found himself back in the small empty room. The brilliant whiteness of the walls and ceiling all of a sudden appeared exaggerated and significant, and instead of smelling perfume, he was now inhaling an overpowering odour of bleach.

Deans stood in the middle of the room and took in the four walls. What was happening? It was as if all his senses were being used properly for the first time.

He faced the wall to the right of the door. He did not know why. An aura of white light glimmered in his peripheral vision, the shimmery movement of something else in the room. He turned that way, his skin crawling with electricity, but saw nothing.

He waited, barely breathing and several minutes went by before warmth returned to his body. He shuffled his way to the stairs and slowly walked down.

The PC stood up from the bottom step. 'Anything up there?'

Deans shook his head and moved towards the door.

The PC followed. 'What do we do now?' he asked.

Deans pressed the heel of his hands into his temples and took several purposeful breaths. 'You go back outside with your mate, and I'll come and see you shortly.'

'Are you okay?' asked the PC.

'Yep. See you outside in a moment.' Deans opened the front door and held it wide until the PC was gone, and then took himself over to the bottom step of the stairs and worked out what to do next.

Emotionally drained, and utterly perplexed, he took out his phone and held the receiver weakly to his ear. Denise answered on the third ring, said she had a feeling something was up. Deans gave her the address and told her to meet him at the house in fifteen minutes, and to wear something businesslike.

He joined the two PCs outside, who were now looking cold and bored. It was time to put his plan into action.

'Thanks, fellas,' he said, doing his utmost to sound normal. 'We're going to need a controlled search of this place.'

Neither PC attempted to hide their reluctance at the thought of staying on an extended shift. *Just as expected*, Deans thought.

'Tell you what,' Deans said, 'your night shift is on duty now, so why don't you guys head back and let nights take over here? I'm not going anywhere and I can cover the place until the search teams arrive.'

'Yeah, that sound good to us,' the second PC said.

'Hit the road while you have the chance, and thanks for your help tonight. I'll call through to the station to arrange your replacements.'

And Deans had every intention of doing that, just not yet.

CHAPTER FORTY-FOUR

Deans watched from behind the mesh curtain and darkness of the living room as Denise approached the front door. She looked smart in a thick black woollen jumper and black trousers. He opened the front door and held out a pair of blue vinyl gloves and shoe covers.

'What's this?' she asked.

'Put them on and come inside,' Deans said, reducing the gap in the door to the outside world.

Denise did as requested and stepped inside. Deans watched with interest as her eyes darted around the space. She was not lying about having never visited.

'Where is he?' she asked after a moment or two.

'In the cells.'

'When will he be out?'

'Not for a while. He's been arrested for Amy's murder, which is why I called you.'

Denise stepped backwards onto the doormat. 'Should I be here?'

'Technically, no. But I need your help. I am kind of hoping

you can do stuff at crime scenes; pick up vibes, that sort of thing.'

'This is a crime scene?'

'You tell me.'

Denise ran a hand through her hair. 'You'll get into trouble for this.' She shook her head. 'No, *we* will get into trouble for this.'

'Only if we're found out, and I don't intend telling anyone.'

She stared at him with hunted intensity.

'It's okay, we're alone,' he said. 'But we only have a short window to play with.'

'Well, whether I like it or not,' Denise said, 'Amy is here with us.'

'I know.'

Denise tilted her head and gave Deans a teacher-like stare.

'What do you need to do?' Deans asked hurriedly, leading Denise by the arm further into the hallway.

Denise stopped in her tracks. 'Upstairs?' she asked.

She turned to Deans. 'We need to go upstairs.'

Deans nodded and led the way.

Denise halted halfway up, and looked around in short, sharp, robotic movements. 'She was here,' she whispered.

Deans checked his watch. It was nineteen minutes since the two cops had left and he figured they had a window of about twenty minutes more, once nights got wind there were no bobbies on point duty.

At the lip of the landing, Denise stopped abruptly and turned to face the door on the left: the empty white room.

Deans felt another arctic bolt of energy smash through his spine, only this time it was seismic. He made a grab for the handrail.

'This room, flower?' Denise asked softly, and positioned herself in front of the closed door.

Deans heaved himself to the top of the stairs, grappling for breath, and waited behind Denise.

She opened the door and tentatively stepped inside. Deans was right behind her. Denise did not move for a few long seconds, and then turned to face the wall on the right.

'Over there, darling?' she said softly, and sucked air in through her teeth. She bobbed and weaved and looked in various directions, and then stood completely still. Deans came alongside her.

'This is it,' she said. 'This is the last room Amy saw.'

'I felt it too, before you came,' Deans said.

Denise nodded. 'I know.' She touched his arm. 'You've done well.'

'What happened in here?' Deans asked.

Denise turned away.

'Denise, what happened?'

'She... she tried to fight him off.' She pointed over to the wall. 'He had a pillow.' Denise's voice tailed away. 'She stood no chance.'

'Go on,' Deans encouraged. He had spotted the subtle twitches and flinches in her face. There was more.

Denise swallowed deeply. 'Amy ended up on the floor. He... he straddled her. Covered her face...' Denise broke away.

Deans stepped forwards and stared at the wall.

'The photographs,' Denise said from behind him.

'What photographs?' Deans asked, spinning around.

'Here, flower?' Denise said, standing central to the room, facing the doorway.

'What?' Deans said approaching Denise. 'He took photographs of Amy here?'

Denise breathed a heavy sigh. 'Not only Amy.'

Deans looked at the four corners of the room. The brilliant whiteness suddenly made sense.

'She touched the wall,' he muttered moving closer. *That's why*.

Denise joined him beside the right-hand wall, both facing it like it was an art gallery display.

'I need to know exactly where she touched this wall,' Deans said.

Denise stepped closer, and dipped her head, as if listening for a far-off sound. With an outstretched arm, she pointed to the wall.

Deans positioned his head side-on, so that he could now see every dimple of paint, and each imperfection in the plaster. His eyes fixed on a shadow directly in front of Denise's finger-tips that had not been visible from head-on. It was a unique feature on an otherwise typical surface. Within this area, he noticed a shallow gouge and spontaneously suffered a ripping, tearing sensation in his right hand. He recoiled instinctively and flapped his hand through the air. Ranford's voice then filled his head.

'The fingernail,' he cried out.

Police instinct took over and he dropped to his knees and searched the edge of the skirting board directly beneath the mark. Could he really be that fortunate?

'He dragged her down the stairs to the kitchen,' Denise narrated in a monotone voice. 'Used the link door to the garage so that no one would see him.'

Deans stood up. 'Link door? What link door?'

Denise was staring into space.

Deans left her in the room and hurried downstairs to the kitchen. Sure enough, on the other side of the fridge freezer was a closed door that he had previously missed. He tried the handle – it was locked.

'He pulled her into the car,' Denise said. She had joined him.

'Any door keys?' Deans asked impatiently, checking the worktops.

Denise had taken a seat, her hair matted to her face.

'Any keys?' Deans said, now practically shouting.

'Under the microwave,' Denise replied.

Deans cased the worktop and settled on a stainless steel microwave in the far corner of the kitchen. He rushed over and lifted it. Time seemed to stop for an instant. He looked over to Denise; she was not even looking his way.

You have to be kidding me, he thought.

A bunch of keys were marooned amongst age-old food debris. He swiped a Chubb key, and it worked.

He opened the door in a hurry – now was not the time for paranormal analysis. The garage was empty. Spotless would be another way to describe it. Even the concrete floor had a recently vacuumed appearance.

Deans heaved a deep, despondent sigh. The whole place had been primed for his arrival. He glanced at the shelving. There were no tools or junk as you might expect to find. Instead, neatly stacked cardboard boxes. Why should he be surprised?

He turned back to the kitchen and for a fleeting moment, took stock of the situation. It would take highly skilled search teams and forensic experts hours if not days to establish what had happened here to Amy, yet, in ten minutes they'd formed a hypothesis. Moreover, he knew exactly where to start looking for the evidence. If he was a reluctant believer before, he would become a fully-fledged disciple if something tangible came from the police search.

'Denise,' he said softly.

She slowly lifted her head. She was tearful.

'We don't have long. Can Amy describe the pillow?'

Denise dipped her head once again. Her body language growing increasingly resigned. She shrugged. 'It was light-coloured, possibly white.'

'Did he leave it here?'

'I don't know.' Denise's eyes were bloodshot. She looked exhausted and emotional.

The scale of Deans' dilemma then struck him; this house offered evidential avenues, possibly enough to place Amy within its confines and suggest signs of a struggle, but the source of the information was a psychic, who should never have been at the scene in the first place.

He pinched the bridge of his nose. He needed to be smart. He checked his watch; 10.55 p.m.

Time's up.

CHAPTER FORTY-FIVE

Deans paced the hallway as he waited for the troops to arrive. He was experiencing a strange excitement; a mixture of knowing he had broken the rules, and overwhelming anticipation, wondering if the search would throw up anything to support his far-fetched encounter. He prayed that Denise had not left a trail that would screw up the forensic examination. Any of his DNA profile could be easily explained away – it would be embarrassing, but he could justify it. Not so Denise.

He was potentially standing in the midst of a forensic-rich environment. Ironic, given the immaculate show home feel. He needed to place Amy at the house, to prove she was there, but more importantly, he needed to show that this was where Amy had been attacked. Babbage must have known this day was coming and been able to prepare accordingly. Deans just prayed he had missed that wall.

The CSI team would not want blind examination of an entire house. They preferred direction, specific rooms, bedding or clothing, but not a complete house. Just like cops, they did not have endless resources or finances in which to luxuriate. Deans knew exactly where to take them. The problem playing out in his mind was explaining how he had come to those conclusions.

He could say that he was looking around and noticed the shadow. It was something unusual, and in a house like this, unusual was a good place to start. He could argue; for the sake of a few quick swabs or dabs, what was there to lose? As for the rest, he would just have to wing it. It was uncharted territory but it was exhilarating.

Moving to the kitchen, Deans attempted to contain his restlessness, by checking on Denise while he was still alone. Rummaging for his phone, he heard a noise in the background. He turned. It was close – muted music – Rihanna, if he was not mistaken. He followed the direction of the sound to the garage, just as the music cut off. It was a ringtone. Why would Babbage have a phone in the garage? Deans frowned. Babbage had not struck him as an R&B, Dance fan.

'Holy shit,' he said, and as he did so, stumbled forwards as if jostled in the back. He turned a one-eighty within the blink of an eye, but no one was there. His limbs stiffened, and he saw his breath once again.

'Amy. Is that you?'

He froze, desperate to hear a response, but he was talking to himself.

'Christ, I need a break,' he said, rubbing his eyes, while diving into his pocket to remove his phone. The screen was glowing – he brought the phone closer to his face – he blinked, and looked again. This was absurd; he was looking at the dialled number for Amy Poole.

It was an old police trick. Input the number of a missing or stolen phone, call it in the presence of a suspected thief or locality, and listen out for a ringtone. It had landed a number of shit-bags over the years and out of habit, he had saved

Amy's number on his phone from the outset of the investigation.

He moved closer to the link-door, his entire body buzzed with energy and his addled mind raced with permutations. *He's only got her phone stashed in the garage*, he thought. *Bingo*.

Deans' face beamed as brightly as the screen before him. He needed to find that phone. Grabbing the key once again, he unlocked the door. His limbs jerked with excitement as he stood in front of the stacked boxes; his thumb poised on the call button. He pressed it.

'Number unobtainable,' a female voice informed him. 'No,' he shrieked, clawing at his hair. He tried it again, with the same result.

The temptation was to wade through the boxes, but he had to be patient. Instead, he rifled through his call history; three recent calls to Amy Poole. He had not imagined things. *It has to be Amy*, he thought.

The sound of vehicles slowing outside of the metal garage door snapped him from his daze. He closed and locked the link-door and dashed to the front room of the house, where he saw a CSI team and uniformed officers gathered outside. There was a knock at the door, and on the doorstep was the CSM, Mike Riley.

'Hello again, Detective. You're keeping us busy,' Riley said.

Deans stared beyond him at the congregating police staff.

'Are you all right?' Riley asked.

'Yeah. Sorry,' Deans said, focusing on Riley. 'I'm just a bit knackered.'

'Anyone else been inside?' Riley asked.

Deans paused for a second. 'Not beyond the hallway, no.'

'Have you had a look around?' Riley said, stepping onto the doormat. 'What do we know?'

Deans stepped aside, allowing Riley to place his equipment onto the floor.

'I've looked at all the rooms,' Deans said. 'On the face of it, the house is spotless…' This was his moment. 'But I've found a patch of oil, or grease on a wall surface up in the third bedroom.'

Riley dipped his head and stared at Deans as if looking over the top of imaginary spectacles. 'Grease?' he mirrored.

Deans nodded.

'Just how much of a search have you been conducting?'

Deans sensed hostility. Time to be wise. 'This room is different. Not like the others.'

Riley scowled. 'Okay. You'd better tell me about this patch of oil.'

'It's on the right-hand wall. About shoulder height.' Deans used his hand to indicate a visual measurement in line with Riley's ear. Deans cleared his throat. 'I also found a small gouge in the paintwork.'

Riley peered over his non-existent specs once more. 'And you think that could be…?'

'If Amy was here against her will, then perhaps it might be a site of disturbance.'

'So you think this stain, or smear, call it what you will, might be some evidential trace of our victim? A facial impression, something like that?'

'Why not?'

'Why not indeed. Conversely, why?'

'Amy had clearly been in some kind of struggle. The marks around her neck, the bruising to her head, the torn fingernail.'

'Ah, so you believe the gouge in the paint is from the victim scratching the wall as she struggled to protect herself from her attacker and the stain will be some kind of body fluid or grease she left behind?'

'Why not?'

'And why do we even suspect our victim was here in the first place?'

'Because I just called her phone and it rang from inside the garage.'

Riley lurched backwards. 'You have the victim's phone?'

'No. I heard it ring. Second time around I couldn't get a connection.'

Riley frowned. Deans spoke before Riley had a chance to discredit Deans any further. 'The search team will find the phone. I absolutely guarantee it.'

'Indeed,' Riley said. He was clearly evaluating Deans. 'Fine,' he said after a long, deliberate pause. 'You'd better show me to this stain.'

Riley had arrived in a white paper suit and handed another to Deans with a black look. 'For what it's worth now, I suppose you might as well put this on.'

Deans opened the door to the white room and Riley stepped inside.

'How the blazes did you find anything in here?' Riley asked.

'Instinct.' Deans wavered. 'And luck I suppose.' He smiled, unsure if Riley was buying into it.

'It's over there,' Deans said with an outstretched arm, inviting Riley to look at the wall.

Riley went over, angled his head to catch the light for a minute or so, and turned to Deans with a baffled expression.

'Instinct?'

Deans nodded.

'I'll get this wall swabbed first.'

Deans looked up to the ceiling. *Yes*, he mouthed.

'Anything else you want to show me?'

'I'd look around the gap in the skirting for traces of the broken nail.'

'Hmmm,' Riley groaned. 'How about we start with you showing me the other rooms?'

Deans complied, but Riley did not comment much, other than to say how sparse the place was. The final room to show him was the garage.

'The search team can start in here,' Riley said, 'while my team are upstairs. We'll start with some photographs.'

Riley accompanied Deans to the doorstep, and ushered in three fully-clad forensic officers and briefed them on what he needed. It was late, but judging by the activity of the locals in the street, word of their presence had obviously spread – that, and the fact that half of the police fleet were now parked in front of Babbage's home.

By 1:36 a.m., organised chaos had taken over. There were easily the same number of staff here as at the scene on the beach. All working diligently, all professional, all determined, and all because Denise had convinced Deans that he was experiencing supernatural contact.

CHAPTER FORTY-SIX

Deans left the scene just after three a.m. The search and forensic examination was well underway and he was now nothing but an onlooker, and in desperate need of some kip. He was impressed with the uniformed team. They were a tight unit and reminded him of his old uniformed days back home; the camaraderie, banter, and friendships, as strong a group as you would find, but it was different for Deans now. He was still part of a team but that brotherhood was not the same – could never be the same. He had watched their interaction with a quiet envy. That was what he needed around him now – his mates.

As he drove through Torworthy, the heaters warmed the air inside the car. He had forgotten to book somewhere to stay and so it would have to be a reclined seat for what was left of the night, and he knew exactly where he wanted to park.

The alarm on his phone woke him at six-thirty from one of the most uncomfortable, cold and crazy night's sleeps he had ever endured. His body was in turmoil; the physical element – completely fatigued, the mental element – entirely wired.

With gummy, bloodshot eyes, he looked at his face in the rear-view mirror. He was pale and unshaven, and his mouth tasted like a tramp's armpit. He had felt better waking up after the office Christmas parties, and that took some doing. He wound the chair to an upright position and blinked moisture back to his eyes. His neck was solid, his back – aching, and his thirst for coffee unbearable.

He checked his phone; no contact since the last time he saw it. He dwelled on the screensaver, and touched the photo of Maria.

There was about an hour's window to freshen up, and drink enough caffeine to feel human again, and not long after, he was at Denise's house.

The smell of a warm coffee maker greeted him as soon as Denise opened the door. She commented on how bad he looked, and smelt. At least she was being honest.

After a rapid shave and wash, Deans was treated to a hot drink and buttery toast, which he devoured under Denise's scrutiny.

'How's Maria?' she asked.

Deans stopped chewing. 'She's moved out.'

'And what do you think about that?'

If his eyes could talk they would be saying, *what a bloody stupid question*.

'I'm sorry,' she said. 'Finish your breakfast. I just want you to know that I'm a good listener if you need me.'

He paused for a moment. 'We've been having fertility treatment.'

She nodded slowly.

'I missed the scan… because I was here.'

Denise stood up, walked to the sink and gazed distantly

out through the window. 'There is no greater gift than a new life,' she said, and turned back to Deans. 'And that takes both of you to create, but it also takes both of you to nurture.'

'I know,' Deans whispered ruefully.

'I know you know. And that's why as soon as all this is over, you must commit yourself to your wife before anything else.'

He nodded and returned to his breakfast. Neither of them spoke until he had finished, and Denise took his plate to the sink. He watched her and waited for his moment.

'Why me, Denise?' he said.

She looked up from the washing bowl. 'Why any of us?'

'Well, you were always going to be a medium.'

'Was I?'

'Your mum and stuff.'

Denise walked back over to Deans and sat opposite him. 'I was just shown a pathway, and I happened to follow it.'

Deans shook his head.

'All Amy is doing is showing you a different course to the one you've known. It's up to you if you follow it.'

Deans grumbled beneath his breath, 'I don't know.'

'I appreciate this is possibly against everything you believe or understand, but everything happens for a reason, Andy.'

'What reason?'

'Isn't that the biggest question for us all? Only time can dictate that.'

Deans huffed. 'Something happened… after you left. Something that couldn't be… chance.'

Denise smiled broadly. 'That would be Amy's way of making you believe.'

Deans dropped his head into his hands.

'Butterflies,' Denise said.

'Sorry?'

Denise had a glint in her eye. 'I bet if you were asked to describe the flight of a butterfly, you'd say: unsteady, fragile, possibly even unpredictable.'

Deans shrugged and nodded.

'A creature at the mercy of the elements,' Denise continued. 'And that may be so, but observe two butterflies, one directly behind the other, and watch how the second butterfly is able to adjust and follow the first butterfly with such precision that the flight can't possibly be as chaotic or random as we believe. It's a chosen direction.'

'So,' Deans said slapping his hands onto the tabletop, 'suddenly I've got some supernatural ability, and I'm supposed to decide if I should pursue it?'

Denise shook her head. 'For some reason, Amy has been the catalyst in the emergence of your abilities. But that's all it is for now: an awakening. My journey began a very long time ago, and I am only in the dawn of the day.' Denise smiled. 'Think about Amy's thesis, her topic; the gift complementing police investigations.'

Deans grimaced. 'It's not going to happen.'

'You were quite right. It is not chance. None of it is chance. You being here now isn't chance.'

'What about Ash? He's got the gift.'

Denise looked away, screwed up her face. 'Remember everyone has the ability, good and bad.'

'And he will know about me?'

'Quite likely.' Her large, dark eyes fixed on his. 'But unlike most other mediums, you are also a police officer.'

'I'm more of a threat,' Deans said, realisation setting in.

Denise nodded sternly.

Deans' vibrating phone shattered the moment. It was a withheld number. 'Could be the office,' he said.

'Can't they give you a moment's respite?'

'It seems not.'

'Don't answer. It's seven thirty, for Christ's sake.'

Deans shrugged. 'No choice, I'm afraid. Psychic or not, I am still a cop.'

He reluctantly accepted the call and heard Jackson's unmistakeable tones. 'Get yourself in the office ASAP. Briefing at eight. The DCI needs an update.' The phone line went quiet. Whoever said the art of conversation was dead?

He swigged his coffee as if it were a cold drink, lifted a triangle of toast from the plate and pecked Denise on the cheek.

'Thank you for your kindness. I have to run, I'm afraid.' He lingered on her face. 'Thank you – for everything.'

She touched his hand. 'Good luck.'

CHAPTER FORTY-SEVEN

The office was a hive of activity. Officers he had not seen up until now were scurrying about busily. In the corner of the room, Gold was sitting at her desk. She noticed him, smiled and waved him over.

'Bloody hell,' Deans said, 'When did everyone suddenly get an interest in this job?'

'Tell me about it,' Gold replied.

'How did you go interviewing Babbage?' he asked.

Gold shook her head. 'What a weirdo. He gives me the willies.'

'Why? What happened?'

'It was a non-starter,' she replied flatly. 'We tried to obtain an initial account but he sat completely silent, just stared back at me with a sick smile. Total freak.'

'You weren't in there alone, I hope?'

'No. But he seemed somewhat obsessed by me.'

'Hmmm. Maybe we should look at that,' Deans said.

'It's the sarge,' she whispered. 'He wants me as OIC. I can't say I don't want to do it now.'

Deans looked around the room to see if Jackson was eavesdropping on their conversation. He was not, and there was no sign of him in the office.

'What's the plan with Babbage today?' Deans asked.

'I gather there have been some results at the home address,' Gold said. 'They are going to be discussed at the briefing, along with an interview strategy.'

'Fantastic,' Deans said. 'Is the CSM coming in, do you know?'

'He's already with the DI and the sarge having a private confab.' Gold leaned in close to Deans. 'Are you feeling okay, Andy?'

'Why?' he shrugged. 'Shouldn't I?'

Gold gave his forearm a gentle squeeze. 'I'm sorry,' she said. 'It's just; you look a bit run down – preoccupied.' She kept her hand on his arm.

'Yeah, well,' he said looking down at her petite fingers, 'life's a bit crazy right now.'

She released her grasp and gave a caring smile. 'What are you doing later?'

He shook his head. 'I don't even know what I'm doing in two hours' time, let alone later.'

'Well...' She looked around. 'Why not come over to mine? We can open up a bottle.'

'Uh...' Deans hesitated, 'thanks. I'll... keep it in mind.'

At two minutes to eight the DCI, DI, CSM and Jackson breezed back into the office and ordered everyone into the conference room. A lucky six people including the bosses, Jackson and Gold secured a seat. Everyone else, including Deans, had to make do with hugging the walls. Deans could have done with a chair. His aching bones were beginning to remind him of his uncomfortable night.

The DCI welcomed everyone and immediately acknowledged there had been progress at the house. She provided nothing more than a précis, but it was enough to leave Deans satisfied and under no illusions that Denise was genuine. The DCI stated that a mobile phone had been located in the garage along with a small purse, void of personal ownership. A search of the study had turned up a series of photographic albums and equipment that was in the process of examination. In addition, the CSM had done remarkable work in one of the bedrooms to locate a micro-scene of disturbance, and the possibility of the victim's recovered fingernail.

Deans listened with interest as the DCI continued.

'I really must praise Mike Riley and his team for finding the scene within the third bedroom. That was truly exceptional work.'

Deans looked at the back of Riley's head. He was about to mark the measure of the man.

'We probably would have missed it, ma'am,' Riley said, 'if it hadn't been for Andy Deans, who somehow identified it before I'd arrived.'

All the faces in the room turned towards Deans, who looked down at his feet.

'Well, in that case,' the DCI said, 'that's even more remarkable. It is instinct and bloody good basic police skills like that which give us a fighting chance against these extremely dangerous criminals. Well done, Andy. You're a credit to your force.'

Deans nodded to the boss and then quickly looked down at his feet again as he sensed eyes boring into him once more. After a few seconds, he peeked up expecting to see Jackson sneering at him. Instead, he saw Gold's beaming face.

Aspects of the DCI's report troubled Deans. A sharps box full of used syringe needles had been located in the bathroom airing cupboard. Babbage had not struck Deans as a user, and the toxicology results had not identified any unexpected substances in Amy's blood samples, so why did Babbage have a stash of needles?

'We need to keep an open mind that the suspect didn't work alone,' the DCI said. 'Intelligence suggests that the property is sole occupancy, however, we must be willing to accept that a partner, friend, or acquaintance could also be in some way involved with this crime. We know that the suspect works at a local holistic clinic. As a priority I'd like an enquiry team to trace and interview this work colleague and gather elimination prints and a volunteer DNA sample.'

Deans' neckline became itchy as his body temperature soared. CSI were conducting a robust sweep – that was good – but that might also mean them picking up traces of Denise. He hooked a finger into his shirt collar and pulled it away from his neck. What had she touched? She had worn gloves, but what if she had taken them off at some point without him knowing, and what if her tears had fallen onto a tested surface? They would find her DNA for sure.

He had put Denise and the entire investigation into jeopardy with his foolishness. Blood drained from his face and his vision tunnelled, but before he had a chance to volunteer for the task, Jackson had already allocated two other detectives.

Deans' head was spinning. What would Denise say to them? He glanced at Jackson, who was smugly grinning back at him. Jackson knew the DCI was talking about Denise, and probably still believed that Deans was engaged in some sordid relationship with her. Once traces of DNA, or fingerprints were attributed to Denise, she would in turn be arrested and interviewed in connection with the murder, and then the truth would surface about her activities with Deans.

. . .

At the conclusion of the briefing, everyone funnelled out of the small room to commence their allocated enquiries. Deans himself was tasked to return to the home address and oversee the search and recovery of exhibits. He slowly walked away from the conference room, completely preoccupied, and had not noticed Gold by his shoulder.

'Andy,' she said loudly, breaking his thought process.

'Yeah,' he replied mechanically. 'Hi,' he said, realising it was Gold. 'Sorry, I'm in a world of my own.'

'So? Tonight?' she asked.

'Tonight?'

'My place?'

'Oh, yeah. Tonight.' He noticed a sparkle in her eyes. 'Um, shall we see how today goes first?'

'So is that a yes?'

Deans lifted a non-committal shoulder. 'Let's see how things play out.'

'Looking forward to it already,' she said and bounded off to one of the other female detectives further along the corridor.

Deans watched her, motionless, until she was out of view. He had neither the energy, nor the inclination to attempt to figure out what was going on in her mind.

Before he reached the office, Jackson caught up with him.

'So the instinctive detective thinks he's got the whole department fooled?' Jackson was looking for a rise, that much was clear.

'Sorry, Sarge, I don't know what you mean,' Deans said, attempting to side-step Jackson, who blocked his path.

'I guess a few truths will come out today then? For you, I mean,' Jackson sneered.

Deans' mouth curled downwards at the edges. Was he insinuating about the so-called relationship with Denise again? Was he talking about Denise being at the scene, or was he talking about whatever was happening with Gold? Either way, Deans did not plan to hang around entertaining the neurotic sergeant, so simply walked away.

He made his way back to the property, ducked beneath the blue and white police tape billowing in the breeze, and booked in with the PC on the cordon. He had already clocked the two press vehicles parked further along the road and recognised the photographer, Nev, from the beach.

One of the CSI team greeted him with a white paper suit, and soon he was back inside.

Most activity was centralised upstairs. The white wall of the small room, now a wispy metallic grey from fingerprint dust. Mini yellow markers denoted points of interest around the room, and one crucially located beside the skirting board immediately beneath the site of the smear.

Deans checked his watch: just gone eleven a.m. His mind wandered; they would have got to Denise by now. If only he could have spoken to her first, but the risk of a phone trail after the meeting with the DCI was too great.

Over the next few hours, Deans followed the CSI team closely, primarily ensuring they missed nothing, but also in the hope of intercepting anything that could implicate Denise.

It was 2:48 p.m. when he received the call.

'Deans, this is Sergeant Jackson. I want you back at the station, now.' The line went dead.

The nausea that Deans had been staving off all day rose in a lump and burned the back of his throat. Taking his own counsel, he waited at the top of the stairs and spoke to the first CSI officer who passed him.

'I've been told to head back to the nick,' he said.

'Coming back again later?' she asked.

Deans shrugged. 'Maybe.'

He left the scene knowing it would be the last time he would be there. He guessed it would be Jackson who would take most pleasure in ripping him to shreds; he would just have to take it and try to remember that at the end of everything, he would be going home. Who knew what the larger ramifications would be?

Each tread of the stairway to the CID office felt like a stride closer to his executioner. At the top, he heard voices inside the office and stopped for a moment to adjust his tie and smooth down his jacket.

He first saw Ranford, who was wading through a bunch of papers, but there was no acknowledgement. A couple of other detectives who had been at the briefing nodded in Deans' direction.

'Anyone seen DS Jackson?' Deans asked glumly.

'Hi, Andy,' Ranford said turning around. 'He is looking for you too. I think he's with the boss somewhere.'

Shit. Deans nodded, and found the corner of an empty desk to perch on temporarily.

'You okay, Andy?' Ranford asked.

Deans was staring at a patch on the floor. He did not look up, but replied, 'Yeah.'

He did not need to wait long before he heard the droll tones of Jackson in the corridor. Deans raised himself from the desk and stood upright, shoulders back, facing the doorway.

'Deans,' Jackson said coming to an abrupt halt. 'With me, please.' He turned and walked back towards the corridor.

Deans followed and patted Ranford on the shoulder as he passed him. His heart was beating quickly. He was culpable for everything, but that did not make it any easier.

Jackson was first into the little bollocking room and this time took the chair facing the door. Deans could not help but smile at the man's comedic value.

'Sit down, please,' Jackson said.

That was twice now he had said 'please'.

Deans manoeuvred the door closed, pulled back his chair and faced Jackson with unreserved resignation.

'It seems we have a problem,' Jackson said, keeping his eyes down on his daybook.

Deans bit down, did not reply. *Here it comes*, he thought.

Jackson looked up, his repulsive beady eyes squinting.

Deans nodded and sank his head.

'I'm not sure what you've done,' Jackson said through tight lips. 'But it seems our prisoner will only speak to you.'

Startled, Deans looked up. 'Pardon?'

Jackson huffed. 'We have had two attempts at interview and all we get out of him is, "Let me speak to Deans". He clearly has something he wants to share with you, and all we are doing is pissing into the wind and getting our legs wet.'

Deans leant forwards in the chair. 'He will only speak with me?' he repeated. *That is what this is about*, he thought. 'Okay,' he replied.

'So, you're off exhibits as of right now and I want you to tie up with Gold, who will run through the two interviews so far.' Jackson prodded a finger inches from Deans' face. 'She is still number one interviewer. But if you are with her maybe between the two of you we might make progress.'

'Of course, Sarge. Certainly.' Deans ran a hand down his face. 'Are there any updates regarding the other enquiries today?'

'Your lady friend, you mean?' Jackson answered as if he had been waiting for the question. 'Seems she's rather shocked about the whole episode. I don't think she'll be anything other than a character witness.'

Deans leaned back in his chair and sighed. 'What about the phone and photographic kit from the house?'

'Still developing the evidence, pardon the pun.' Jackson tilted his head expectantly. What was he after, applause?

Jackson narrowed his gaze. 'We should have it by end of play today.'

'Good,' Deans said.

'Right,' Jackson said, standing up. 'You need to get your arse over to custody. Make sure you grab some grub en route. I think we're all in for a long day.' And with that, he left the room.

Deans remained seated. He did not know which he was more surprised at: not dropping in the stinky stuff, or actually having a civilised conversation with Jackson.

CHAPTER FORTY-EIGHT

His strategy was risky, but so far, so good. It would only be a matter of time before the forensic results would trickle back through to the office.

Deans arrived at the charge desk just as a young-looking PC was reluctantly patting down a dishevelled vagrant. An obscene smell hit Deans the moment he walked into the room. *Those were the days*, he thought, and gave the PC a sympathetic smile, while trying not to inhale too much of the choking air. Behind the charge desk, the custody sergeant was less convivial, holding a wad of tissues over his mouth and nose. A detention officer further behind covered his face with a sleeve and held a can of air freshener high above his head like an air horn, ready to marinate the room with an equally toxic plume of artificial fragrance.

The detainee appeared to be having a drunken conversation with himself as the PC ran his gloved hands down the inside of each leg.

'Just stay there, Charlie. Stop moving forwards, mate,' the PC directed, his head as far away from the prisoner as his elongated neck would allow.

Deans then noticed the damp patch down the inside of Charlie's left leg – like a balloon strung to his unlaced boot.

The sergeant turned to Deans and gave a shrouded welcome with his eyes. 'Be with you shortly,' he muttered from behind the muzzle of tissue paper, and the three of them watched in pity as the PC completed his routine and stepped back away from his prisoner, who was still chuntering incoherently. The PC was the only one of them not covering his face. He had probably already spent so long with Charlie that the pungent cocktail of ammonia and excrement had killed off any sense of smell.

The sergeant completed the formalities in double-quick time and sent the prisoner off to a cell with the PC following behind clutching a pair of custody-issue tracksuit bottoms. Not far behind him, the DO was emptying a can of Wild Orchid into the room, and further back the custody sergeant and Deans were spluttering from the heady mixture.

'Welcome to my world,' the custody sergeant said with outstretched arms.

Deans chuckled. 'I'm here for Babbage.'

'Ah, another quality guest in our humble establishment tonight,' the sergeant joked. 'Your colleague is through there.' He pointed to a nearby door.

Deans found Gold in one of the interview rooms, amidst piles of case paperwork.

'Hi,' Deans said and sat on a chair next to her.

'God, what's that smell?' she replied.

'Nice to see you too.' He must have dragged the nasal cocktail in on his clothing. 'So, how's it going?' he asked her.

Gold screwed her face up. 'Not too well, but probably better than the poor bugger dealing with whoever dragged that stench in.' Both of them giggled.

'Jackson actually had a civilised conversation with me,' Deans said. 'I understand Babbage isn't playing ball?'

'No. He apparently only has eyes for you,' Gold said mischievously.

'It's about time someone did.'

'I'm sure you have lots of admirers,' she replied with a toothy grin.

Deans rolled his eyes. 'Jackson told me to come down and tie up with you if that's okay?'

'Yes, of course. Thank you. This was starting to do my head in.'

'So, what's been put to him so far?'

'He's heard the grounds and reasons for his arrest. I've been able to explain the interview process and he has been given an opportunity to give an initial account, but all he does is ask to see you, before being censored by the solicitor.'

'Well, that's better than nothing, I guess. Has he been given any detailed information, or been asked specific questions regarding the murder?'

'No. We haven't got that far,' Gold said.

'Good. Until we get the forensics back, the interviews will need to be benign. How has his brief been?'

'She's been no problem.'

'His brief is a woman? Has anyone been chaperoning their contact?'

'Not to my knowledge. She's been on cell camera during their chats.'

'Was she requested by Babbage or is she a duty solicitor?'

'Requested, I think.'

'Have you seen her before?'

'No. I think she's from Plymouth or somewhere down that way.'

'Interesting,' Deans said. 'Has he been put through Livescan yet?'

'Yes, we've got his fingerprints, and DNA, and a photograph.'

'No issues?'

'Not that I've been informed of.'

Deans frowned. He had expected something to show up. 'Okay. How has it been left with the brief?'

'We are to call her once we have a better idea when the next interview will get off the ground.'

'Excellent. Call her now. Let's see what Babbage wants to tell me.'

The solicitor requested at least an hour to return, which was perfect for Deans. His energy reserves had depleted days ago and now he was running purely on caffeine and adrenalin. There was not much he could do about one of them, but the other was definitely in his control.

Gold took him to a cafe in the back streets of Torworthy near to an indoor market. It was the best in town, she told him. There were benches rather than individual seats but they still managed to find a space in the corner of the room.

'Tell me your impression of Babbage,' Deans asked.

'Creepy.'

'Why?'

'I don't know. The way he looks at me. The staring. The calmness. Especially considering he's been arrested for murder.' She shook her head. 'There's just something about him. His... oh, I don't know.'

'Do you know what bothers me?' Deans said. 'We didn't find him.'

Gold leant forward, a confused look on her face.

'He was stopped by traffic cops for something completely unrelated. Something random and insignificant,' Deans said. 'He could have driven away and we would be no closer to finding Amy's killer than we were when all this began. Instead, he makes a big deal about asking for me, and then assaults one of the cops. Why would he do that?'

Gold shrugged.

'That's what bugs me,' Deans said, and took a long swig from his Americano.

They both fell silent; Deans concentrating on his mug, and Gold staring out of the window, chin resting on the back of her hand.

'Do you mind if I ask a personal question?' she said after a few minutes.

'Fire away,' he said looking up from his mug.

'Does your wife mind you being away from home for so long?'

'My wife?' He turned away. He had never been comfortable discussing personal matters, let alone with a relative stranger.

Deans huffed, wiped his mouth and ran his fingers along the contour of his chin.

'Yes,' he said after careful deliberation. 'In fact... Maria moved out earlier this week. Just couldn't take it any more.'

'Oh, I didn't know. Sorry,' Gold said, blushing.

Deans chuckled. 'Why would you know? It's not something that I have wanted to share.'

'I'm sorry,' she repeated.

An awkward silence followed, and then Deans opened up to put Gold at ease.

'It's probably been a long time coming, to be honest,' he said. 'CID should be the acronym for Crawling In Divorce.'

He had not taken his eyes away from his mug, and did not

notice Gold place her hands on the table, fingers pointing towards him.

'I guess this investigation was just one straw too many,' he continued, 'on top of many other straws accumulated over the years.'

Gold wrapped her hands softly around the back of his as he cradled his coffee mug. Deans glanced up. The pooling of his eyes betrayed the emotion he was battling to conceal. She pulled one of his hands away from the cup, and clasped it tightly between both of hers.

He looked back down at the table awkwardly, but Gold did not let go. And, if he was being honest, he did not want her to.

They sat like that for several minutes. No words. Just comfort, and in those moments he realised the state of his current vulnerability.

Deans forged a wide smile and pulled his hand back. 'Thank you. Do you know? I don't even know your first name?'

'Sarah,' she said tenderly, 'and you're very welcome.'

He sighed deeply and downed his coffee. 'Right,' he said, placing the mug firmly on the table. 'Let's nail this son of a bitch to the wall.'

CHAPTER FORTY-NINE

Sarah led the way to the interview room, which was number four of six identical rooms within an annex off the custody reception area.

Deans compared this facility to his own, where only two interview rooms meant he often spent an inordinate amount of time waiting in queues. Back home it was a case of first come first served, unless the job was juicy or custody time limits were a factor. The new breed of super custody unit might lack character but they won on practicality.

Deans followed Sarah into the room. A smartly dressed woman in her early forties with fresh-out-of-the-salon styled hair was sitting at the table, an empty note pad open in front of her. *The brief,* Deans thought. She had a po-faced expression as they made their greetings but Deans gave a warm and friendly welcome, as he always did.

It was a personal curiosity of Deans' how clothing could differentiate the detectives from the solicitors. It was tougher with the women, but for the men, as a rule, it was all in their ties. He first discovered the trend when he initially joined CID and he estimated his theory to be around eighty percent accurate. Solicitors liked to attire themselves with dots or spots and shirts that were not necessarily compatible, whereas your average detective preferred bold diagonal stripes and soft pastel or white shirts. In simplistic terms, it was the spots versus the stripes.

He looked down at his own combination; a red, white and black diagonally striped tie over a white shirt and his M&S off-the-shelf, washable suit.

This solicitor was in a black trouser suit and a white blouse. Obviously no tie, so this comparison was invalid. There was nothing obvious between the women. They were both in trouser suits, but one was looking a hell of a lot more appealing than the other.

'I do hope you have something a little more substantial for me this time,' the solicitor said. 'My client and I have yet to hear any evidence remotely implicating him in this grave allegation.'

'Well, for starters we now have Detective Deans,' Sarah said.

Deans raised a hand and smiled. 'Your client asked for me, so here I am.'

The brief maintained a hard exterior. 'So, I take it that you still have nothing to put to my client?'

Deans dropped his affable facade. 'Why don't we wait and see what he wants to talk to me about?'

The brief tutted loudly and placed her pen firmly onto the pad.

'Detectives, this is a waste of my time, and my client's time.'

'Evidence is still being collated,' Deans snapped. 'Now, your client has gone out of his way to demand that he speaks with me. And we intend giving him that opportunity.'

'This is a joke,' the brief scoffed.

'I'm not laughing,' Deans said, his glare intense.

'Fine,' she said, standing up. 'Expect any responses from my client to be appropriate to the deficiencies in your investigation.' Clutching her paperwork, she tugged at the door and stormed out of the interview room.

'She is right, Andy. Until we have the forensic reports we have nothing to put to him,' Sarah said.

'I need to see Babbage.'

'But he'll make no comment.'

'Maybe, maybe not.'

As they waited for the solicitor to return, Deans glanced around the interview room. It was larger than those he used back in Somerset but decorated with the same pale green paint. A relaxing colour, allegedly. The verdict was still out on that one, but he was sure Dulux, or Crown, or Farrow and Ball had done quite nicely out of it, thank you.

The table was butted end-on to the far wall and he noticed a small video camera fixed above the entrance door. That was the modern way. Somewhere there would be a hub; a place for all the recording equipment, and chairs placed in front of a TV monitor, for as-it-happens assessment of the action. Helpful if a defendant gave an account that another officer could corroborate while the interview was still in progress.

Deans had not seen the satellite room yet, but imagined Jackson and possibly even the DI to be interested enough to be watching once the show got started. In any event, one of the nameless DCs would be in there operating the recording equipment.

The interview room table and chairs were bolted to the floor. Sarah sat closest to the wall, maybe subconsciously using Deans as a barrier between herself and Babbage. Deans did not like the fixed chair setup. It meant suspects could not use them as a weapon, but it also prevented a chair being used in self-defence; it is quite tricky for a shit-bag to fight when they are pinned against a wall by four chair legs.

The door opened inwards and Deans turned to see Babbage walking in with the brief. The custody sergeant was following close behind, giving him instructions where to walk.

Babbage was still wearing his own clothing, but Deans noticed that he was wearing black custody-issue plimsolls, similar to the ones Deans used to wear as a six-year-old at junior school. He had not identified it before, but Babbage had unusually small feet.

Babbage locked onto Deans the moment he saw him and took the seat directly opposite him with composed confidence.

'Would you like to sit here, please, Mr Babbage?' Sarah said, her arm outstretched towards the chair opposite her.

'No,' Babbage said, still looking at Deans.

'Would you like a drink of anything?' Sarah asked.

'No,' he said, and finally faced her for the first time since entering the room.

Deans remained silent as Sarah completed the introduction to the interview. He studied Babbage and began working on a theory that could account for quite a lot.

'Andy,' Sarah whispered, interrupting Deans' concentration.

Babbage was smirking.

Deans nodded. 'So,' he said. 'Here I am.'

Babbage did not speak, just continued grinning.

'Why did you ask for me?' Deans said.

Babbage stretched his arms out slowly to the side, and then rolled his neck in a deliberate circular motion. He placed his arms lazily back onto the table, interlocking his fingers, his eyes closed.

Deans waited ten, maybe fifteen more seconds for a response. It did not come.

'You've expressed a desire to speak with me. So, what do you have to say?'

Babbage drew air in deeply through his nose, and out again slowly through his open mouth. Opening his eyes, he slowly tracked an imaginary line between himself and Deans until they were once again eye-to-eye.

Deans flashed the palms of his hands. 'Well?'

'Do you like your life, Detective?'

'Mr Babbage,' his solicitor interrupted.

What sort of a question is that? Deans thought and frowned. 'Something on your mind?' he asked.

Babbage grinned – the broadest yet. 'I wouldn't worry so much about my mind, Detective.'

'Mr Babbage,' his solicitor barked.

Everyone, including Babbage looked at the solicitor.

'I don't think I need you any more,' Babbage said to her calmly.

'Mr Babbage. It would be a good idea to cease this interview, so that we can have another private consultation,' the solicitor said.

'Are you saying you'd like to seek alternative representation?' Sarah asked.

'No,' Babbage said.

'Mr Babbage,' the solicitor said impatiently. 'I would like this interview—'

'I. Don't. Need. You. Any. More.'

'I'd like this interview suspended,' the solicitor said rising to her feet. 'It would benefit my client to have a further consultation in private.'

'I just said, I don't need you,' Babbage repeated, baring his teeth.

'Fine,' Deans said, now also standing. 'We'll have to inform the inspector, while you both sort out what is happening.' He looked up at the camera, used the universal cut gesture, and walked out of the room.

Sarah followed him into the corridor. 'Well, that was another waste of time,' she said.

'No, it wasn't.'

CHAPTER FIFTY

They left the custody reception and asked for a call in the unlikely event they would be required any time soon. Deans found an empty office, slumped down on a chair and hooked his feet up onto another. Tilting the seat, he closed his eyes, concentrating on nothing more than the sound of his own breathing. The chairs were vaguely comfortable and, desperate for a nap, he felt himself drifting off.

'How long have you been on the go?' Sarah asked.

Deans groaned silently. 'I really don't know any more,' he said. 'Everything's starting to become a blur. I don't even know what the date is.'

'Saturday the eighteenth,' she replied.

Deans rocked his head.

'So, are we still on for later?' she asked.

'Later?'

'Opening a bottle? It is the weekend, after all.'

'Do you really think we'll be out of here tonight?'

After a beat Sarah asked, 'Where are you staying?'

'Hmmm, me?'

'You. Are you booked in anywhere?'

'Bollocks,' he shouted, sitting up.

'Well, you're more than welcome to stay over at mine. I've got a couch not doing much tonight.'

'Wouldn't your partner mind me crashing over?'

'No. I live alone.' She paused. '…And I'm single.'

Deans rubbed his face and flopped back onto the chairs. 'Let's just see if we make it out of here first.' Everything was becoming all too much to comprehend with an addled brain.

They remained in silence for the next thirty minutes and then the peace was broken when Sarah's mobile phone rang. She answered – it was custody.

'That was quick,' Deans said disappointedly. 'I was well away then.'

'I know. You were snoring.'

'And you still want me to stay over?'

Sarah laughed and gave him a playful twitch of the eyebrow.

'Come on,' Deans said, heaving his body up from the makeshift lounger. 'Let's go find what awaits us at custody.'

'You're going to like this,' the custody sergeant said as they arrived.

'Go on,' said Deans.

'Babbage has sacked his brief. Apparently thinks he is able to represent himself. We can't force him to have a solicitor and now I need his detention reviewed, but the inspector is tied up for the foreseeable at a griefy job.'

Deans worked it over in his fatigued mind. For an offence of this magnitude, not having a brief was self-destruction. But it was also conceivable that Babbage knew exactly what he was doing.

Faced with a further long delay, they headed back to the station at Torworthy. Deans was quiet throughout the journey.

An envelope from the intelligence department was waiting for Sarah on her desk. She opened the package and removed a report.

Babbage had no history. No previous convictions, no cautions, no logged calls to the police, no census details, DSS or social housing records. He was off the radar.

'Clean as a whistle,' Sarah said.

'Maybe,' Deans replied, and took the sheet from her.

Jackson came into the office. 'What are you both doing here?'

'Gathering further evidence before we go into the next interview,' Sarah said.

'How did it go?' Jackson asked.

'He's sacked his brief,' Deans said. 'He's going it alone.'

'He's doing what?' Jackson's pitch climbed.

'Any other updates for us?' Deans asked.

'Yeah,' Jackson said, 'the phone belongs to Amy.'

'Yes,' Deans shouted, clenching his fist. He turned away from them both and mouthed *Thank you, Amy*.

Jackson threw another envelope onto the table. 'Phone reports from high tech crime,' he said.

Deans removed the papers and spread them out onto the table. The report included all call and text history one month prior to the date Amy went missing and up to the date the phone was located. These reports usually took much longer to come through. Jackson had done well and pulled some useful strings.

The last outgoing call was at 18:41 hours on Saturday the 4th October, to Scott Parsons. Probably their last meeting arrangement, but certainly Amy's final call.

Deans scanned the text data and read the last message sent

at 22:36 hours that same day: *Hi Mummy, hope all is well with Aunty Jayne, you and Daddy. Having a great night. Speak soon. Love you all loads XXX.*

Deans bowed his head and imagined how Mrs Poole had probably read that message a hundred times over since Amy went missing. If that was their last contact then at least it was a loving message. Few bereaved shared the same fate.

Deans called over to Sarah, 'What have you got for the last incoming call?'

She flicked through the back pages. 'It looks like the battery died on the fifth; nothing since then.'

Deans fell silent. That was impossible.

CHAPTER FIFTY-ONE

Babbage was clearly confident that he no longer required a solicitor. The inspector had already been into his cell, attempting to tick all the policy boxes by convincing him that each solicitor was independent and working for his best interests. Ultimately, that was all he could do. The police could not suggest or recommend what Babbage should do, and Deans did not care one way or the other, so long as nothing was going to come back and bite him on the arse twelve months down the line at court.

Although it was late, Jackson had directed them to interview Babbage again before the end of the day, and so they had all returned to the interview room.

What is going on in your head? Deans thought, as Babbage grinned his way through Sarah's introduction. Why was this all so inconsequential to him? It was baffling. Just as much as why he had asked for Deans in the first place.

They had already agreed not to hold back – hit him with the new evidence. Give him some sticky answers to find. He had messed them about, and now at last they had something concrete to put to him.

'Tell us about the iPhone found in your garage,' Sarah said.

Babbage did not acknowledge her, let alone answer the question. He was facing Deans, unnervingly emotionless. Not even blinking.

Deans had two options. Let it slide and indulge Babbage with his moment, or hit it head on, meet eyeball with eyeball and show that he was not intimidated. He decided on the latter.

'Ash,' Sarah said, trying to break the checkmate. 'Ash, will you look at me, please?'

Deans bet that was something she had not expected to say after the first couple of interviews.

Babbage smirked, and turned towards Sarah.

'Tell me everything about the phone,' she said.

Babbage pursed his lips and waited for half a minute.

'No,' he said calmly, and tilted a look back at Deans.

'Explain how the phone came into your possession,' Sarah continued.

A sinister laugh spewed from Babbage.

Deans could feel an up-surging lump of revulsion in his chest.

'Who does the phone belong to?' Sarah said, doing her best to stick with the interview plan.

Babbage's left eye narrowed in a millisecond twitch. Deans leant forward. The thought of Amy had brought about an emotion. Had he pictured her face in that instant? Or, was his reflection full of far more disturbing images?

'Explain how the phone came to be in your garage,' Sarah persisted.

Babbage studied her face, taking in every aspect of her features, and then broke his silence.

'Very pretty,' he said softly. 'Very pretty, Detective Deans. Wouldn't you agree?'

Deans noticed Sarah fold one leg over the other and turn slightly towards the wall.

'I wonder what Maria would make of this?' Babbage continued.

Deans did not react, outwardly.

'Haven't you got lovely eyes? Detective Gold, isn't it?'

Sarah shifted in her seat once more and hooked wayward strands of hair behind her ear. It was time for Deans to join the party.

'What's this all about, Babbage?'

'Don't you know, Detective?' he hissed, turning towards Deans in an instant.

'Enlighten me.'

'"Enlighten me"? Just like that, Detective? "Enlighten me"?'

'The phone my colleague has been asking you about belongs to Amy Poole.'

This time there was no visual reaction from Babbage. A more emotive description was required if it was to stir his indifference.

'Amy Poole, who was murdered, mutilated, and dumped on a beach.'

Babbage's attention resumed onto Sarah.

'You're too pretty to be a police officer. I bet you are very popular with the boy police, am I right?'

Sarah was unable to maintain eye contact with Babbage, her cheeks increasingly flushed. Deans needed to regain control.

'This isn't her interview, Babbage, it's yours,' he said, his voice wavering on aggressive. 'You've been arrested on suspicion of murdering Amy Poole and you're being asked to account for why her mobile phone was found in your garage.' *You piece of shit.*

Babbage ignored Deans and spoke to Sarah again. 'Are you two getting it on yet?'

Sarah twisted her body and faced the wall.

'Okay, that's enough,' Deans said. 'The time is now twenty-two sixteen hours. This interview is being suspended.'

'What? Have we finished already?' Babbage said jovially. 'But I haven't answered my questions.'

'You're going back into your cell,' Deans snarled. 'I think that'll do us for the night.'

Sarah nodded approval from behind her daybook.

'But I'm not finished,' Babbage replied, holding his hands out in front of him.

Deans got to his feet and moved towards the door. 'It's over. No more questions tonight. You had your chance, but instead you wanted to be a prick.'

Babbage walked directly over to Deans. Babbage was significantly shorter, but still stood toe to toe. Deans tensed up, his vision tunnelled. Fight, flight or flirt. He was certainly ready for one of those options and it did not involve running or shagging.

'Poor Maria,' Babbage said under his breath, but loud enough so that Sarah could hear. He lifted himself onto the toes of his plimsolls. 'No wonder she left you.' He sidestepped Deans and tugged at the door. A detention officer was already waiting to take him away.

Deans was raging inside, bursting for just ten seconds alone with Babbage away from the cameras. That was all he needed to feel a whole lot better.

'You okay?' Sarah asked.

'Fine,' Deans snapped, and then noticed how withdrawn Sarah appeared.

'Hey, how are you bearing up? You did well,' he said.

'Sorry,' she said shaking her curtains of fine blonde hair. 'He's freaking me out.'

'I completely understand. Come on.' Deans put his arm around her shoulders. 'Let's see if the others are around.'

They left the interview room and met a determined Jackson in the corridor.

'Why the fuck did you stop it there, Deans?' Jackson seethed. 'He was at least speaking, which is more than he has done up to now.'

'He was pissing us around,' Deans bit back. 'We still have plenty of time on the clock to play with.'

'Oh we do, do we? This is just a game, is it? There are people depending on you getting results.'

'Well, unless you have an update for us, we're still waiting on the forensic results. At least then, we could put a proper interview to him. In the meantime I'm knackered and I need some sleep.'

'Or maybe you didn't want Gold answering his question?' Jackson said snidely and turned away. 'Seven a.m., sharp. Both of you,' he said over his shoulder and walked briskly back the way he came.

'Since when does that knob-head care about other people?' Deans said, watching Jackson vanish around the corner.

Sarah shrugged.

'Can you just give me ten minutes, please?' Deans asked her.

'Sure… of course. I'll wait in the car shall I?'

'Thanks.'

'See you in a bit then,' she said, and glumly trailed in the direction that Jackson had taken.

. . .

Deans had not spoken to Maria for what seemed like an age, which was her decision, but right then he really needed to hear her voice. He returned to the quiet room and dialled her mobile number.

The person you are calling is not available. Please leave a message after the tone. 'Oh, come on, give me a break,' he said to the screen, before the beep prompted his message.

'Hi, Maria. It's me. I know you said you didn't want me contacting you, but… I'm missing you.' He ran a hand down his face. 'It'd be nice to talk; to know you're okay… nothing more than that.' He swallowed deeply. 'Things have gone a bit mental for me these last few days and I want…' his voice faltered. '…I need you to know that I love you.'

CHAPTER FIFTY-TWO

Deans met up with Sarah at the car in much less than ten minutes. He sat on the passenger side, dropped the seat and closed his eyes. Sarah waited silently for a moment and then started the engine.

They drove for several minutes before she spoke.

'So, where are we going after we drop the kit off?'

Deans kept his head back and his eyes shut. 'I hope you've got lots of alcohol at your place. I really need a drink.'

'I have more than enough,' Sarah said obligingly.

They continued the journey in silence until they reached the station. The time was nearing midnight. Seven hours until it all started again.

Deans followed Sarah in his car towards her address, providing him with undisturbed time to think. Sarah was very attractive, but the thought of chit-chatting for hours really was not appealing, though a shot or two of something strong most certainly was, along with a few good hours of shut-eye.

.   .   .

Soon they were on the other side of the estuary pulling up outside of a semi-detached town house with a parking space that Sarah took.

Deans checked his phone. No messages, but more frustratingly, no signal.

Sarah held the front door open; Deans followed her inside to a flight of stairs and a hallway large enough to store a push-bike but not much else. As they ascended the steps, he could not help but notice her bottom, only inches from his face, the tight-fitting light grey trousers leaving nothing much for him to imagine. At the top, Sarah provided a courteous explanation of where each room was and then dived into a large refrigerator and pulled out a chilled bottle of Sauvignon Blanc. She poured two generous glasses, and handed one to Deans.

'Cheers,' he said, took a large mouthful and glanced around. The room was decorated in vibrant colours with numerous foreign-looking knick-knacks and tribal facemasks attached to the walls.

'Take a seat,' she said, removing her jacket, and walking towards the bedroom.

There was only one seat in the room – a bright-red two-person sofa. He tested the resistance of the leather, sat down, and took a swig from his glass. *Am I supposed to sleep on this?* he thought.

Sarah walked back into the room and sat beside him. She had not changed, but the top two buttons of her blouse were now undone to reveal the youthful firmness of her cleavage. Deans identified the waft of freshly applied scent as she turned to face him, legs tucked up yoga-style, accentuating her taut lower limbs. She took a cushion and hugged it between her glass and body.

Deans looked away and slugged another mouthful. The

wine tasted good, and if he was being honest, so was being there with Sarah.

'Nice place,' he said.

She smiled, and sipped her wine. 'It's nice to have some company. It can get lonely living here and having a job like ours.'

'I'll drink to that,' he said, and gulped another mouthful.

'So how did you get involved down here?' she asked.

'I guess I'm lucky.'

'No, seriously. How's it you came to be on this case?'

'I was involved from the outset.' He paused – that already felt like so long ago. 'The job came to me as a MISPER. You know how they start, and before I knew it, I was down here.' He sank the remainder of his glass. 'And then not long after that, the body was found.'

'So, why do you think Babbage is interested in you?'

Deans winced. The name alone irked him beyond comprehension.

'I met him in the early stages of the investigation. He works in an alternative therapy shop-cum-clinic. Whatever you want to call it.'

'Rayon Vert,' Sarah said.

'That's right.'

'Tell me to mind my own business,' she said, squeezing the cushion, 'but were the rumours right about you and the woman that works there?'

'Absolutely not. Denise has been very helpful to the investigation.'

'Oh, okay. Good.'

Deans recognised the possible significance of the word 'good' and felt the need to clarify.

'She made me some food, we chatted and I stayed over because we had some wine. Just like now, really.'

Sarah smiled, and took a sip from her glass without taking her eyes off Deans. 'Can I ask another… personal question?'

Deans nodded. 'Go ahead.'

'How do you feel about your wife moving out?'

That question again. His eyes glazed over. How did he feel, and did he want to disclose it tonight, with Sarah?

He lifted his empty glass and Sarah responded by pouring more wine. He took another large guzzle before answering.

'Numb. Sad …Responsible.'

Sarah fiddled with the stem of her glass. 'I admire how you're able to carry on,' she said. 'I'm not sure I could cope as well if it were me.'

'Well, it seems that thanks to Mr Babbage, I don't have much choice in the matter.'

They both chuckled.

'Do you mind if I ask you a personal question?' Deans asked.

'Please do.'

'Jackson. I notice he is very… how can I put it? …close to you. Are you guys—'

'God, no,' she barged in. 'Has somebody told you that we are?'

'No, I promise. I kind of picked up on a vibe, from him anyway.'

'I can't lie. He has made advances my way, but I think I have made it abundantly clear he has no chance. After all, he is my skipper, and old. I mean, he must be almost fifty.'

'Easy. I'm not far off that myself.'

'No comparison,' she said quickly, hugging the cushion a little closer.

Deans made a face. 'How so?'

'Well, you know,' she said coyly. 'You're no letch, and

you're a gentleman... from what I can tell so far.' She twitched an eyebrow and grinned.

Deans looked away, touched the pocket of his trousers, and felt his phone.

'I should go,' he said.

'You can't.'

Deans raised himself from the sofa.

'You've had some wine,' she said.

'I'll be fine.'

'You've had quite a lot,' Sarah insisted, now following Deans towards the top of the stairs.

'Thank you, Sarah.' He touched her arm. 'I'll see you in the morning.'

'You'll never find anywhere to stay at this time of night.'

'I'll be fine,' he repeated.

When he reached the front door, Sarah was still at the top of the stairs. He offered a wave, and was gone.

Little did Deans know that the following twenty-four hours would change his life forever.

CHAPTER FIFTY-THREE

Deans woke early, cold, disoriented, and aching. A disciplined few were already out on the water. He did not want Denise to think that he was taking advantage of her kind nature, so not long after, he was doing his best to freshen up in the cruddy sink basin of a nearby twenty-four hour garage.

He arrived at the nick just it in time for seven. Sarah was at her desk.

'Good morning, Sarah,' he said.

She gave him a fleeting glance. 'Hi,' she replied.

'Anything good,' he said, referring to the documents she was looking through.

'Where did you stay last night?' she said, and swivelled in the chair to face him.

'Just my usual.'

She turned back to her desk.

'So, what've you got,' Deans said, coming alongside her chair.

'Wallet of photographs, and forensic data.'

'Cool. I'll have a look at those in moment.' Deans picked up a mug from the desk. 'Fancy one?'

'Thanks.'

He left the office, but on his return, Sarah and the papers had gone. He found her in the bollocking room, documents spread over the table. He handed her a hot drink.

'Thanks for the invite last night,' he said.

She nodded.

'I'm sorry I had to go.'

She nodded again and hooked hair over her ear. Deans lifted a report by the high tech crime analysts.

'Shall I take a look through this?'

'Sure,' Sarah replied, but did not look his way.

Deans moved his chair to the narrow end of the table, closer to Sarah. 'Excellent,' he said, and gave a sideways glance. Sarah did not look up from her documents. 'As expected,' he continued, 'Babbage's prints are all over the camera, and there's a partial lift from the rear housing. Could be Amy's.' He looked up from the paper. Sarah was paying attention now. 'All the photos have been taken within a twenty-three-day period, ending on Monday the thirteenth. Looks like we also have a breakdown of the albums found in the study. Good job, high tech guys.'

'That's good,' Sarah said and returned to her papers.

'Can I see the photo album?' Deans asked.

Sarah handed him the A5 sized, ring-bound wallet, each page numbered 1 to 83; a single colour print to each page. He flipped through the first forty-four but did not recognise any of the outside locations or any of the different females contained within. He then stopped at number 45. It was Amy.

She was sitting on a high-armed wooden chair and her head was slumped forward. Her arms draped over the elbow rests and her hair covering her face. If it was not for the extensive bruising she sustained whilst being buried, Deans would think he was looking at a snuff photo.

As he turned the pages in sequence, his mind's-eye created a virtual replay. He saw Amy, and he saw Babbage. It was if he were a free moving entity in the room and they were unaware of his presence. He watched Babbage position Amy in the chair and could detect a palpable excitement in the room.

Deans pulled away from the album and looked over at Sarah. She was doing her own thing. He screwed up his face, shook his head, and nudged the album away. This was insane.

He could not ignore what was happening to him and pulled the album back. He opened the pages, his hands trembling. Another picture; Amy's face. He brought it closer. *My God!*

He touched the side of his right temple, his eyes burning on the page. *The headaches*, he thought. He raced through the subsequent pages, and then at number 71, his skin blanched and he stopped dead.

He was looking at the driveway, front garden and front door of his own house. Frozen air stiffened his neck and shoulders and goosebumps spread over his body like a pestilence of locusts, gnawing at his skin. He hurried through the pages, unable to turn them fast enough, but it was alone. A solitary image.

He returned back to the page and blinked uncontrollably as he took it all in. His car was on the drive.

Sarah had been watching him. 'Are you all right, Andy?'

He did not answer.

'Andy? Are you okay?'

The door opened and Jackson burst in. 'There you both are. Briefing in ten. Don't be late.' He slammed the door and was gone.

'Andy?' Sarah said with more urgency.

'Yes, what?' he replied sharply.

Sarah flinched, a look of surprise on her face. 'Shall we get some thoughts together for the briefing?'

'Briefing?'

'The one Sarge just told us about.'

Deans shook his head.

Sarah snatched the documents away from him and bundled them up together. 'Come on,' she said pushing her chair away from the table.

'I'm going to give Babbage what he wants,' Deans said in a monotone voice.

'What do you mean?'

'Me. He wants me. So he's going to get me.'

'I don't understand.'

'I want to go solo in the next interview, Sarah.'

'The sarge won't go for that. He will want both of us there. The policy stipulates—'

'Fuck the policy and fuck that wanker, Jackson.'

Sarah took a backward step. 'What's happened, Andy?' she asked nervously.

'Babbage has happened.'

'What do you mean?'

Deans did not answer. He was already walking out of the room.

CHAPTER FIFTY-FOUR

Deans and Sarah were the final two people to arrive at the conference room. There were no seats again so they stood against the wall. Deans sensed urgency in the room, the taste of progress in the air.

The DI explained that Sarah and Deans would put another interview to Babbage and hit him with all the new evidence. Jackson would arrange the extension of custody time from the magistrates' court, and he hoped by the end of the day that they would have the full forensic package.

Deans did not mention the photograph; in fact, he failed to speak throughout the entire briefing.

Jackson followed Deans and Sarah out of the room. 'I need a detailed report from you within the hour,' he demanded.

'About what?' Sarah asked.

'Everything. Unless you want to bow and scrape to the magistrates? No, didn't think so.'

'We need to prepare for the next interview. Ask the disclosure officer,' Deans said.

'Just get me that bloody report,' Jackson snapped. 'If we

don't get this extension we can kiss the next interview good-bye, along with the job.'

Deans had not seen him this flustered before. Angry – yes, stressed – no.

Jackson glared at them both. 'I need it like yesterday, so get on with it,' he said and stomped away.

Whether Deans liked Jackson or not, he had to agree with something he had said; they were scuppered without the magistrates' approval for longer detention. Therefore, he and Sarah set about knocking up a typed précis, which just less than an hour later was in Jackson's ungrateful hand.

Deans imagined Jackson would read the summary word for word like a script. He so wished he could have put something in to screw him up and make him suffer. He would have loved to view the spectacle in person but alas, the interview of Babbage was waiting.

They arrived at the custody suite and set about preparing the new evidence for interview. The duty inspector had already conducted a welfare check on Babbage and it was evident that he was still refusing legal representation, but that could still change with the looming prospect of another couple of days banged up.

Sarah took Deans along a narrow corridor to show him the video satellite room and found the DI inside talking on the landline. Five empty plastic chairs squeezed tightly into the width of the room, beneath a TV monitor fixed to the wall.

Deans looked at the bright image on the TV screen. It was the familiar view of their interview room.

Sarah raised a hand and quietly apologised to the DI, and closed the door again. She pulled at Deans' arm before they reached the interview room.

'Are you angry with me about something?' she asked.

'God, no. Why?'

'You just seem quiet today.'

'Sarah, seriously. I'm fine.' He hesitated. '…I'm sorry. I've got a few things bothering me right now.'

She dropped her head. 'I shouldn't have invited you over. I'm sorry.'

'Sarah, don't be sorry.' He reached out and touched her hand. 'I promise it's nothing to do with you, or last night.'

'Are you sure?' Her doleful brown eyes combed his face.

'Come on,' he said, giving her a one-armed hug. 'Shall we get this show on the road?'

Two and a half hours later, they were ready. Jackson had succeeded with the extension and Deans and Sarah waited for Babbage's arrival in the interview room.

Deans had scribbled a note to Sarah; she would start the interview but he would indicate when the time was right for her to leave.

Babbage walked nonchalantly into the room sporting a wide grin, a detention officer close behind. Deans looked away.

Sarah commenced the interview, and as before, Babbage stared at Deans throughout.

'Tell us everything about the camera found in your study,' Sarah asked.

Babbage leaned on the table towards her. 'No comment.' He sat back and faced Deans once again.

'Tell us who the camera belongs to.'

'No. Comment.'

'Describe the images stored on the camera,' Sarah continued.

Babbage closed his eyes, emitted a slow, hushed groan, and formed a satisfied smile. 'Why don't you tell us, Detective Deans?' he said darkly.

The bastard was trying to wind him up, and doing a good job of it too.

'I'm asking you,' Sarah interjected calmly.

'Come on, Detective?' an increasingly-animated Babbage said. 'Was there anything on the camera that you'd like to share with us?'

Deans did all he could not to vault the table, strangle Babbage and enjoy every second of it. Instead, through clenched teeth he responded, 'It's not my interview, Babbage, it's yours. And you're being asked a question.'

Babbage leaned closer towards Sarah, who simultaneously pushed back in her chair. 'I tell you what, pretty,' he said. 'I will talk with Detective Deans now. So you can toddle off and do your nails or something.'

'You don't tell me how to run this interview—'

'Sarah, it's fine,' Deans interrupted. 'That's fine. If Mr Babbage wants to speak with me, then that's okay.'

Sarah looked up at the camera.

'Go on, Sarah, it's fine,' Deans encouraged.

'Mr Babbage,' Deans said, 'for benefit of procedure, would you please confirm that you'd prefer that it was just myself present during this interview?'

'I believe that's what I asked for. Go on, Sarah – off you go.' Babbage turned to face the camera. 'I hope you're paying attention out there.'

Deans scribbled a note on a scrap of paper: *I'll be OK. Stay in the video room.*

Sarah stood up and reluctantly announced, 'The time is twelve twenty-three hours. DC Gold is leaving the interview room at the request of the defendant.' She gave Deans another look of concern and headed out of the room.

Babbage appeared very pleased about things, and strangely relaxed.

'So finally, Detective,' he said. 'Here you are, and here we are... alone.'

Deans said nothing, rested his elbows on the desk and interlocked his fingers, his stare penetrating.

'I must say, I'm surprised at your constraint. I had you figured for a man that didn't have much in the way of... self-control.' Babbage forced a brief smile. 'I was very sad of course, to hear of your dismissal when the *affair* came to light.'

Deans scowled, his fingers melding together as a molten fury surged through his body.

'Oh, sorry, Detective. Has it only just dawned on you who the concerned member of the public was that alerted your sergeant to the entire sordid liaison? One can only imagine what poor Maria must've thought when she found out.'

Deans was taut with rage.

'Oh, forgive me,' Babbage said dramatically. 'How is the delightful Maria? You must miss her terribly.' His tone was sickeningly patronising.

Deans steeled himself and broke his silence. 'This is neither about me nor my wife.'

'*Au contraire*, Detective. You haven't figured it out yet, have you?'

Deans' eyes flickered.

'What's wrong, Detective? Have you lost your voice without that little tart by your side?'

If Babbage was digging for a reaction, he got one.

'I don't want to hear another murmur from your trap about me, my wife, or Detective Gold. Do you understand, Babbage?'

'Hit a nerve, have we, Detective? Maybe Maria should know about this little temptation too... *ooh*,' he covered his mouth with both hands, just like a child exposing a secret. 'I almost forgot,' he whispered.

Deans wriggled in his seat and tugged at the inside of his shirt collar.

'You see, Detective,' Babbage said, now increasingly animated. 'You don't necessarily need to kill someone to ruin another person's life. Although, you could argue it's much easier if you do.'

Deans broke eye contact for the first time and clenched his fists beneath the table.

Babbage did not take a backward step. 'Why do you think you're even here, Detective? Eh? It's because I wanted it to happen. Because all along I have been playing you.' Babbage's face twisted with a look of utter contempt. 'I didn't have to end up here. I *chose* to be here.' He stopped talking, his lips twitching as if he was practicing a kiss. 'Think about it. You're on a thin thread my suited friend, and you're dangling – from my fingers.' As he grinned, the tips of his ears lifted. 'You were here, then you weren't, then you were again.' He leant on the table and stood away from the chair. 'How do you enjoy living alone, now that Maria's left you?'

Deans turned from Babbage, and twisted his body away.

Babbage then spoke with an infantile voice, 'Has she told you you're special? Hmmm? Has she said you have *the gift?*' He laughed heartily. 'You and Denise think you've got me sussed. Well I have news for you suckers; Denise is an old has-been and I have taken the gift to a completely different level. You? ...You don't even know you're born. Do you think it was a mistake punching that traffic cop? Course it wasn't. I planned it. I *made* it happen. I got you dismissed and I got you back. You are nothing but a pathetic lackey. I have been dissecting your crappy existence piece by piece for my personal entertainment right from the start. Look at you – you are tragic. You don't even realise it yet, but I've *ruined* you.'

Deans was now huddled in his chair, his hands covering his ears.

Watching from the satellite room Jackson was on his feet.

'What the fuck's he doing? Why is he allowing Babbage to speak to him like that? Deans is having a fucking breakdown in there.' He started to make towards the door. 'I'm putting an end to this joke.'

'Leave it, Jackson,' the DI snapped. 'Sit down.'

'He's fucking this up,' Jackson frothed.

'Sit back down and watch this develop,' the DI demanded.

Jackson flung his arms down by his sides and returned to his seat like a stroppy teenager. 'He's making a mockery of this investigation, and all of us.'

Sarah could not look away from the screen, her face aghast. She wanted Jackson to rush in just to save Deans from the humiliation unfolding.

Back in the interview room and Deans was curled up tight in the chair. A tingle passed through his spine.

Donna. Donna. A child-like voice captivated his senses. He held his breath and attempted to shut out a raging Babbage.

Donna. Evil, little Donna. There it was again, only this time louder; the unmistakable voice of a child, calling out.

Babbage suddenly stopped ranting and for a brief moment, there was respite. Deans sneaked a glance; Babbage was flapping his arms as if he was fending something away.

Evil, little Donna. Evil, little Donna.

Was Babbage hearing this too?

Mummy loves me more than you. This time the voice was accompanied by gushing laughter.

'Donna?' Deans repeated with barely a whisper. Babbage was now in full tirade, his behaviour more hostile than at any time before.

'I can't believe you're jumping through hoops for that little slapper anyway,' Babbage snarled. 'Prancing around like royalty. Thought she was so privileged with her *perfect* little life. She thought she was better than me too, but I knew her dirty, slutty secrets.' Babbage began to laugh. 'At least she had more spirit than you. Had some fight in her. You are pitiful. I was at least hoping for some sort of opposition.'

Deans lifted his head. 'Evil, Donna?'

Babbage faltered, steadied himself with the table. 'What?'

Deans faced him for the first time in minutes and noticed Babbage blink uncontrollably. 'Donna,' Deans repeated loudly.

'You?' Babbage said, and took a noticeable step backwards. He then erupted with uncontrollable ferocity. 'You don't know me. You don't know anything about me. You've got no idea,' he bellowed. 'Don't ever think that you can get the better of me. That's not ever going to happen.'

Deans slowly uncurled himself and rose to his feet.

'That other little princess?' Babbage shouted, teeth bared. 'She thought she could get into my head, and look what happened to her…' In an instant, his anger turned to laughter. 'Not so clever was she, when she was *pleading* for me not to end her inconsequential existence. You're all—' Babbage stopped abruptly.

The room fell still.

Deans straightened his shoulders, turned to the camera and reached down the lens, eyes wide. A minute went by and neither of them spoke.

Deans approached a now sedentary Babbage and rested his knuckles on the desktop. 'Your eyes tell you what you want them to believe, Babbage.'

'You bastard!' Babbage shouted.

'Who is Donna?' Deans asked again.

Babbage narrowed his stare, the crow's-feet ever prominent.

Suddenly, involuntary images flashed through Deans' mind; the pebble ridge, Amy, Babbage's house, and then a collection of old family pictures he remembered seeing from the photo albums recovered at the scene.

Jesus Christ, he thought.

Babbage was searching Deans' face and had obviously picked up something in Deans' expression.

Deans looked away, put both hands to his head and paced the room. He stopped and turned towards the camera once again.

'You know, at first I was surprised by the position of the body,' Deans said. 'Either side, there must have been hundreds and thousands of tonnes of rock to conceal Amy beneath.' He turned back to face Babbage. 'Initially, I thought I was looking for someone with a self-admiration complex: allow the discovery of the corpse, and then revel in the media frenzy.' He paused. '…And then I looked at motivations, and I have to say that I was somewhat thrown to learn that sexual contact was unlikely. After all, Amy was a good-looking girl… no, take that back. She was an absolutely beautiful, intelligent and warm-hearted young woman—'

'She was nothing but a little slut,' Babbage interrupted.

'And you took it upon yourself to remedy that particular situation.'

Babbage did not reply. Instead, with a broad smile he began to snigger.

'What's so amusing?' Deans asked.

'You. You are so amusing, Detective Deans.' Babbage's eyes narrowed to horizontal slits.

I've got you now, fucker, Deans thought. 'Tell me about your brother,' he asked.

Babbage scoffed and turned away.

'You know,' Deans said. 'It was confusing at first, but now? Makes perfect sense.' He looked up at the camera again and spoke as if directly addressing the audience in the satellite room. 'If only we had put you in a forensic suit.'

Babbage shuffled in the seat for the first time. Deans had him.

'You were taunted weren't you?' Deans said. 'Did your little brother make fun of you? Did he reinforce the deficiencies in your mother's love?'

'Are you a detective or a fucking psychiatrist?' Babbage seethed, full of loathing.

Deans chortled. 'I must admit, sometimes it is hard to distinguish the two.'

Babbage stared down at the table with a crazed, fixed grin.

'So, let's for a moment get back to Amy,' Deans said. 'What was it, her popularity? Her looks? Her devoted family life? Your shitty life?'

'What would you know about shitty life?' Babbage bit.

Bingo, Deans thought. 'So tell me about it.'

'Fuck you.'

Deans could feel Babbage simmering with angst – on the brink.

'I suppose you had a perfect upbringing?' Babbage said, unable to contain himself.

Deans shrugged. 'Not particularly.'

'Well, I bet you weren't always second best.'

'I'm an only child,' Deans said, and noticed Babbage watching him closely.

'I get it,' Deans said. *"See No Evil. Hear No Evil"* – her cheeks – the glue. You were referring to you.'

Babbage grinned.

'Where is your brother now?' Deans asked.

'Somewhat indisposed,' Babbage said disturbingly.

Deans waited and silently debated the appropriateness of his next question. He couldn't give a toss about being 'PC' anymore.

'So, what are you, post-op, or just playing at it because you've got no tits?'

Babbage glared at Deans and oozed resentment. 'Whatever happens to me now,' Babbage said calmly, 'at least I have the satisfaction of knowing I destroyed you.'

Deans laughed, and closed the covers of his daybook. 'Don't flatter yourself, it's my job. And unlike you, at least I'm getting paid for being here.'

Babbage broke out into riotous laughter.

Deans shook his head and bundled up his papers, as the insidious noise from Babbage intensified. That was enough. He could not remember dealing with anyone more detestable at any time of his career. *Why did it have to be Amy?* He thought. It saddened him to think that Babbage was the last human being that she had encountered.

'The time is now twelve zero-eight hours,' he said disconsolately. 'I'm concluding this interview.'

Deans pulled on the door handle and as a DO entered the room, he took a prolonged look over his shoulder at Babbage before making his way towards the satellite room, from where he saw Jackson exiting.

'You can leave it for us to deal with now,' a deadpan Jackson said.

Deans had not expected hugs and kisses, but that was a strange reaction.

'Okay,' he replied warily. 'But he's going to need working over. All that stuff about family—'

'No longer your concern.'

Deans hovered, waiting for Jackson to say something else – he didn't.

'Fine,' Deans said, pointing at Jackson. 'Make sure you follow that stuff up.'

'Last I heard; I was wearing the stripes around here,' Jackson snarled.

'Last I heard; I was the only one Babbage was talking to.'

Jackson's steely glare lingered just long enough to become awkward.

'I'd better say some goodbyes then, I guess,' Deans said.

Jackson turned and walked away, clearly not wishing to be the recipient of one of them.

Deans entered the satellite room. Sarah was watching the screen. He looked at the monitor and saw that Babbage was still laughing and defiantly resisting two DOs who were attempting to remove him from the room.

'Was that all an act in there?' she said.

'It's all about the body language,' Deans smiled.

Sarah stood up. 'What happens next?'

'Well, it seems I'm leaving. Jackson just relieved me of my duties.'

'No!'

'It's fine,' Deans said. 'At least you guys now have something to work on. Besides, I've got important things to do back home.'

'Andy, how did you know that stuff in there?' She shook her head. 'We didn't have intel for that.'

'Hmmm.' Deans smiled. 'It's been staring at us throughout. Make sure you finish this off. Don't let Jackson fuck it up.'

'Will I see you again?'

'Well, hopefully there'll be a trial some way down the line. Maybe I will get to see you then, if not before.'

'I hope so.' Sarah lunged forwards and embraced Deans with a firm hug.

'Take care of yourself, Sarah,' he said, and gave her a kiss on the cheek.

He was more than ready to return home. Ready to sort things out with Maria and ready to return his life to normality. First, though, he felt compelled to see Denise.

She was in the shop behind the counter. She appeared restless.

Deans bounded over. 'My time here is up. I'm heading home.'

'Did he admit anything?' she asked anxiously.

Deans rocked his head. 'Kind of, though I don't think you need worry about Babbage coming back here any time soon.'

Denise looked away.

'I just wanted to thank you, before I head off... for everything. You're a very special lady.'

She gave a half-hearted smile and held out a hand, which Deans took.

'Maybe I'll get to work with you again sometime?' he said.

'You will.'

Denise had tears in her eyes and her voice was brittle.

Deans kissed the back of her hand and gently pulled her into an embrace, which they held for a long, silent minute.

'I really must get going,' Deans said. 'It's been an eye-opener, and an absolute pleasure.'

She snatched for his hand and held it firmly in her grasp.

'Promise me you'll keep going,' she said.

'Of course.'

'I'm serious. No matter what.'

He laughed. 'I promise.'

Denise looked disturbed.

'Don't worry, Denise,' Deans said. 'He's not coming back.'

She shook her head and released his hand.

Deans walked to the door and stopped at the exit.

'Goodbye, Denise. Thank you.'

She raised a hand and wiped tears from her cheeks.

As he closed the door, he looked back in through the glass and privately admired the woman standing on the other side.

Denise had shown him a side of life he never believed existed. But that was already in the past. All he cared about now was his future, and how he was going to make amends with Maria.

FREE NOVELLA

Join the VIP Reader Team and receive a *free and exclusive* offer.

Read the prequel novella to the Detective Deans series for free by joining the VIP Reader Team.

Visit www.jamesdmortain.com and click *START DEANS FOR FREE!* to receive this exclusive offer.

No spam, guaranteed. You can unsubscribe at any time.

DEAD BY DESIGN PREVIEW

DEAD BY DESIGN

A DETECTIVE DEANS MYSTERY
- BOOK TWO -

PROLOGUE

BATH 1975

George Fenwick leaned back against the cushions of his new cane Peacock armchair and admired the stonework of his freshly crazy-paved patio area.

His daughter, Samantha, had made fun of him ever since he purchased the wicker furniture, saying it looked more like a royal throne. Now that the final concrete slab was laid and set, he could finally take his place upon his 'throne' and enjoy the delights of his lush and verdant garden.

He smiled to himself and returned a lit pine match to the tip of his imported Montecristo cigar and sucked his cheeks until the leaves glowed orange once again. He inhaled a lungful of the sweet tasting Cuban smoke and watched Sammy playing on her bespoke oak swing at the far end of the garden, under the shade of the majestic weeping willows.

Her mother died three years before. It was sudden and shocking, and as a six-year-old at the time, it knocked the stuffing out of the poor little girl, but now, she was able to have fun again. When the time was right, he would too.

George tapped his shoe on the thick paving slab beneath his chair and a smile curled upwards from the corner of his mouth. Life was good, life was great and now, things would only get better.

Sammy came running over to him. 'Daddy, can I have a bottle of cola, please?'

George smiled, 'Of course you can, Sammy. Why not bring one back for Daddy, there's a good girl.'

Samantha skipped off towards the house, leaving George to his thoughts. He was making significant improvements to the home, Sammy was doing well at school and tomorrow, George was taking the new E-Type Jaguar Coupe for a test-drive. It had long been a desire of his to have a flash set of wheels to drive along Pulteney Street and impress the neighbours even further, and now that he was able to, nothing was going to stop him.

He scratched beneath his ear. *Where is Sammy*? He looked back towards the house, but there was no sign of her. He leaned his head against the high fan of the tall wicker chair and closed his eyes.

A fly buzzing around his face caused more than a degree of annoyance. He swatted the air, took a satisfying deep breath and listened to the birds chirping happily in the nearby trees.

Samantha returned soon after. 'Daddy we haven't got any Coke.'

'We do, Sammy. Look closer.'

'But Daddy, there isn't—'

'Sammy,' George said glaring at her. 'Look in the pantry, you will see a crate on the floor, I know it's there, I only bought it yesterday.'

'But I did look there— '

'Look harder,' George said. 'I'm hot and I want a drink. You really do not want me to have to get up out of this seat…?'

Sammy stood in front of him. Her arms rigid by her side. Her eyes wide and unblinking.

George suddenly sprang up from the seat and grabbed Sammy by the shoulders. 'Come on, Samantha, step out of my sunshine and get me that ruddy drink.'

Samantha let out a squeal, turned quickly away, and her long tousled hair slapped her in the face.

Standing two paces away from him, she huffed loudly and stomped back towards the house.

George sank back into his chair, shaking his head and

mumbling something beneath his breath about a 'lazy, ungrateful brat', he returned his cigar to his lips and puffed with more vigour, creating a blur of smoke around his head.

This was turning into a very pleasant day, if only he had that drink!

The flies continued to bug him, buzzing close to his face. He puffed more smoke and blew it in the general direction from where they appeared to be coming – which unusually was beneath his seat. Several insects were getting through the shield of smoke and pitching around his neckline. It was a warm July day, and he was perspiring. He could feel the dampness of his skin around his collar and continued to waft his free hand around his head as he did his best to relax, leaning back in his luxurious new armchair, eyes closed and face turned towards the sun.

'Daddy, I can't get in the pantry, the door is locked,' Sammy shouted running back towards him.

'Jesus Christ!' George spluttered and sprang up from the comfort of the seat. 'I said to you, that if I had to move…'

Sammy stopped dead in her tracks and covered her face with her hands. She looked at him and let out a shrill scream.

'What the hell is wrong now?' George said making his way with a heavy foot towards her.

Sammy cowered away and screamed again.

'The pantry is not locked. You were in it five minutes ago! For Christ's sake!' he shouted. His teeth were bared and his shoulders were tight.

'Daddy what have you done?' Sammy mouthed, breath-lessly, taking two steps backwards.

'What the hell are you talking about?' George seethed as he stomped beyond her towards the concrete steps leading up to the back door.

'Daddy you're bleeding—'

'I am most certainly not bleeding.'

Samantha screamed again and George turned angrily.

'Daddy, your shirt has turned red.'

George looked down and frowned as he shook his head, his shirt was fine.

'Right,' he snapped. 'I've no idea what has gotten into you, but you are no longer having a Coke. I'm not going to tolerate any more of your nonsense.'

George climbed the steps and looked back towards his daughter. She was standing ten feet into the garden and she was still clutching her mouth.

He grumbled and walked into the kitchen and made direct for the pantry. He opened the door and there on the floor was the unopened crate of cola that he had picked up the day before.

How the hell could she miss that? He sighed deeply and removed one of the bottles, yanked off the cap with a nearby bottle opener and made his way back towards the door.

'I bloody meant it,' he mumbled to himself. 'She's not having one. All this fantasising—'

George suddenly stopped. His eyes were wide and gaping. He took several backwards steps the way he had just come, turned about, and looked at his reflection in the window.

Mouth ajar, he leaned in closer. His shirt was crimson red; in fact, it was seeping with blood. He cautiously looked back down at himself and he shook his head. His shirt was still pale blue. There was nothing on it. He quickly looked back into the reflection of the window and the bottle of pop dropped from his hand and splashed in an arc of exploding bubbles.

He leaned in again and looked at his throat. Small wells of blood were oozing from under the surface. He reached for his

neck and rubbed beneath his ear as another small balloon of
red gloop burst from his skin.

Frantically he rubbed the area, but the more he did so, the
more the blood leached out.

'Daddy, Daddy, are you okay?' Samantha's voice came
from outside the door.

George quickly turned. 'Stay there, Sammy. Don't come in.'

'But Daddy—'

'I mean it, Sammy. Stay the hell outside...' George turned
back to his reflection and saw a perfect line from ear to ear of
weeping blood under his jawline. He gripped his neck with
both hands and tried to stem the flow of blood, but the more
he tried, the quicker it flowed.

'Daddy!' Samantha screamed. She was in the kitchen.

George faced her with horror in his eyes. He cried out
'Don't see me' and waved her away with a completely blood-
dripping hand. He turned back to the window and his heart
stopped.

Written on the glass in his blood, were the words:

IT BELONGS TO ME.

'Peter?' George breathed.

He turned and ran to the top of the steps. He looked over
to his chair on the patio – the entire area was now infested
with flies and the sound of buzzing filled the air. He noticed
Sammy two steps below him, pointing up at him, her other
hand across her mouth.

George followed the direction of her finger, it was pointing
at his chest. He looked down – his shirt was pale blue once
again. He rubbed his neck – there was nothing. He looked back
towards the chair – the flies had gone. He settled on Sammy.
She was now crying and laughing at the same time. George
held out his arms and Sammy came running into his secure
grasp.

George looked around him in slow motion – to the patio – over his shoulder at the doorway to the kitchen and finally back down at his hands. He rested his chin on the top of Sammy's head and directed his eyes once again on the patio area.

'He's back...' George whispered. 'Oh God... Peter... Peter.'

CHAPTER ONE

Driving back up the M5 motorway, the sound of Detective Andrew Deans' ringtone interrupted his music.

'Hello?' he said.

'Deano, it's Mick. Where are you?' There was urgency to Detective Sergeant Mick Savage's voice.

'On my way back up from North Devon. I'm no longer required on the murder investigation.'

'Good. I need to speak to you.'

'Yeah, that's fine, but I was hoping to take a few days off. I've accrued a boatload of—'

'I really need to speak to you now, Deano,' DS Savage interrupted.

'Okay. That's fine. I'm on hands-free.'

There was a silent break in the conversation.

'Hello, Mick? I must be in a bad area – try me again in a few minutes.'

'No... I'm still here, Deano.'

'Come on, Mick, stop messing around. I'm too tired for games.'

'There's no easy way to say this, Deano.'

Deans waited.

'We've got another missing person.'

'For Christ's sake, Mick. Give me a chance to settle back into the office will you. I've been away from Bath for ages.'

'No... Deano. You don't understand. It's... Maria.'

DEAD BY DESIGN

Available now!

FROM THE AUTHOR

Thank you for reading my first published novel. I hope you enjoyed *STORM LOG-0505*.

You may have taken a chance on reading this book. If so, thank you for discovering my work.

For those of you coming over from my DI Robbie Chilcott series, I hope you enjoyed this introduction to Detective Deans!

James

BOOKS BY JAMES D MORTAIN

DETECTIVE DEANS MYSTERY SERIES
STORM LOG-0505
DEAD BY DESIGN
THE BONE HILL

DI CHILCOTT MYSTERY SERIES
DEAD RINGER
DEATH DO US PART
A WHISPER OF EVIL

ACKNOWLEDGMENTS

There are many people I must thank for their assistance in the creation of this book: Doug Watts of the Jacqui Bennett Writers Bureau, being the first professional to view and critique my work – for his encouragement, tact, wit and direction. Thanks also to the team at Cornerstones Literary Consultancy for their editorial talent and expertise, and to Jessica Bell, for her imagination and skill in creating the cover image.

For Barbara Olive, the *real* Denise Moon, whose guidance and influence on my family has been substantial. To my beta readers: Clare; Liz; Fiona Staddon; Lynne Webster and Terry Galbraith – thank you for the time and effort you afforded to me. The story would be poorer without your input.

To all the police officers and staff who have served the community of Bath and the surrounding areas, but particularly those that kept me safe during my time in service.

Finally, to my wife, Rachael, who encouraged a whim, and supported a husband through uncertainty, obsession, anguish and desire. Without you, this would still be but a dream.

ABOUT THE AUTHOR

Photograph Copyright of Mick Kavanagh Photography.

Former British CID Detective turned crime fiction writer, James brings thrilling action and gritty authenticity to his writing through years of police experience. Originally from Bath, England, James now lives in North Devon with his young family.

Visit: www.jamesdmortain.com

Email: jdm@manverspublishing.com

facebook.com/jamesdmortain

twitter.com/@jamesdmortain

instagram.com/jamesmortain

Printed in Great Britain
by Amazon